SINGING BONES

S. G. ULLMAN

ISBN: 979-8-9867610-4-6 (eBook)
ISBN: 979-8-9867610-5-3 (Paperback)

Title Management by BookWhisperer.ink

PROLOGUE
FALL 6262 BCE

A light breeze sent a few early fall leaves skipping between the Téuta huts in the dark on a night that, where the Téuta lived, was simple and beautiful. It was a year, and a day, of deep consequence for the world, but nothing in the Téuta village seemed out of place.

The wanderers, the Kujoté, hunter-gatherers who sometimes lived nearby in the forest, were also sleeping, and they also knew nothing about how much the earth had suddenly changed. They slept often in the day as well, but at this time of the year their days were full. They were preparing for the end of summer. Preparing to move. Some of them, a few, would come for a last visit for the year at the Téuta festival that marked the year's end, harvest's end, and the approach of winter. But soon after that they would leave the mountain. Soon they would begin their long walk down the river to the lowland where they lived in the winter for warmer winds and easier hunting.

The Téuta, though, did not move. That was its importance. That was the gift it gave to the people in other, smaller villages around them. It was a stable strength in the whirl of life there.

Even the Kujoté felt its stability. They continued the life they knew, summers on the mountain and winters on the plains, and sometimes took long excursions to meet other wanderers for feasting. At their feasts, the feasts of wanderers in all their gathered hundreds, they did not think about the Téuta. They took joy in the days of the feast: they ate to their capacity for eating, and drank, and loved each other and fought with each other and ate and drank and ate again.

But the Téuta was a still center even for these untamed wanderers. That's why, year after year, they returned to make their camp in the low mountain forest near that great village, and why they kept and valued their friendship with the Téuta people. The Téuta village was a still center for everyone on the mountains then, even for people who had never seen it.

Stable. Changeless. That had meaning for them. It was their identity, one that the Téuta people felt in their marrows. The Téuta had been in its place for so long that the time before people settled there was no more than stories and legends told over and over from each generation to the next. They were wisps of memory nearly lost, those ancient times. The great cliff with its carvings for the ancestors, and the Téuta village itself, were their only remnants.

Nestled contentedly in their safety, dawn still far distant, the Téuta slept. The cliff to the north and the wide river to the south protected them—and because of these, and because the village was so large, predators, either human or animal, were wary. Such dangers kept their distance. Unless pushed to desperation they looked in other places for their prey.

With all these things to protect them nothing threatened the Téuta people beyond their tolerance. Nothing within the memory of any living Téuta ever had threatened them as much as that.

So the Téuta people in their village rested in innocence. They rested confidently, ignorant of the profound violence that had occurred far to the north, and which would ride for many years across the earth to reach them. Disaster was like the distant ocean; they could not imagine what it might be, or that so great a violence could ever come to them. They had no inkling of it.

Most, at least, had no inkling. Only young Eini, perhaps, had her first sense of it. She had, perhaps, the first ghostly edge of a fear that would chase her through all the following years of her life.

Perhaps.

Maybe.

Or maybe it was something else that pestered her. I don't want to imply too much. How could she know about these things that were so distant from her across the earth, things happening in places she had never seen? Places that, so long ago, she could not even have believed were real? How could she know about a village calamity so distant from her across time? How could these things trouble her when the night was so calm and the early leaves blew quietly through the village, and the night smelled sweetly of them, and of fire pits newly stoked, of the cool surface of mud bricks that made the huts nearby, and smelled also of the wide river and the forest around her?

No. Are we children to believe such things? It was something else that bothered her dreams. Of course. Of course it was. It must have been something else.

It *must* have been.

PART I

Eini

CHAPTER 1
FALL 6262 BCE

ⱀⱀⱀ

In a soft evening in early fall, the last evening before Eini had the first of her great visions, the wolves did not care that Eini loved them. They did not know it. But she did love them, and that helped her through the night.

Do you sing for us? Eini thought to the wolves. *No, of course you don't. Why would you? You sing for yourselves, and for each other, and for the world. You help us by your song, though. Even after you have gone, we still hear your voices in the dark. In our sleep we hear you.*

Much earlier, when evening was only a fresh scent on the wind, the wolves had come to the plateau across the river from the Téuta village. They came just as the day was at its most brilliant grace, with a deep ochre blush thick and bright at the peaks to the west but also dusted in lumped patches under the clouds that still covered much of the sky. Eight wolves ran without warning from the trees. They were lured by sheep grazing on the remains of the grasses after harvest, wandering too far from the huts and the people around them.

The morning had been full of rain and gusty wind, which slowly left as the day went on. By late afternoon the rain had slowed almost to a mist, and the clouds were longer, thinner ones that moved quickly across the sky. By evening, the rain had stopped completely. Everyone on the plateau was glad of the morning rains with the heat of summer still lingering, and then glad of the rain stopping so they could do some work before dark.

But then wolves came to interrupt them.

The wolves had picked a poor time for a raid on the plateau's livestock, though. The sheep were enticing, spread wide across the field, but the fields of wheat and barley had been harvested a week before, so at the side farthest from the forest, near the steep slopes down to the river, a large cluster of people from the village were gathered to laugh and chatter and work. Most of them were threshing and winnowing the harvest, and others filling great sacks with the clean grain to carry it on their backs, or baskets to carry on their heads, down to the village below. The wolves had only a fleeting moment before the sheep reacted, and the disturbance among the sheep drew the attention of those who were alert, and those facing the fields.

"Ho!!!"

The call was loud, clearly not just gossip, so people looked at the man who yelled it. He was pointing to the field, pointing to the sheep running and bunching together. He needed no more words than that to tell everyone on the plateau what was happening.

The reaction was practiced, and quick. This was not the first time wolves had come. Men with spears, bows and slings ran toward the wolves almost as soon as they were seen. The wolves were sent back to the forest nursing bruises from sling-stones. One wolf at least had been wounded by an arrow fired on the run. But one sheep also lay dead from the attack, and one bleeding and stained red across its back. The rest of the sheep huddled together in the center of the field, looking at their keepers with eyes longing for safety.

With other tasks now preempting it, work on the wheat and barley was done for the day. Those carrying clean grain continued down to the village, and the rest put their work away for the night and took time to help care for the sheep.

The people always up there, those who stayed there on the plateau and slept there, did that partly to care for the sheep and goats, and the fields of grain during the summer, but also because wolves and other dangers do sometimes come. This evening's attack by predators looking for an easy dinner was disturbing but not shocking to them. The loss of two sheep was bad, of course. Sheep had value. But there were many sheep. They and others working up on the plateau would eat well this week, and that was good. Theirs was long work, sometimes hard work, so they deserved their bit of unplanned feasting.

Of all the Téuta, only Eini had expected the wolves. She had dreamt of them before the harvest even began, and had told her father and her mother and others that this would happen. Her dreams, as always, were dismissed, in part because she knew so little about what they showed. She knew only that wolves would come to the plateau. That much and no more. Not the day or the time of day—or even the year. She knew only that they would come sometime.

But the adults already knew that wolves would come *sometime*.

"I'm busy," adults had said. The most accepting might continue with "That's all you can say? That sometime wolves will come?"

"They will kill a sheep," Eini replied when asked this. "Maybe two sheep."

But that was not enough to make the grownups listen. She was a child, everyone said, a nervous child. These were only a child's dreams. People often thought of her as an anxious girl, tall at ten winters, with big eyes and long soft hair a lighter brown than most others, but a girl who was too thin and was sometimes frightened by things she couldn't name.

Eini and her father had been working up on the plateau with the others, winnowing the grains, bundling clean grain into sacks to be taken down to the village below. When the wolves were gone, her father came to her. Together they walked along the steep slopes and looked out across the river, across the forest that began not far from the cliffs opposite them and extended up onto the mountain. When the forest rose across the mountain, they could see the tops of the trees. Eini liked that. Usually, when you are in the forest, you don't see the tops. So she stood with her father watching that. He placed a hand on her shoulder.

"What are you seeing, Eini?"

"The tops of the trees."

"It's beautiful from here, isn't it?"

"Yes. There is a tree there," Eini pointed, "that is really tall, really big. It's so tall next to the other trees there."

"Yes."

"I wonder how long it has been there. I think it must be very old," Eini said, and then glanced at her father with a little mischief on her face. "Maybe as old as you? Can it be that old?"

Her father looked at her, but he knew her. They had played this game before. He laughed at her effrontery, and replied, "Maybe, possibly as old as me." Then he was more serious. "I do know that tree. It was tall, almost like that, standing above the other trees, even when I was your age, Eini."

Eini gazed at the tree, and then said, "I want to see it at night, with a bright moon."

"The moon is just new tonight, Eini. Maybe we can come back when the moon is full, and stay in that hut there," and he pointed. "I've stayed with them before when there is work in the morning." And then, returning her mischief to her, he continued: "They snore very loudly so you won't be able to sleep, but otherwise they are nice."

Eini looked up at her father. "Do you mean it? We really could come back when the moon is full? Promise!"

"Yes, Eini. We'll do that. I promise. We'll come to work the day here. You are already good with the garden below, the peas and lentils. It will be good for you to learn the barley, and the sheep."

Eini leaned against him, deep in thought. Then she said:

"I like old things. I like to know about them." She looked up at him. "Even things as old as you!"

Eini jumped and laughed when he tickled her, and then the two stood watching for what seemed like a long time. It couldn't have been as long as it seemed because it was still light when they walked down the path toward their hut. They were thinking only of the trees as they walked, and the great age of trees, and perhaps of the wisdom of trees. They did not think of wolves. The wolves were gone, they thought.

But that was not quite true. When dusk had filled in and night was almost full, the wolves sang. They howled their sorrow at their lost meal and their joy in living in the world, living in the company of other wolves. Because they sang, Eini felt them, felt all of the meaning of their song.

Wolves often sing in the mountains. There is nothing special in that. What made the songs interesting in the village that night was that they were so close. The wolves had crossed the river to the side where most of the village huts were found. They sounded their grief and their joy that night just over the heads of the Téuta people. They sang from the top of the great cliff with carvings to honor the Téuta's ancestors, carvings to give the dead a place among the people even after they had gone to Dhegm. They sang from a place very close but out of sight, just over the cliff's top edge. From there, just up above the village, the sound of their song settled into the wide river basin between the cliff and the steep slopes across the water, echoing back and forth between them so that the eight wolves almost sounded like twenty. The music they made seemed to come from all around, almost as though the wolves them-selves were just next to every person, or just behind every hut. Several times Eini saw someone start and look around, thinking the wolves would be at their feet. But no wolves were as close as that. None were visible.

All through the village, it sounded as though it was not the wolves, but the Téuta itself that sang. No one could remember wolves singing from that place before. It was close enough to amaze those who heard it, and to make some of them afraid.

On this night, though, on the night of the wolves, Eini heard them as though they were just beside her and she had no fear. She knew where the wolves really were. Others could be afraid of these wolves if they liked. But when Eini heard the wolves singing around her in all direc-tions, Eini only loved them. Her first thought was that their song was beautiful, always, and even more beautiful so close, so clear.

Later, the wolves were silent. But the beauty of the wolves sounded in her dream during the night, and that lightened her sleep. It might have been the light sleeping that allowed a vision of a darker, more distant danger to enter her mind. She felt cold in her sleep, long cold, but after the cold she thought she felt an empty Téuta. She felt the quiet huts. She thought they watched her, the dark huts in the night, as though they were hoping she could bring those who should live in them back from wherever they were. Through a mist in the darkness she felt it all. She listened. She heard the river's burble, the wind, the wolves. But no people. Even her own hut was empty. Even she was not there.

It was not a dream. It was a vision, one of the visions that made her different from anyone she knew, because visions like this one held a real future in them.

Even as she slept, Eini knew that the strength of what she saw and the lightness of her slumber would allow her to remember this vision when she woke.

The vision, mysterious and dim, seemed terrible. But Eini did not feel despair as she slept. In the song of the wolves, she seemed to hear their hearts, which lifted her. But she also thought she heard another song, a song of hope, a song of relief like a bright thread of light woven through the danger, as though the wolves, or something else that sang with them, came to help the Téuta.

In her dreams Eini wondered: *help us with what? What is this terrible thing?*

She disliked the visions that came to her in her sleep, that showed her glimpses of what might happen. She disliked *that* they showed her what might happen. That made her strange. And they were ugly, the future-dreams. They were clumsy. It was a floundering, graceless, murky future that shook her awake far too soon. It shook her from her sleep while night was still deep. There was no hint of morning.

The room was quiet except for the sighs and snores of the others around her. Waking annoyed her; she wanted to be asleep, as all the others were. She closed her eyes and slept again. Her new sleep still was light and restless. The distant, ugly vision was gone, and her dreams became different.

But the new dreams were almost more disturbing. In these new dreams she saw ice and she saw fire, and in the fire there was a girl burning. Strangely, though, Eini did not feel only fear or anguish in the girl. She did feel those things, but also something else. In the agony of the burning girl, Eini felt the lonely, joyful music of the wolves. Laced into that dream, through all of it, she felt hope as wide as all the earth she had ever seen, and as enduring as all the time she could imagine.

The night was lingering still when Eini woke for good. After a dream so strange she knew she would not sleep again. She still felt the agony and the beauty of the burning girl inside her heart. But in the waking world, the girl's thread of hope seemed more fragile.

Eini rose, dressed, took her cloak and stepped outside the hut.

CHAPTER 2

Dawn was not so far away that *all* the village slept. Other early risers were waking in the dark. But most were sensibly inside their huts, well wrapped against the cool of early morning. The cloaks they draped around them even indoors were one more hint that cold winter, while not here yet, was not many moons away. Light, fluttering dimly out of the doorways of huts from newly stoked fire-pits, spotted the ground here and there. But only two people were out of their huts in the cold: Eini and one other.

Across the Téuta village from Eini's hut Seneks, just over forty-three winters old, stepped briskly and with purpose in spite of his age, intending to spend a long day gathering honey, mint and garlic, and leaves or bark or roots to steep for healing tea. No one was deeply sick just then, and there were no wounds or broken bones to mend, but some of the older Téuta had bones that ached at this time of year, and as winter approached, he would want a store of these things to help people with coughs and runny noses. He might also gather foxglove, pomegranate and sage, and any other medicines he could find on his walk.

He passed through the slowly waking town and kept on along the river until he came to the trail that forest animals had made when they came to the river to drink, a trail that led up the banks and into the hills where he could find what he needed.

Eini stood outside her hut, her cloak held tight around her for warmth, and watched sky with all its pre-dawn opulence of stars. She wore a frown, a worried look, but said nothing so she would not disturb the others in the hut behind her, or any others in the village.

A night fear. Nothing more than that, Eini thought. *There is nothing really here once morning comes. The grownups are right. I am just a silly child with dreams that frighten her in the night.*

She listened to the dark and almost silent village.

But it is still night, not morning yet, she thought. *And I am still frightened.*

She waited, knowing what she would do but first letting the night's beauty calm her if it could. The cool air brushing against her helped, and the stars in their multitude, and the leaves. Trouble and fear from her dreams still were weights inside her, though.

The burning girl. As morning approached, that was the dream that troubled her most. She loved the burning girl, and she felt her agony. The girl, and the wolves—they captured her thoughts, and her emotions. Eini felt them.

But she did not fear them.

No, she did not fear the girl, or the wolves. It was her vision-dreams that she feared. They were dreams that came in mumbled whispers she could not quite hear that spoke of things that might happen in a future she could not quite see. And she feared this one more than any she could remember. She feared it because the shape it showed her, the thing coming toward her through the fog, was so dim and so distant that she could not tell what it was.

Eini's mother would still sleep for some time. Waking to find Eini gone, her mother would worry, but she would also understand what had happened. Eini had done this before, rising early and leaving her hut. Whenever she had a night like this, a vision in the night, Eini woke early and walked.

Usually she walked in the village, among the huts, random walking through the great Téuta village until others woke and came out for the day. By then, by the time the village was up, her night frights had usually faded and she could go back. She did that on this night too. Eini walked first to the river and splashed her face with its cold water to rid herself of the image of the burning girl. That dream did fade a little. It did not completely leave her.

She walked on in the blackness, listening still, sometimes to the breeze or the leaves blowing across the ground, sometimes to muffled conversations of those awake in this new day, sad or sleepy or worried or happy, talking of their concerns, or of their plans for the day, or making quiet, whispering laughter within the privacy of their huts. And always, always in her hearing there was the soft soothing sloosh of the river as it brushed the shore. Eini walked, listening to the Téuta.

Listening to her people. Listening to her home.

Barely visible glints appeared along the mountains to the east. The pure dark in that direction began to form familiar silhouettes of the clifftops and of the peaks beyond. On the peaks there was snow; there was always snow there, although much less in hot years like this one. But still there was snow in great patches along the slopes, and it began to show its mottled coral and gray hints of morning.

Maybe I am not so different, she thought. *The pink, the shadows that show very dimly now on the snow, that is knowledge of the future, isn't it? Knowledge that the dawn goddess will be here soon. Everyone can see the future in that. Can't they? Maybe the dreams I have are no more than the hint that is given by color on snow in the mountains to the east. No more than an outline of the coming dawn.*

People slowly emerged from their huts. The village came alive with the dawn, as though the dawn goddess brought all the village's energy with her in the folds of her clothes. Several times Eini saw adults she trusted, adults who had status in the village, and tried to tell them what her visions had shown her. And as always, they dismissed her.

"What could be a danger to the Téuta?" they asked her. "We are too large; we have been here too long. There is nothing that can hurt us. Go back to your hut Eini, do your chores. Your mother will worry."

But this vision would not fade. The thing she saw so dimly through the fog, the thing that stumbled from the future toward the Téuta, would not relent. And the burning girl too was still there, and the cold river still could not completely chase her away.

It bothered Eini that others scoffed at her visions. But she scoffed at them herself. "No one can see the future," they told her. *And that is truth*, she thought.

But in the part of her that did *not* think, that only felt, she believed that what came to her in the night, her visions, were also truth.

They're also a sort of truth, she thought. *A kind of truth. A part of truth. But what good are they, these things that come in the night?*

Although they seemed to be only mood and feeling, like a whispering breeze blowing through her, sometimes the feeling was specific. And like the wolves that had come to harry the sheep, sometimes it happened. She felt that a crock would fall and break, or that there would be a very large fish in the trap, and then the crock would fall, or the fish would be there. But sometimes the crock fell but didn't break, and sometimes the fish was only large, not *very* large.

And she might say that two sheep would be killed by wolves, and then only one would be killed by them, and another wounded—and the wounded one killed instead by the village for feasting.

Fog, yes, she liked that image; the future is hidden from us by fog. For most of the Téuta people, most of the time, the fog is so thick they can see almost nothing through it.

But for me, Eini thought, *maybe the fog that hides the future becomes thin, and I sense some blurred thing within it.* Then, still walking, she thought, *maybe everyone sees things like that, but they just don't notice or don't know what it means.*

Eini continued, winding between huts, clutching her cloak tight around her. She felt the wind on her as morning rose around her, and the east became brighter. And she thought: *I notice, and that makes me different. But I don't know what it means either. Most of the time I don't. I just notice that it is there. I know it is there, and that makes me strange.*

Eini meandered through the village until morning was well along and then returned to her hut. Her father was already out. He was up on the plateau taking part in the work there. She should be with him. She was not, which was annoying; the winnowing was fun. That was like a big party up on the plateau, with many people working together. Eini would go to do that tomorrow. But she knew that today it was better that she work alone, do chores alone. On the plateau she would chatter about her dreams, and the others there would try to ignore her.

Her mother had made rounds of bread for breakfast, and had autumn apples too, and Eini was glad of both. She was hungry, and mostly happy, after her early waking and her long walk.

But as the morning passed, she still felt restless. Just that: not good or bad about it, or truly afraid anymore, but restless. What she felt from this dream seemed too big, and too strange, for a morning walk to ease it.

"I need to walk again," she told her mother.

Her mother paused and looked closely at her, seeing her unease in her face. She watched Eini for a long moment, then said "Ok."

"I might go outside the village a little."

"OK, but don't go too far away," her mother said. Then, thinking of the events of yesterday afternoon, remembering the wolves, she changed her mind. "No. Take care where you walk, Eini. Stay inside the village."

Eini walked then, distracted and lost in thought. And, like any child, once she was out of sight, she paid no attention to what her mother had told her to do. She was lost in her own heart, in her memory of her dreams, and in the lingering sense of the song the wolves sang to the Téuta. And lost in her fog.

To Eini, the sense of the wolves was happy. But the memory of her dreams would not leave her alone.

CHAPTER 3

Seneks walked barefoot among the oaks and willows and cedars; the ground was warm, and the day, unexpectedly after the morning cold, was also quite warm. Summer was over, leaves were falling and late-year rains had come at last. The leaves under his feet were wet. They were soft and silent under him as he walked. *In a moon, the leaves will be dry and cool, and they will crunch under my feet*, he thought. *In two moons the winter will come. It will be cold then, and I will need shoes and leggings and a heavy cloak out here.*

But today was quiet, and the sun was bright over the trees. With his summer-calloused feet, he needed neither shoes nor cloak nor leggings today, although he had with him the cloak he had worn when he started this walk.

He was not really that far from the village—a slow morning's walk but no more. But neither was he so close that he would expect to hear a child nearby. To hear anyone nearby. Out here gathering herbs, he was almost always alone. Here, the sounds of the village were far too distant for him to hear. Only the forest sounds reached him. So, a child crying softly to herself sounded strange and out of place. It took him some time to realize what he was hearing. Once he understood, though, he took time to look for the source.

He found her, a girl of ten winters, whose name he almost knew after a moment of thinking. It was a name he should know but could not quite find. She was sitting cross-legged among the fallen leaves, her knees high and her arms resting on them. Her chin was down on her arms, and she seemed to be looking into the forest ahead of her for something she could not find. Her face was quite wet with tears.

Seneks knew many of the village children because he was asked often for medicines to help them—or their parents—through some difficult time. This girl he had seen in the village, but she had never needed his remedies yet. *Tall for her age,* he thought. *Both hair and complexion not as dark as most, and with eyes very big and very light blue. Not the greatest beauty, but her eyes will interest the young men when that time comes for her.*

The girl, lost in her thoughts, started when Seneks spoke to her.

"What is your name, daughter?"

She turned and raised her head, sitting straight up to see him.

"I am Eini," she said. "And you are Seneks. You are a shaman."

"Yes." Seneks smiled; she was bold for a child. She was not, perhaps, quite as well trained as she should be in reverence for those older than she was. Seneks liked that. It was a failure he shared with her.

It took her a moment of thought before she realized her rudeness and bent her head lower to honor him. To himself, Seneks might say he was *only* forty-three winters, but he knew that forty-three winters seemed like a very great age to a girl with only ten.

"Are you hurt?"

"No. I mean I didn't fall or anything. I don't usually get hurt."

"Why are you out here so far from the village," Seneks asked her, "And why are you crying? Are you lost?"

"No. I don't get lost."

Seneks again was amused at her boldness.

"Never? Even this far from the Téuta?"

"I don't get lost." She said this with unbreakable confidence. It was simply a truth she knew.

Seneks watched the girl. She did not seem injured, and said she was not. *Something else has happened to her,* he thought. *She is not crying for nothing.* He was a gruff man who did not respond well to stupidity, but this girl did not seem stupid. And he was a healer. It was his instinct to try to fix what he could.

Seneks knelt down, his knees on the soft leaves, dappled sun across them, and across his arm too. The light speckled him, and the warmth of the sun did also, warm where the sun fell directly on him and cool where there was shade.

"What troubles you, then, if you are not lost and not hurt? Why do you cry?"

"I didn't mean to cry. I wouldn't have if I had known you were here. I am afraid, but of nothing."

"Nothing?" Seneks sat, then, just in front of the girl, and crossed his ankles, leaned against his knees as she was doing. "I don't think it's nothing. You don't look like someone who would cry for being afraid of nothing."

"Well, maybe it is something. I mean I think it is not only being afraid that makes me cry like this, it's that I don't know what I'm afraid of. If it's something and not nothing I don't know what the something is. I think I was crying for not knowing. But it's silly to cry anyway. A silly child's reason for crying."

"Everyone cries sometimes Eini. That's not so silly."

"Well, but I am a silly child. Everyone says so."

Seneks was not sure she was joking, but he came very close to laughing at that. He kept his laughter inside, though, because he didn't want to seem like the 'everyone' who said such things to her. He was learning very quickly that he liked this girl.

"When did you start feeling this thing you cry about so far into the forest?"

"Early today. I had a—a dream."

"You don't—" Seneks was going to say *you don't look like someone who cries about dreams*, but he looked closely and was not sure that was true.

"A bad dream, then," he said.

"Very bad dream. I call it a dream. And very bad, I think. I'm not sure."

"But dreams fade away in the sun, child. They do you no harm, do they?"

"My dreams do. Sometimes they do. Sometimes my dreams happen really."

A long silence followed that. Seneks tried to decide whether she meant that, and whether she was crazed if she did. And also, as another more distant thought, whether there was anything true in it. As a shaman, he had seen many things that most others couldn't see; he had, in earlier years when he was still awed by such things, spoken to gods, and to the dead. And he had met others, not just shamans, who could sense special things, although most of the time they didn't know they could do that. Their sense was too gentle, or too fleeting, for them to treat it as real. Those who had such senses often dismissed them, or ignored them. But Seneks never did. When he met someone like that, he listened to them.

"What did you see in your dream?"

"I don't see the things."

"In your dreams you don't see things?"

"In these dreams, the true ones, I don't. Mostly. Usual dreams I do. In the true dreams I just know something is there. A future thing. Sometimes I know futures when I am awake, little futures, and near futures. But even then it still seems to be dreaming."

"What kind of things?"

"Like now, I know that is not a good way to go," and Eini pointed through the forest, toward the path that Seneks intended to take back to the village. The path led to a dry creek that, during heavy rains, sent water to the river, and walking down it was steep but not really hard. Coming up that way, though, was a venture for the young.

Eini was still pointing. "I came that way, but it isn't good now."

"Why not?"

"I don't know. I just know it's not good."

"But that was not your dream last night. What was true in that dream?"

Eini was quiet, clearly nervous.

"What is it? Is it something you can't say?"

"Don't laugh at me if I tell you."

"I never laugh at girls I find crying in the forest."

Eini looked to see if he was mocking her, but he seemed completely serious. There was no part of a smile on his face.

"Ok. I will tell you. Something will happen, or is happening now but it will be happening for a long time. I can sense it there," and she started to point before she realized this time there was nothing to point to. What frightened her was the future, and that has no direction or every direction. Sometimes there was a direction to point, as there was when she pointed to a close danger, one in the near future. But the thing that frightened her now was distant, and strange, and had no direction.

"In my dream from this morning everything is different than it is now. Or *some* things are different, not everything. It will be hard for us. It will be cold."

"Yes," Seneks said. "It will be cold, of course. Soon it will be winter, and there will be snow. There will be ice on the river."

"No, not that. Not *just* that, I mean." She paused. "Or maybe it is that. I don't know." Another pause. "I wish I knew, then I might not be afraid of it. Even bad things are not as frightening if you know what they are. To me, anyway."

And a pause again, her face drawn close and frowning as though she were peering hard into a dark space.

"Sometimes I will be hungry. *We* will be hungry. I know this. I know. Maybe I am afraid of that."

"We—you mean I will also be hungry? The two of us?"

"The whole Téuta, I think. More, even, everyone on the mountain. All the mountains."

Eini paused but looked like she was not finished. Seneks waited for her.

"And after that something else, something worse, something terrible, but the cold thing is hiding what is behind it."

CHAPTER 4

गा

Seneks rose and held his hand to her.

"I am finished here; my sacks and skins are full of what I need. Let's walk back together."

So Eini stood too, and she gently pulled him away from the way that was no longer good to walk in. Seneks smiled, but humored her, and took her back the longer way, back across the more overgrown path he had walked to find her. By this path, it would take them until evening to get home, but he was enjoying her company.

Along the way he did find a few more things to stuff into his bulging sacks, and when that happened, Eini waited patiently and watched. Their walk was pleasant, and cool, and Seneks was affirmed in his judgment that Eini was not stupid. After the first time he found each kind of plant to collect, she would sometimes point to the same plant growing in other places along their path. When he saw that, he thought she might take an interest in healing, that perhaps he could teach her, that perhaps she might even become a shaman. It would be an unusual ambition for a young girl, but not impossible. Of course, she was a bit old to start that training. She was a smart girl, though. Maybe he could mentor her if she chose to do that.

But when he asked her about it, she told him she wasn't interested in shaman stuff, speaking to dead people and all the other things.

"Oh. What interests you, then, Eini?"

"Stories."

"Stories?"

"Yes. Old stories. About where the Téuta came from and stories like that."

So he spent their time on that walk telling her what he knew of those. While they spoke about these things, her fears evaporated, and she seemed light, full of wonder and energy, walking with her eyes seeing everything. She was odd, perhaps, with her dreams, but he enjoyed her company. Maybe he enjoyed her *because* she was odd. Odd and smart was always a fascinating combination to him.

When they had descended to the river's edge, the burble of the water quieted them. They walked for some time listening to it, both deep in their own thoughts.

Then Eini stopped. Seneks still walked for a short distance before he realized she was not beside him. Then he turned back. She was twenty or thirty steps away, looking dazed and again a little frightened.

Seneks walked to her and drew her to some rocks they could sit on, near the water where, if they wished, they could put their feet into the river after their walk.

"What is the trouble Eini?"

"I lied, or I mean, I didn't lie I just didn't say everything."

"What didn't you say? Something from your dream. That's right? From your dream?"

"Yes."

Seneks waited; he had found that sometimes silence was as good as a question. In this instance, it was more than as good. Her face showed last night's fears, and she spoke quickly.

"The farthest thing, the thing that was hiding behind the cold, felt like it wanted something. The true things in my dreams don't want anything, they *never* want anything, they don't know enough to *want* anything. They just are showing me they are there."

And then: "But this one seemed different."

Seneks did put his feet into the river for a moment, to cool them, but a moment was enough in water as cold as that. He waited again.

Eini spoke then. Her thoughts flowed from her then as though they were poured from a spouted crock. She told him much more about her visions and her dreams, and about the wolves and how she liked them, and all of her day before her visions. She talked about the burning girl, but she left that topic quickly. That was not where her thoughts were. That dream was just a dream, or so she thought it was just a dream because she could see the girl. She wanted to forget having seen that.

So she kept to the thing that she truly found disturbing: that something in her dreams, in her visions, felt like there was desire in it, that it saw something it wanted, and that what it wanted might not be a good thing for the Téuta.

"What did it want," Seneks asked? "Can you tell in your dream what it wanted?"

"No. No. I can't tell. Maybe it wanted the end of the Téuta. Or maybe it wants not-the-end of the Téuta. That's what it felt like. I mean the last end, nothing after. It seemed like that, anyway. But it was so far, so I don't really know. But it frightens me a little. I guess that was what I was afraid of in the forest. My dreams never have frightened me that much before, so I'm afraid of being frightened."

"The end of the Téuta." Seneks looked hard at her. She still did not seem crazy. He wanted to dismiss what she said and was sure that anyone else *would* dismiss it. The end of the Téuta? But with Eini beside him, seeing her face when she said this, he couldn't make himself dismiss it.

"What is this end? A fire? A sickness?"

"I don't know. I can't see, the cold stuff is in the way. And also, I usually don't know very much about these things, just good or bad usually. But not a sickness I think. Maybe fire, I did think about fire yesterday morning. But I don't know."

"But next year, or after?"

"I think much longer. After many winters."

"Then there is time to change it."

"I don't know. Really, I don't know what happens I just know—I— I guess I don't know what it is I know. I know to warn people, but of what? What are we supposed to do?"

Eini shook her head hard then, her eyes closed and her hands made fists in frustration. But that passed after a moment. Then she went on.

"And maybe, what you said about changing it, but I don't know. Sometimes there are other paths, like today, one path is a bad way but there is a different path that is not."

They sat quietly then, listening to the river, and watching the day. Seneks was soothed by it. But when he looked at Eini, it seemed again as though she were close to tears. One hand was holding tight to the other.

"What is it, child? Why are you tense?"

"I don't know how to go now." She turned to him. He was the first grownup that had ever really listened to her when she spoke about these things. She was not sure how to tell him. "I don't know the way," she said.

"The way? The way to your hut?"

That brightened her a little. She half-smiled and looked at him as though he were making a joke.

"I know how to get to my hut. Of course I know that. I know how to do my chores, how to sleep and wake up. But then what? What do I do then, after that?"

Seneks realized she had been wondering about her frightening vision. Wondering what she should be doing to make it better. A bigger wonder than that, really: this tall, thin girl of ten winters wondered how to *live her life* to make that frightening future better.

Now he truly wished that she would consider being a shaman. But this was not the time to ask again.

After a long look into the river, he said, "Maybe there is a way you haven't seen yet. And maybe it is not something for *you* to do, maybe someone else has to do it. You say it is far in the future. Futures change, don't they? Things happen to change them."

Eini looked up at him as though he had said something important and clever. He didn't think he had, but it seemed to raise her spirits further.

"Chermesh," she said.

"Chermesh?"

"She is a friend."

"Yes, I know Chermesh. She brought me a bird once, an injured bird, asking me for help with it. An interesting girl. Who brings a bird to a shaman?" Seneks thought quietly for a moment. "She is your friend?"

"Yes, a friend, and sometimes she makes things seem better. Maybe she can make this better."

"Maybe so."

"And the other girl too. The burning girl. From my dream."

Seneks said nothing to that. The other girl was just a dream. But she was *Eini's* dream, and Seneks knew that her dreams mattered to her. He said nothing.

They stood then and continued their walk home.

The village when they returned seemed surprising because it was utterly normal, with busy people and resting people and cooking and walking, as it always was this late in every day. It also seemed hotter than the forest, because the sun warmed the ground and the huts.

It was ordinary. But after the walk through the dappled forest together in each other's good company, and after Eini's confession about dreaming the Téuta's end, ordinary was surprising to both of them. The late afternoon sun threw long shadows across the bright rosy white of the cliffs, making the carvings for the dead stand out.

For the first time today, Seneks saw Eini really smile. Her fear seemed to have left her during their walk.

Seneks was busy for the next two days tending to some sneezes and coughs in the village. In a moon the autumn would be full of them, if they were starting this early, so he again walked along the path he knew well, gathering bush leaves for tea, and honey where he could find it. At the day's end he hesitated before returning along the shorter path to home, remembering what Eini had said, that it was not a good way. He smiled and shrugged it off. A little over halfway back to the village, he paused and backed up. He had noticed an odor he knew well in the brush between trees, well off the path.

It took some time to find it, but it was not a surprise: he knew it would be there. The evidence was strong even on the path, and the sounds and smell grew much stronger as he got close. Meager remains of a deer carcass lay there, bones mostly and some hide, but buzzing with flies. The bone was fresh. The deer had been savaged by wolves. From the look of it and the smell, this had happened only two or three days earlier.

Strange. Wolves don't often come so close to the village, he thought. *They are a danger seen more on the plateau where there are fewer people and more sheep.* But they had been close the night before he met Eini, and clearly they did visit this trail not long ago.

Seneks walked on, more alert now, less sure about walking alone through this seemingly peaceful place—and also thinking long thoughts about the smart, brash girl that he had found crying in the forest, and who had warned him away from this path home three days earlier.

CHAPTER 5
SPRING 6161 BCE

W inter came and left for the Téuta, offering mild snows and cold but gentle days. Birds of a kind they had not seen before became common in the skies. Their cries were strange to the Téuta. Despite last year's good harvest and the gentle winter, many in the village felt an edge of wonder, of change—and for many who were open to such feelings, foreboding.

These last found support in news from distant places.

At the festival in the spring, Eini heard Seneks speaking with some of the Kujoté, two men and a woman. Eini had really never thought very much about where the forest people went in the winter. She just knew they went south, down the mountain, but that had little real meaning for her. They were somewhere in the forest nearby. In the summers, they came to the festivals at the start and end of the summer's work, and that was all she really knew about them.

The conversation was in the Kujoté language, so Eini did not understand what was said. But to Eini they looked intense and concerned, and people were gathering to listen. These wanderers often brought stories about events beyond the mountains. She liked stories, so she wondered what they were saying that was so serious.

Eini looked around for someone who could translate for her, and found two of the older Téuta women, including one who had lived among the Kujoté for many years. The last of these, who knew the forest people well, had been there through the whole conversation, sometimes taking part, but she didn't mind talking to Eini.

"They are saying there has been a big flood," the woman told her. "Very big, with many dead, entire villages sinking in the water."

The woman paused to listen for a time. Eini was getting frustrated listening to the long conversation, and thought she had been forgotten, but the woman finally continued.

"They said there was a wonderful lake far to the west, so big no one could see the other side of it. There were villages along the shore of the lake, villagers whose lives had been easy with so large a pool of fish to feed them. The Kujoté themselves have not seen these things, but other groups like them, groups that wander and do not grow grain, have seen them and told the Kujoté about them. This winter those others were frightened by what they had seen."

Seneks asked something then. The Kujoté replied to him, and Eini's translator explained what had been said.

"These new birds we see here are common near the lake, the Kujoté say."

Again the woman paused to listen, but resumed quickly.

"Over this winter the water in the lake rose very high. It flooded all the villages that were close to the shores. Some villages were drowned in this great flood, but for all of them their huts were soaked and sometimes covered by the water, their fields were flooded until they were under the lake. The villagers had seen floods before. In the past there had sometimes been floods after heavy rains; we know about that even here. Even the Téuta has seen floods when the rains are too heavy in the mountains above us."

A pause to listen, then the woman, moved by what she had heard, continued with more emotion, and more eloquence:

"But normal floods recede, and the land comes back. This one did not. Those villages, those fields, are still under the lake. Villagers, expecting the rising water to stop and then recede sometimes waited until the water was deep inside their huts before they left. And the waters rose high, so high that the huts these villagers had built were now filled with it, and with mud, and with swimming fish. Their hearths were now in deep cold water. Places they had used for meeting, for feasts and other gatherings, even places that were sacred to them, were swept away or buried as the waters came, relentless and deep."

Eini listened carefully, wrapped in this news. She saw Seneks looking over at her.

"Some of the wandering clans who had made camps on land too low had to pick up what they could and move inland; but for them it was easy. They were used to moving. But the villagers who live always in the same place have lost that skill."

Seneks was frowning, listening still, thinking his own thoughts.

The woman continued."Some villagers had travelled inland, some had sought help from the wandering tribes and learned to live not by farming but by wandering in the world; in truth the wandering people do not understand why the farmers had ever chosen to do anything else. But now, at the end of the summer with all of their grain fields under the lake, many are hungry, and many are desperate. Angry. There are sometimes violent fights among them."

People in the Téuta were troubled by these stories told by the Kujoté. The spring festival was more somber than usual. And Seneks came to Eini late in the day to ask her what she thought.

"Is this what your dreams told you? That this would happen?"

"Maybe," she replied. "Maybe this is part of it. But not all. There is something else. This has happened to others, but something in my dream is about the Téuta, I think."

"You think—you don't know?"

"I never know. Not exactly. I just see that there is something in the fog."

But it was spring festival, and there was food and beer, and the joy of the feast overcame all dread.

Summer was sweet that year for the Téuta, nestled so snugly far above these troubles. It was sometimes hot, but not unbearably hot on the mountainside where the village was, and in the early part of the day it was shaded by the great cliff with its carvings for the dead. Rains came frequently that year to nourish the wheat and barley, to fill the basins with water for the sheep and goats to drink. Harvest was plentiful. At the end, after the threshing and winnowing, every hut had a store of grain to last through the winter and spring, and the large common stores were also full to their tops.

Life was good for the Téuta that year, and the Kujoté said that even on the flatland below the mountain all was still well.

For some in the west, the Kujoté had told them, life was not good. For them, life was hungry. It was brutish, and filled with sometimes terrible violence among the people. The Téuta believed their friends. Yes, they believed. But these things were happening far away. Far, far away, near water the Téuta had never seen, among people they had never met. These were sad stories, even frightening stories. But they were not the story of the Téuta, or of the Kujoté either. In the fall, the Téuta and their wandering friends celebrated the year's good harvest. They ate their fill, and drank festival beer, and went on with untroubled and bountiful life.

⊓⊦ ⑴ ��

Winter passed, and the next winter. Each year was peaceful for the great village, but each spring the Kujoté returned with news of desperation and occasional violence in places the Téuta had never seen. To the north, the Kujoté said, there was wide land beyond the mountains, and the flooding in that place had been as bad as it was around the big lake. There was no news about any people to the north of the flooding, so the Kujoté didn't know if anyone lived that far north. But on this side of the floods, the rising water was still drowning villages and pushing their peoples south. Some of those people, the Kujoté told, fought with other villages to take their fields, or if not their fields then the grain from their fields. And the violence, they said, was nearing the steep hills, and even the mountains. Villages on the northernmost mountains had been raided for food, and many killed.

These stories still seemed like fables to the Téuta. They were still a distant problem that others must face. Nothing had changed around them other than the new birds. Those had caused some worry the first year as the people wondered why they came, wondered if they foretold some trouble. But no trouble came to the Téuta, and as the years passed the numbers of the new birds dwindled, so the Téuta decided that they had been a good thing. Summer in the village that year was still peaceful, the crops of grain healthy and the harvest sufficient.

Winter came; the snows were heavier and the winter colder that year. But Eini liked that. Snow cleaned the world. That year, ice formed more often than in past years at the river's edge and over puddles across the village.

The next spring was Eini's thirteenth, the spring after her thirteenth winter. It was the year she became an adult.

Eini's visions remained with her, sometimes coming to her in the night, but with waning force as time passed. She became used to them, so they didn't trouble her anymore. She never again dreamt of the burning girl. And doubt seeped into her, about what they all meant and even about whether they meant anything.

All of that, she started to think, was only childhood. Nothing was special or different about her, she told herself. They were just a child's dreams.

And, too, she took Seneks' remark on the day they met into her as reality. She held it. If her dreams did mean something was moving toward them, whatever it was still was far in the future. It was not really her worry yet, even though she was now an adult. Let it be a worry for those who were older. For those who had long responsibility for the Téuta, who might find a path away from whatever it was. *She* did not have to find every path for every single Téuta.

Eini was busy with her new adulthood. With new tasks, or at least with new expectations for her to take her share of larger tasks, although the tasks themselves were not new to her. She knew already how to do them. She was already very good at the work in the communal garden, and was a good spinner of threads and a good weaver once the threads were made. She had gone to the plateau with her father after harvest to spend weeks threshing the grain and then winnowing to clean it. She had not tended the large fields of grain, or the animals on the plateau, as much as some others. But she had done that sometimes, and she could learn more about that too. Nothing was very hard for her to do.

And she felt the changes in her, and in the world, which suddenly seemed bright enough to distract her. New interests captured her. For Eini and all the friends of her childhood, the spring festival, a warm and nearly cloudless day, was a new playground filled with games they had not played before. Eini danced a swirling dance in the afternoon that made her a little dizzy. She danced with food and beer and youth and laughing windy sunshine in her.

The day after the feast, after the festival beer, everyone in the village slept late. Eini still felt full, and still felt sleepy after a late night, her first festival night as an adult, and also still happy. She walked in the early morning to wake up. In the distance, between the mountains she could see, there were clouds building. Maybe it would rain. That would be good. The wheat and barley up on the plateau always needed it.

CHAPTER 6
SPRING 6159 BCE

Through the village, up the steep slope of the dry creek bed near the village and into the forests she walked, as she often had as a child, not for any purpose except to walk free and to see what was around her. She had no hesitance in this; she knew the forest well, and was always aware which ways were safe.

After a time, she knew where she was going. There was a place she knew where the trees were thinner, where the sun could reach through the branches above to reach the ground. The place where she had first met Seneks. A good place, and a happy memory for her, since Seneks had become a friend in a way. He was so much older, but a kind man and full of knowledge she found interesting. In that more open place the sun would warm her pleasantly in the cool of the forest. As she walked, the memories of the prior afternoon's music, the songs and drumming in the festival, and the dancing in the afternoon sun, all came back to her as an exhilaration. A few times she stopped to dance with closed eyes to the memory of yesterday's music.

The joy—and the beer—of the prior day, her first spring festival as an adult, filled her enough to dull her warning sense a little. But enough remained of it to keep her on the safer paths.

When she reached her sunny break in the trees, she sat. She leaned with her back against a flat-sided rock, the spring grasses thick under her. Eini's mind was full of many things, of the sounds around her, of young men, who increasingly and pleasantly occupied her mind, of her mother who by now probably sat stitching hides together in their hut. That last thought reminded her she should return soon to help with anything that needed her help.

Chores. Yes, there were things to do, even the day after festival. Soon, as spring became warmer and the plants began to show themselves, she would be expected to help with the peas and lentils in the small garden near their hut, and also now to help more fully in the larger community garden farther away. She would be expected to help with that and preparing skins, and to go again with her father to help with the harvest in the fall. But it was hard to remember that with the sun on her skin and the contrast of that heat with the cool rock behind her, and the tall trees around her. Nothing was urgent for her, with all the Téuta being lazy and sleeping late on that day, and with spring rising up around her.

The drowsy morning, the warm sun, the morning insects zuzzing their busy way through the grasses, through the trees, and the more distant birdsongs, felt too sweet to give up so soon. It had taken time to get to this place. Eini was reluctant to leave it. She sat thinking, dreaming really, but good dreams, joyful dreams, with images she could see. There was little danger to her, even this far into the forest: she had still no sense of danger nearby, and if that changed, the village was close enough if she went back through the creek-bed.

Eini did not intend to sleep so far from home. But she let her eyes rest, listened to the breeze in the branches, and that was all that was needed on a warm morning. Her waking dreams continued as sleep came, quiet at first, with the wind-sounds and the buzz of spring around her, and the branches above her dappling her eyes with sunlight as the wind pushed them one way or another. She heard, in her sleep, all the sounds of the forest. She heard the creaking branches and the air moving through them; she heard insects moving in leaves now richly molding after the winter, and squirrels, birds, and also what, in her sleep, she imagined might be a fox rustling in the brush. This last interested her but did not rouse her from her sleep. She liked foxes. Foxes are luck, she thought as she slept; they mean good things to those who see them. Maybe even when we see them in a dream. Or maybe it's even better if they come in dreams.

Through the long warm morning, Eini dreamt and kept dreaming.

As the sun rose far overhead, the sunlight was dimmer, as though evening had come early, and her dreams turned darker. The ebbing of the light disturbed but did not yet wake her. It was rising noise that finally opened Eini's eyes. The forest smelled sharper and wetter than it had when she had come, and something which she could not identify felt strongly of danger. It had no direction, not this path or that one; it seemed to be everywhere, under the earth and in the now more vigorous tossing of the treetops overhead.

A storm was coming, Eini realized as wakefulness came. A storm was almost here, in fact, and would be over her very soon.

If Eini's eyes had opened when the sun was just overhead, or just past overhead, she would have seen what was coming in time. But by the time she was fully awake and aware of her surroundings, the gusts were already bending trees, and sun-bright lightning was far too close. It was almost on her. Her senses were suddenly full and alert, with danger over her and under her, and in all directions. There was no path she could feel that would avoid it. No direction was really safe. The village was close, but not so close that she could get back before this storm came to her.

Suddenly she was very slightly, but distinctly, frightened. She rarely came so close to danger.

But I was dreaming of a fox, she thought. This should not happen now. Foxes are luck!

Eini looked around for some shelter. Trees might provide a shield from the rain, but they would not be a certain defense against the lightning, and if the winds were strong enough, they might also drop broken branches, large and small, around her.

Standing where she was seemed very wrong, though. She moved into the forest. She moved in among the trees because that thing inside her that moved her toward the safest path told her to. Now, though, it was not toward a safe path. It was toward the least unsafe one.

She didn't run—what would be the point? Toward what, or away from what, when danger was in every direction? She did not dawdle. She set out in a direction away from the village, since that seemed less wrong than any other. She had not moved more than a fifty steps, though, when the rain came down like a waterfall, and the dim afternoon was suddenly dark—and then so bright it was white; it was like standing inside the sun. Behind her there was a crash so loud that it nearly knocked her down. Eini dropped to a crouch and covered her head, but a second sound came a moment later, something striking the ground behind her. When she looked back through the trees, she saw a branch the size of a small tree lying, still rocking and steaming slightly, all across her resting place. It had not come down directly where she had been sleeping, but it was very close to it.

Eini felt the pounding in her chest and her breaths, deep and fast, and she realized that she was feeling something she did not remember ever having felt before: fear. Real, immediate, tremulant fear. Fear for herself. The sense that had always turned her away from danger was gone.

She stood again, watching the wind as it rose high among the trees, with whole treetops bending in heavy gusts. Then, afraid of going but more afraid of staying, Eini walked into the forest. Soon she was walking in places she had never visited, among trees she had never seen, all wild and tossing above her. Trees and brush leaping and twisting, frantic and wild, was all she saw around her. She had followed no trail to where she was. From the evidence of her ears and eyes, the deeper woods seemed safer. The sounds were less deafening and the lightning less bright. But no matter where she went, Eini knew it was not really safe. And she was cold. Even in the deepest forest, she was wet, soaked by the rain.

Her sense had not deserted her entirely. It still drew her toward the least dangerous path—and that path almost always led away from home, away from the Téuta.

Afternoon storms that came quickly were often over just as soon, creating sudden havoc as they moved across the land, then passing on to create havoc elsewhere. Eini hoped this would be true, and the storm would pass. But it did not. In her rambling flight from dangers behind her, this one seemed to last forever, loud and terrible. This is a very big storm, she thought. Very big.

In her chest, she felt all the danger of the storm—and the presence of another danger as well, smaller, perhaps, but unnamed.

She had seen storms as strong as this one before, and even enjoyed them—but always from the doorway of her hut. Then she had been inside, where the sounds were softened, not out among the trees, where every gust, every crack of wood, carried threat, and where her own foot-steps sounded loud and uncertain in the deepening mud. Each moment demanded a choice of direction in a forest without direction, tall trunks closing in on all sides. Often, when she chose the least dangerous path, lightning struck or a violent gust tore through the branches somewhere just behind her as she walked. Once she saw a fox—perhaps the same one that had entered her dream that morning—trotting down a path Eini sensed was dangerous. After the sharp sound of a falling branch, she saw it again, running hard the other way, toward a direction that felt slightly safer.

The trees were shelter, but not nearly enough in rain as hard as this. Very quickly the upper branches were soaked, shedding water around her as she took one path and then another, searching for a place that felt safe. Twice she found small nooks that offered some shelter, less threatening than what surrounded them—until she drew near. Then they changed. As she approached, they resolved into danger, almost shouting it, and she moved on.

At times she ran for short stretches, to keep warm and to put distance between herself and the danger she felt behind her, but running meant dodging branches that sprang up without warning. Most she sensed before she saw them; twice, they struck her painfully, once near her eye and the next leaving a gash along her arm.

Streams of water flowed downhill across ground that had seemed level before she noticed the runoff. Eini saw this, and after that she took paths that led upward when she could, walking rather than running when that seemed right, hoping to find places that were not only safe but drier, places not turning into mud. As she walked, she realized that the ground tilted more, and she was walking up into the steeper hills. The danger from the storm began to seem smaller as the ground rose. Eini had never before been this high, or this far from home.

The third place she found seemed safe—and continued to seem so as she approached. It was a rocky area on one side, with ground raised above the surrounding forest. Mud would not be a problem there. Overhanging rock gave relief from the rain and blocked the wind. It would not be as warm as a hut and a fire pit, but to Eini it seemed like perfection after her twisting flight through the stormy forest below.

Eini had to crouch to get into the hollow. She clasped her arms close around her for warmth and waited for the storm to pass away, heading southeast toward the river. The other danger she sensed was still around her, but her sense of it was not so strong that it drove her from her shelter.

As she sat huddled in her rocky refuge, Eini felt a tremor beneath her, and then another slightly stronger. She heard pebbles bouncing down the rocks from above. Both the tremor and the sound startled her. She watched some of the pebbles, and a few larger rocks, skitter across the ground, but they did not fall into her shelter. She was still wet, but also still well. Still safe. Still filled with a sense that this place was a haven from danger, even with trembling ground and a storm raging through the forest.

As she watched the treetops below bend like blown grass in the gusty winds, she saw one tree bend and tilt, and then just continue, as though the trembling earth had loosened it on purpose, just so the gusts could blow it over. Then another fell far from the first, and a third far from that one.

One tree, very tall, stood high above those around it. It is the tree we see from the plateau, she thought. It must be. Because there were no trees around it tall enough to block the wind, the storm was whipping it wildly back and forth, but it was enduring, unlike some of the younger, smaller trees. Such an old tree has learned its tricks. It knows how to hold the ground, Eini thought, and huddled into her shelter again.

Late afternoon skies, when they came, seemed less dark than the storm skies had been, and the wind less brutal. From this, Eini knew the storm was moving away. Dazed by her flight and chilled in her shelter, she found herself watching the light around her, curious which way it would turn—toward darkness as night approached, or toward brightness as the storm withdrew. In the end, the retreating storm won. She would have at least a little light for the walk back to the Téuta.

The rain stopped. Eini crawled back out of her shelter and realized it was not as late as she had thought. Evening was coming but was not here yet; the sun was still well above the rim of mountains to the west. But the vision around her made her pause. From this higher place, Eini could see the river curving down the mountain, much farther than she had imagined before this. She could see the tops of the forest, dripping and glinting in the sunlight, the color of day's end shining through them. She could see glimpses of other mountains to the north, mountains that she had heard about but never seen. The land below her on her hill looked peaceful and very green, and silent, very calm and safe after the gusty storm.

The old tree, the great tree, was still standing. It tilted oddly; it was not perfectly straight anymore. But it had not fallen. As she had many times before, Eini marveled at it, and bent her head to honor it. You are strong, and ancient, she told it. The other trees must worship you.

She wanted to stay to watch the sunset from this place. The world she could see was beautiful. But it would still be beautiful tomorrow, and tomorrow she would be dry. Right now she was cold, so hut and fire lured her. After a last long look, Eini started down the hills, using the location of the sun to find her way back to the part of the forest that she knew.

She had covered what she thought was about half the distance home when she saw the fox again. It was lying near a fallen tree. It watched her warily but did not move as she approached. When she was nearer, she saw why: the fox's leg was pressed against the ground by one of the tree's branches. The fox had been digging, and probably would dig again once Eini left. But it looked like the branch had been sinking into the ground as quickly as the fox dug under it.

Eini thought she might be able to help a little. The branch was long, so Eini could hold the end of it without getting too close to the animal. And she was on slightly higher ground. She took the branch in her hands and pulled. At first, the fox reacted with frantic thrashing, so she stopped. But the fox started again to dig under the branch. Eini held the branch back and up, gently.

With Eini helping, the wait was not too long before the fox managed to dig its leg out. When it was free, it moved very slowly, watching Eini carefully. She kept still. A moment passed, and then the fox decided she was not a threat to him. He paused, sniffed and licked his leg for a moment. He looked again at Eini. Then he trotted into the woods and was gone.

Eini spoke out loud to the dark between the trees, to the shadow the fox had vanished into.

"Thank you, fox, for the luck you gave me in the storm."

She meant her thanks. She had survived. She had found a shelter, and no branches fell to trap her leg, or any other part of her. She knew luck had been with her. The fox had been with her.

And the sense she had always carried was with her still.

When Eini walked back into the Téuta, the people were still cleaning debris from around their huts. Eini's mother saw her and yelped with relief, and then immediately scolded her for something, for just being worrisome, for being somewhere else when a storm created so much havoc in the village. But she drew Eini to her, and then, realizing how wet the girl was, hustled her into the hut to get her wet clothes off, and to wrap a warm fur around her inside by the fire.

Eini was an adult now. She had thirteen winters. But mothers are mothers.

CHAPTER 7
SUMMER 6258 BCE

Not the prettiest, Eini thought, *but I am not a goat either.* At fourteen winters, at the end of a late summer day, Eini felt whole. She felt good. She laughed with the other girls, and played her part, glancing at the young men with her great eyes to coax them. She had learned that her eyes were the most enticing lure she had for them. When the young men saw her eyes, they forgot that she was too thin.

For right now there was the feast, and everyone was chatting, drinking weak beer, beating a hollow log that one of the men had brought, talking nonsense to the rhythm just to make music, and waiting to eat. The smell of roasting pig was everywhere. Eini's young neighbor a few huts away from hers, the lean young man Sntodi, had killed a fat boar, his first when hunting alone, although others had been nearby to help him carry it home. He had dried and salted some small bits of the meat and was throwing a grand party with the rest. His status would be higher for the rest of the year. Among the young men who watched her, he was her favorite right now.

Eini's fears from four years ago, from her tenth year, had been at least partly real, she had decided. The years *had* been getting colder since then, not just a little colder, but enough so people were beginning to notice. A single cold year would just be a cold year; some years are colder than others. But for four straight years the winters had each been harsher than the year before. Much harsher. People were wondering if they had offended the gods somehow.

It was not all bad, though. She liked the colder, snowier winters, and the summers were still hot enough. Crops grew on the plateau above them; they had their sheep and goats; game ran through the forest; and fish swam deep in the wide-pooled river. No one was hungry. Nothing really terrible had happened. And of course at fourteen years she had other interests to divert her mind from any fretting.

The dreams had not *completely* vanished. At night, or in calm times away from feasts and playing with friends, when the day was filled with chores, gardening or weaving or caring for her young brothers, at times when her mind had idle space to wander, she had them still, but small ones now about small things. They intruded even here, at the feast, in glimpses just out of reach, just too far to the side to see.

I hate them, Eini thought. *They are ugly pests that will not leave me alone. Tiny hopes or fears, as tiny as the sparks from the fire when a log falls in, tiny little sparks of fear or hope in the air. But like the fire-sparks you just avoid them and then they disappear, and nothing is hurt and nothing is helped. Why can't I enjoy just this one day without them, if they mean so little?*

She had not forgotten her fear in the storm, but a year had passed, and she had not found her sense to be useful since then. The opposite, in fact; it was an intrusion when she preferred to give her attention to other things.

Smoke from the fire rose to smudge the blue of the sky. Eini watched it, in good spirits because of the day, and the sun, and the smoke rising to it. In some small ways she was still bothered by something that was just beyond her ability to sense, but on this day, lifted by music and beer and roasting pig, and with all the young men watching, she could dismiss any vexations.

How can you tell something to be quiet when it already makes no sound? Eini thought. *How can you tell something to go away when it isn't really there, when it isn't even really a thing?*

Finally the smell of cooking meat was so distracting that it overwhelmed every other thought. Eini breathed it deep, and let her breath back out. Then, free from her dreams for this moment, she stood to dance to the drumming, humming to herself, and sometimes, through half-closed light blue eyes, glancing at Sntodi, who was watching her with the hint of a smile on his face, and with his eyes wide open.

CHAPTER 8
LATE SPRING 6253 BCE

"In the forest I spoke with a young man who said that Saurig had only eighty winters in age before she died. And that she had only twenty children, no more," Seneks said. Eini smiled at that. Everyone knew that Saurig lived two hundred winters and had many children, but only two that mattered in the stories: her twins, the one who stayed with the Téuta and the one who wandered. Even the forest people knew stories about them, as they should, since the second twin is said to have traveled with them. It was a legend they shared: one twin for the Kujoté and one for the Téuta.

Eini was happy. The morning was bright and cool enough that she welcomed the warmth from her fire pit. Her son Assa played and made small mischiefs, glancing at her to see if she watched. Sntodi was outside working flint to make arrows and other tools. His skill at that kept him busy many days because others, less skilled, asked for his work. Not just hunters. Those who needed to work with wood or skins also asked him to make axes and awls, knives and scrapers. Sntodi could coax useful tools from a flint core that others would break.

Inside the hut, Seneks was here to talk with her about the oldest of old Téuta stories. It was one of their best and most frequent topics. The old shaman had young Welo with him. It was hard to remember that this young one was still a child. He was very thin, but he was already, at nine winters, taller than Seneks. Taller than many of the men in the Téuta. He was, she thought, embarrassed and awkward about his height, at least with children his own age.

But this child of nine liked Seneks, who had more than fifty winters now, and he seemed to follow the old healer often. He was a curious boy. The work that Seneks did interested him. And also, he enjoyed walking in the forest when Seneks went out for medicines. Often he walked alone in the forest, this strange boy who loved solitude, and loved the world around him.

And like Eini, Welo did not seem troubled about dangers that might be around him. She had spoken to him about this before. He was not like her. He did not know futures at all. But he knew *something* that kept him safe.

Others also sometimes forgot that Welo was a child: he was popular on hunts, particularly in winter, because of his size and strength and because he seemed always to know where the game was. Those who had been out with him on a winter hunt had slowly overcome their skepticism about this. He had an instinct for it, they said. Welo would point, sometimes toward a distant place around hills, and always when they followed his pointing finger they found the game they sought.

The company made Eini happy. The conversation made her happy, because she liked to talk. And a pleasant edge of hunger as she baked made her happy too. It was the smell that made her hungry and made her boy restless. Her son had four winters so far, and he still lived, and was in robust health except for a runny nose at this time of the year. He lived, and would live for a long time still. Eini felt that in her bones. She felt it in her dreams. And Seneks also said so.

The baking smells made Assa active in spite of his spring sniffles. The child was always hungry! Eini was making six flat barley-breads. Three were on the hearthstones already, three were only dough-balls waiting. One flat loaf she made for herself, one for her son, one for Sntodi, one for old Seneks—and two for Welo, who, as Eini knew from past visits, had an appetite like a bear. The first three were for her guests, as was proper, and then she would bake the breads for her family.

Seneks had come with a tea to help with Assa's runny nose, but even more to bring Eini stories of the ancient times. He was her scout for these stories, finding new bits of them from time to time: he enjoyed them, and enjoyed sharing them with her—in part because it was simply a pleasure to talk to her, and in part because she was grateful. She was avid for the old stories, all of them, in all their variations. The Téuta had their versions, but sometimes those told by the shamans were a little different from those told by others, and those told in some parts of the Téuta varied slightly from those told in others. Seneks believed that the versions among the shamans were more right, since the shamans, some of them, memorized these stories word for word from one generation to the next.

The forest people had their versions too, which were even more different. Sometimes they had stories told by other peoples too, other wanderers or other villages, and they had just returned from their winter in the lowlands. Seneks had gone to them, as he did every year, because he knew them well and liked them, and also to see if they had need of his skills as a healer. He had brought some of these forest-stories back to her today.

Seneks finished his story, the version he had heard in the forest. There was a pause while Eini turned the bread, Seneks and Welo letting her work without disturbance. Her son was less considerate. Assa pestered her legs, bumping them as he played underfoot. Eini scolded him—again—for being underfoot so near to the fire-pit. She reached down, picked Assa up, and handed him to Seneks, who received him with calm efficiency.

But Seneks seemed to have something else he wanted to say. When the bread had been turned, Eini looked at him, waiting.

"Do you remember, Eini, the day we met first, out in the forest? The day you cried a little bit because of a worry for the future that you didn't understand?"

Eini remembered well, but she was reluctant to talk about it. She did not want Seneks to remind her of this. Those memories had been and were still a discomfort, so she had pushed them away, and had become accustomed to depending on others to solve whatever problems the Téuta might face. She liked talking about the old stories better. Since that first meeting with Seneks in the forest nine years before, Eini had been curious about her Téuta village, curious about where they came from and how they came to be who they were. She was interested in the stories of the forest people too, but in the Téuta first. Her interest in their past might have come from her worry about what would happen to them in their future, a worry she had carried with her also since that same day. But she had not had that same dream again.

So instead she told stories about the Téuta. Eini loved hearing these stories, and loved telling them to the children, so that they would know where they came from, know what made them who they are. She told them that: "the future is what you have," she would say to them. "It is really all you ever have. But the past is what you are". Then she would ask them: "Which is more interesting to you?"

For many of them that is what made them listen, just that she would ask that, because it was a curious question and they didn't really know the answer, and also because most grownups just told things but never asked anything. At least not anything real.

Neither did Eini know the answer to her question. For nine years, since she was only ten winters old, the past had been a great pleasure, and the future a small worry to her. She *preferred* the pleasure. But both mattered. Each had its own interest to her.

For now, though, the worry was silent. Today thoughts of the future, and even the pleasure of the past, were smothered beneath the joy of the present.

"Yes, of course I remember Seneks."

"Not of course, Eini. You were very young then, a child. It was half of your life ago."

"Yes. But I remember," and she was smiling at him. "It was a great day: it was the day I met Seneks the Wise, a teacher and a healer to everyone and a friend to me."

"Oh—yes, yes, but that is—" and then he paused for so long that Eini spoke again.

"We walked through the forest back to the village together. It was the first time we talked."

"Yes. We did. What you said before we walked, though. About the cold. Do you remember? That you dreamt it would get cold. You said it was the kind of dream that sometimes came true after you dream it.

And now it has been nine years, and each year since then has been colder than the last. The snow is more in the winters. Much more than when I was young. And the summers have less rain than they did. You said we might be hungry, and the harvests are less now. What you said then is happening, Eini."

Eini had given him his bread, very hot, and given two flat rounds of bread to Welo, and both held their bread ready, waiting for her to finish bread for herself and her family. She was quiet as she tended the three new loaves, thinking to herself as she turned them. She gave one to her son, then took one out to Sntodi, then returned. She was testy when she spoke.

"I remember that, Seneks, I never forget it really. I felt it then, and I still feel it, a great thing, maybe a bad thing is moving toward us, or we are moving toward it. Yes, it has been colder. And I feel that it will still get colder. Maybe for a long time. That is what you want to know. Right? You want to know if I still feel that."

"Yes. That is what I wanted to ask. The wheat does not like the dry summers. The barley is better, but the wheat suffers. In the summers we sometimes have to lift water up to the fields from the river, lift it in skins and it is long and very hard work."

Seneks paused before going on.

"Does your dreaming tell you the cold will continue, that it will not stop? This change will not stop?"

"I don't sense a stop for it. But it is just a feeling, Seneks, and I don't feel it much anymore. I don't think about it. I don't know. Everything might be ok, and it is ok right now, right? It is ok, just a little more work. We are ok."

"We are ok. I've heard that there are villages that are not, though, not only the drowned villages north of the mountains, but also villages that never saw that flood. Mountain villages. The Téuta is big, and we have big fields up on the plateau. We are ok. But I've heard that smaller villages are troubled, some of them. For some villages their small crops have failed enough, because of the dry summers, that the cold winters are hard. The Kujoté tell me about them."

"Villages we know?"

"No. I think they are far away from us. Far to the north, on other mountains than ours." Seneks paused for a time, thinking. "I think violence makes more violence. The drowned villages raided to their south, and into the mountains there. Then the villages there became violent in return, against the raiders from the north, yes, but sometimes also against each other. I don't know what is going to happen, Eini, or when it will stop."

Eini didn't want to think about that. She didn't want anyone to be hungry; winters were becoming hard even here. That was always true, but more true now. There was more snow, and game was scarcer. There had been times in the winter or early spring when some of the Téuta were hungry too. She had sympathy for that. But she had no sympathy for the violence. That seemed insane to her.

We can't fix every problem on the earth, she thought. *If they are hungry, let them help each other. Let them come here, work here and share with us. They could help us in the summers to take water to our fields up on the plateau from the river below it.*

For now, the day was enough for her. Assa played and ate not more than a step or two away, and Sntodi worked just outside the doorway. She heard him chipping and striking rocks against flint.

She did not want to think about problems that were so far from her. Spring was here, summer was coming, filled with sun and hope. She wanted to hold hope close for a while and let worry go.

CHAPTER 9
LATE WINTER 6248 BCE

In her twenty-third year Eini found that she enjoyed the nights, or at least the dark in evenings and the dark in early mornings, even more than the brightness of the days. The sudden return of night-fears was a shock for her. She listened to the others sleeping in her hut, to Assa and Sntodi and Juwo, the young man that Sntodi was teaching, the one who was learning flint work. This young man, barely an adult, had a young woman named Ceneta with him, which pleased Eini. The young woman was good company among the plentiful supply of men in the hut, and was a help to her.

Eini listened to all of them sleep, wondering how much of the night had passed before whatever it was in her dream had lumbered toward her through the mists, whispering things she could not quite hear. Even though she had not had such dreams for years she remembered the sense of them very well. Something was coming toward them from the future. The only thing in all of her dreams that seemed to want something.

What do you want? Eini thought. *What do you want from us? Are you the hungry people? Do you want food? But we don't have enough food now even for ourselves and our forest friends.*

She lay in the dark trying to find this thing while she was awake, trying to talk to it. But she couldn't find it, and it would not listen to her. Maybe it couldn't listen to her, or to anything. Eini thought it wanted something, but she was not sure it *knew* it wanted something. Like all the others it simply wandered toward the Téuta through the foggy future as though it were drunk, unaware of what it was doing, unaware of itself, unaware of any want it might have. Simply unaware, of anything.

All the paths, good or not, she thought to herself as she lay, her eyes still closed in the dark. Eini felt them, all the paths from now. Like walking through a forest. Choose a path, a new one at each step. Avoid the tree branches. Find the safe place.

There must be a path to hide us from this thing, Eini thought.

She opened her eyes, but there was nothing to see inside the hut. There was still some light from the fire pit, very little but some. She had not been asleep very long before her dream roused her.

And if the step away from this thing is hard to take and 'us' is more than just me, can I convince others to take it?

Eini had no way to answer the first questions. The answer to the last seemed clear to her: no. No one ever listened when she told them what path was safe. Almost no one. Seneks and Welo. No one else. She was just Eini, just a young mother with one child, the boy Assa, still healthy as a bull, and a second who died soon after birth and so had no name. Perhaps the second child would come again and decide to stay this time. But even then she would still be just Eini, and no one would listen to her dreams.

She rose from her sleep-shelf. She knew what to do after fear dreams: she had to walk her fear away. Assa was young still, just nine winters now, but he was strong, and very independent, and the others in the hut would care for him if he needed anything. So Eini left her hut and walked in the cold night. There had been snow, still deep in the forest but only the depth of a single finger's width in most of the village. The cold in the night had made even that snow hard on top. The walking was easy.

Solitary, cold, and the sky clear and bright with stars. Eini was still walking slowly, a frown on her face and eyes seeing only enough to keep her from stumbling. She was thinking to herself, wrapped in that, when a voice startled her.

"Why are you out here? It's cold."

Eini turned. Assa was close behind her, and might have been behind her for some time before she noticed him. She looked back at her path in the snow, and Assa's steps were on the same track as hers.

"Assa, why are you awake?" Eini looked at her son. Then she looked again. "And why are you outside without a cloak?"

"I woke up and you were gone. I came to find you."

Eini's thoughts disappeared, and her fear with it. Her walk had not helped her, but her concern and amusement about Assa did. She shook her head at him, and smiled, not sure whether to scold him or hug him.

"Tch. You are frozen. Come with me, Assa. We will get you home and stir the fire to warm you."

Eini took the boy's hand and walked back toward the hut. But Assa was young and very healthy. He did not really seem frozen. What seemed very cold to Eini seemed to him to be almost comfortable. It didn't trouble him. He seemed warm even outside; Eini could feel the warmth of him when he was close to her. She thought he might have been running for pleasure as he roamed the village to find her. As they walked he jumped sometimes instead of putting one foot in front of the other.

So Eini walked and Assa jumped, but neither hurried. They found their way back to the hut, and entered, but once inside Eini felt no need to stir the fire up. Assa was all the fire that was needed, even on a cold night. She did wrap her son in a cloak, and kept him with her to sleep, thinking she would warm him as he slept, or he would warm her, but either way she was happy. Assa had, for a moment, saved her. Because he was here her fear had passed. He had shown her in the snow that the present was beauty, and the future was far away.

But as she held Assa she realized without warning that the fate of the Téuta was Assa's fate too. Her dread came back hard to her, and she could not dismiss it. She discovered, very suddenly, that the future mattered to her. Not an abstract thing, not the whole village. Not just the fields on the plateau, and the huts huddled between the river and the cliffs.

Assa. This future might take Assa. And Sntodi, she thought. And Chermesh, and Welo, and Seneks, and Juwo, and Ceneta. Now this thing was not just stumbling toward all the people, if that was what it was doing. It was stumbling toward *her* people.

Without warning she felt the weight of it. The whole of if it was abruptly on her as though it had dropped from the sky. She felt, suddenly, as though one of the great forest pigs was draped around her shoulders.

Hunters needed many men to carry a great pig home. But she did not have many men to help her. This one she had to carry by herself.

Through the years worry had ebbed, and on this night walk with Assa it had vanished for a moment. But Eini knew now that worry would not go away as easily as that. Not tonight. Or tomorrow.

Eini thought to herself, about this future thing, and thought *to* the thing as though it were a displeased god. *What do you want? What can we give you?*

But Eini's mumbling vision would not tell her that.

CHAPTER 10

Bright sun filled the hut's doorway when Eini woke again, and the hut was empty except for her. Sntodi and his young apprentice were outside the door, a short distance from the hut and to the side. The boy was knapping away at flint, chatting with Sntodi and occasionally cursing when the piece he worked on did not cooperate. The apprentice was learning how to work the flint, but he came already well trained on how to curse. Sntodi was working on that—not to *eliminate* the cursing, which seemed a natural part of the work, but toward a softer and gentler cursing, and an acceptance that sometimes the flint did not do exactly as the knapper intended.

Assa and Ceneta were working or playing a little farther off. If what they did was work, it didn't seem to be burdensome, since Assa and the young woman were a contrast to Juwo: instead of cursing, they were both laughing frequently. Ceneta seemed older; at thirteen winters she was an adult, and Assa at nine was still a child, but the difference between them was really only a few winters in age. They understood each other very well, and what they did together generally felt like play even when it was intended to be work. Even when it truly *was* work.

A bowl with grain and fish was staying hot just on the edge of the fire-pit, clearly intended for Eini when she woke. She picked up the bowl, crouched to exit the doorway, and stood upright just outside, feeling the village's busy murmur around her, relaxed and satisfied in the morning of what would be an unexpectedly warm day after the cold of her night-walk. Snow had thinned, so that ground showed through in most places. If the day continued warm, the snow in the village might be largely gone when the night came again.

The cliffs were still in shadow; the day was still young. But Eini had slept longer than was common for her. The shadow would soon be gone, and then the wall of the dead would be dazzling with sunlight, the carvings lit with white and rose on the surface and standing out in contrast with deep-etched grooves that were still dark.

Eini walked to the river as she finished eating. Once there, she washed her bowl, and feeling the warmth of the day around her, she removed her parka, stepped fully into the water and washed carefully but quickly—the day might be warm, but the river was not. Despite the warm sun today, it was still end of winter. And in any case the river's water wound down the riverbed fresh from mountain ice far above, and still felt like ice. Even in deep summer, the water was cold. The bath woke her completely.

When she felt clean enough, she lifted herself from the water and dried herself with her hands as well as she could, then stood in the sun to let the sun and breeze work to dry her further. She was still slightly damp when she pulled her parka over her head and walked back toward her hut. The clean, and the breeze, and even the cold of the river, all felt brilliant on this day.

Streaks of cloud moved across the sky far above the Téuta through much of the day, the whole day warm and good. Sntodi and his young student worked through the morning, but after the sun passed its peak they tired of smacking rocks together—and in any case, the young man had produced a short but very well-formed knife with guidance but not help from Sntodi, and he had bound it into a temporary wood handle. That was enough success for a single day, they decided, so the two men wandered away to try the knife in various uses.

The young man was good at carving wood. Toward late afternoon they returned with the knife now wrapped in a simple bark sheath, and the two of them presented Assa with a small but realistic carved goat made of wood. That his student was as skilled as that in wood was apparently a surprise to Sntodi.

"He is learning the flint, learning how to feel it. Given time he will be good. But in carving wood with a knife he is master, and I am student."

By that time, the clouds overhead were lower and thicker, but still white, and the sun still showed through them and between them. Warm wind from the southwest, and thickening clouds getting closer—Sntodi grunted watching them.

"Rain tomorrow. Good rain, soft rain, maybe long rain I think."

"Yes. Today has been good for walking outside, but rain tonight, or tomorrow," Eini replied. She watched her son play with his new goat in the patchy sun. Then she and Assa went inside to prepare something for everyone to eat.

That night her dreams returned, but not the same dreams. Something big and dangerous, like a great fish in murky, muddy water, swam toward her from the future. But this thing was not the cold, or the one behind the cold. This one was close. It troubled her in her sleep, so that she moved and rolled toward the wall, and thought she must have said things aloud because Assa was shaking her. She rolled back to find him, glad to be out of the dream.

When she woke, she realized that it was nearing morning; still dark, but much of the night had already passed—and Assa was not the only one awake. There was hubbub outside, and a light flickered through the doorway against the ground inside.

What was happening? It didn't take Eini more than the time to open her eyes to understand. The light she saw could only be one thing, and that thing was a terror.

Eini was up almost as soon as she was awake. She grabbed two pots, one large and one smaller, and she and Assa stepped outside. The roofs of two huts not far away were smoking heavily, and one had flames rising well above the walls. There were many people, and more arriving every moment, already busy dowsing the nearby huts and roofs with water. Eini and Assa, and Sntodi, and now stepping through their more distant doorways other people as well, joined the tumult of people running to the river and back with water. The next hours were solid work, and often she lost track of her family in the effort to keep the fire from spreading across the village. Once she found Assa nearing a hut as the wall of the burning hut behind him collapsed, and once she found Sntodi in a similar situation. Both times Eini ran to them to pull them aside. And both times there were burns, some small and others much larger, among them.

And once the thatch of a roof slid down onto her, burning hard. She leapt aside, but the pain was instant and sharp, almost unbearable, and she smelled her burning skin it was so close. The smell might not have been unpleasant if the pain were not so terrible. But strangely, the pain seemed to pass almost as quickly as it came. She ran to the river to immerse her arm. She felt sick, wanted to be sick but could not.

Then, since she could, she returned to work. Sometimes she ran to the river again when the pain was too great; the fires were lessening in the rain, and much of the village was there controlling them. But after each trip to the river, she returned to work with the others.

Raiders had made the fire. They were a recent thing in the near mountains, new, at least, on *this* mountain, as the world became cooler and the summers drier. They were desperate, hungry people whose crops had withered and whose villages had withered with them. Now they tried to gain food—and other things—by violence. They had tried to steal sheep and goats on the plateau, but it was a small group of them. The Téuta people, who lived on the plateau, were enough to dispel and discourage them. But they were angry, it seemed. They had come down to the Téuta village itself to take their revenge.

Luck and weather had been with the village that night. Light rains had started even before the fires did, and became heavier as the night wore toward morning. By the time dawn was full, the fires were out, and the rain came down steadily to quench any remaining embers. The village had done its best, and they were holding the fires back with their efforts, but it was the god of rain and storms who had done the most work. Perkunos had put the fires out.

People far and near, when they realized the danger had passed, sank to the ground exhausted, but also to bow low to thank the gods, and mostly to thank Perkunos, for the help he had given them. They would need to thank him with sacrifices, and with a feast, but later, after they had rested and seen to their injuries.

Eight huts were damaged, and two were destroyed completely and would have to be rebuilt. Eini noted this but found that she was unable to concentrate on it. Assa had a blistering burn on the back of one hand. Sntodi seemed fine. And Eini stood with her arm out, letting the cold rain ease her; she had large blisters down her right arm from near her shoulder to her wrist. She fought the pain as well as she could; she had known pain before, as everyone did. But this pain was very strong. She found it very hard to attend to anything else.

Seneks appeared as though he leapt from the earth beside her, took her arm to look at it, but she shook him off. The pain was too great for any touching, and the rain was already the only relief from it. But also, she wanted to take care of Assa. She herded Assa toward the river. The river's cold, which had been a joy the day before, was now a kind of medicine: she remembered from her childhood that the cold of snow or the river gave some relief from the agony of burns.

Seneks was busy for much of what remained of the night. As light began to show, and the dawn made brazen color along the highest peaks, he finally reached Eini and Assa again. He spread a cold mud across their burns, mud that smelled of honey and willow bark and some other things, flowers she thought, that Eini couldn't identify. The mud, and that it was cold, seemed to ease the pain. He wrapped this in strips of woven grasses to set the mud in place. And finally he made a tea that also eased the pain, and left a bowl of the tea leaves with Eini to help her through the next days.

It took Assa only a few days to heal, and he healed with only a tiny scar. But Eini's burns did not heal as quickly, or as well. Seneks came to her often, and he gave what remedies he could to help with the pain, and with the healing. The final remedy for her injuries that Seneks advised was easy to say but very hard to do: he advised sleep. The tea did seem to make that easier, and for Assa it seemed to work well. But for Eini, nothing really seemed to work, because awake she was in pain, and asleep, the few times she could sleep in the first days of her burn, she had dreams she did not like.

When Seneks finally removed Eini's mud and willow, when she then washed in the river and saw her arm, there were long, rippled and twisting burn scars running from wrist to well above her elbow, almost to her shoulder.

It was ugly, but Eini did not resent it. She was grateful that it was no more than that, and that Assa was safe, and Sntodi was safe, and all in her hut were safe and well. And the village too, most of it, was also safe and well.

But even though the village was safe for now, Eini woke and walked on many nights. The village knew now that the rumors of violent men on the mountains were true. The raiders that night had been badly beaten by the Téuta with its great size, its great numbers. Still, they had come. There was a general alertness among the Téuta people, a general awareness that the raiding people might be desperate enough to return if they sensed a chance.

As Seneks tended to her burns, and then later, she had talked to him about all her fears, but he had seemed unconcerned.

She spoke finally to Sntodi about it. She spoke about the dread her dream pressed into her, because there was no safety from it. Perkunos had helped them put out the fires this time. But if the hungry and violent came again, when Perkunos was not near them? What would happen if they came then? Eini could not find the path to safety.

Sntodi held her, tried to soothe her. He told her, as Seneks had many years before, and had repeated when she spoke to him now: "You should believe there is a way, Eini. There is no good in doubting. You will find it. And we will take it."

Eini let herself be soothed.

But she was not sure a way was there for her to find. And she knew that no one else would even look for one. No one else in the Téuta *could* look for one.

Only Eini could have her visions.

CHAPTER 11
LATE SUMMER 6244 BCE

The weather looked fine and sunny, the prospects good for a cheerful and successful day.

Three times in the early morning Sntodi saw red deer through the trees, but the hunters did not want deer that day. Juwo, with his sharp young eyes, had seen tracks of both deer and bear, and had pointed them out to the group. But neither bear nor deer was their goal.

They wanted pig. That was what they had come so far from the Téuta to find. Deer were easy. They were everywhere. Boar were scarcer, and more interesting because they were dangerous. And for some reason this year they were scarcer than normal.

The men — seven of them, Sntodi, Assa and Juwo among them, and two boys with them — walked as quietly as they could in the forest. The group had walked through the morning, farther and farther from the Téuta, but so far they had seen no sign of pigs. But a boar would be a proper gift, and a proper feast, for the end-of-year festival in the Téuta. That was what they wanted.

It was the time of year when leaves were beginning to drift down from the trees, but those that had fallen were still soft on the ground. Walking quietly was not difficult. The mood was high, with autumn festival only a few days away, so after a long morning of looking they were sweating, and a little muddy, and entirely happy. Whispers and laughter were a temptation. The men had to keep their goal in mind to remember to keep their silence.

Several times during the prior year, boar had been seen in the area where they walked. This year, if there were any boar were in the area they were not showing themselves. They found no sign of them throughout the long morning. After the sun had risen to its highest point and moved beyond that, the day grew hotter; in the shade of the forest it was a little cooler, but the heat was felt even there.

They were watchful, but their concentration was on the ground and forest around them, and deep in the trees it was easy to overlook the changing light. But soon they heard thunder in the distance and increased the pace of their walk. Now they looked for boar, but also for shelter.

They found none before the storm reached them; they were in a forest with no known caves, and none of them knew of hollowed or fallen trees nearby large enough to shelter seven men and two boys. When the storm passed directly over them and the thunder sounded close, they simply sat in the highest and most open ground they could find and covered themselves with their cloaks. If the storm was quick, as usually they are, and rain light, as even at the end of summer it often was, then the cloaks would keep them dry enough.

Rain, when it arrived, came down on them like a waterfall, though. It soaked them. But it didn't soak their good humor. They were happy to be out in the world; they held their cloaks over their heads and joked about the downpour.

"We will be washed down the hills and into the river!"

"Well, we will be clean then!"

"I'm cold enough! I would rather be dirty and happy than clean in the cold river water!"

Laughter and light chatter went on until one of the strikes of lightning hit very close and very loud. That startled the men and quieted them for a moment. Chatter was just starting again when the day grew much darker, and a sudden and angry wind shook the trees around them, making the tops bend and buck.

Then Perkunos sent lightning, getting always closer as though Perkunos was hunting the hunters. But the last the hunters remembered was the loudest. All who heard the burst were deafened. They bent low and covered their heads with their arms. They closed their eyes and could hear nothing.

That last strike, so close it took their senses from them, so loud that they could hear nothing else, split a tree only steps away. With no hearing and closed eyes, they simply stayed still in the storm for the falling half-tree to find them.

Only four of the hunters and one of the two boys returned without injury. One man and one boy were dead. Another man had deep cuts on his leg that the others had bound hard with leaves using the string from his bow. Many had bruises that would take time to heal. On the way back, they carried the dead, and the wounded man walked and hopped, resting his weight on the shoulders of a friend.

Assa and Juwo were only bruised—but Sntodi was carried back for most of the walk, because both his left leg and arm bones had been broken. Seneks was called, and the bones were set as well as Seneks could set them. Seneks did well, very well, but broken bones never healed perfectly, never as they were before the injury. By the year's end Sntodi's bones had set, but his left arm was a little bent, and it was weaker than it had been before, and he walked with a limp. Sntodi found it hard to hunt then, or to knap flint as quickly or as well as he used to. When tasks were necessary, he did them. He ate when food was ready for him, and spoke with those who spoke first to him, and was cheerful. But other than those things, he withdrew into himself.

No one from their hut was dead, which relieved them all. But they lost one part of their household. Only one, but that loss made the whole group different, and a little sadder. Juwo left them. He was not injured, but he also seemed changed by his experience in the storm. He had learned all he could from Sntodi, he thought, and Sntodi did not seem interested in teaching anymore. Juwo moved back to the hut where he had been a child.

Ceneta did not want to go there with him. Something in that hut seemed to frighten her. So Ceneta chose to stay with Eini and Sntodi and Assa.

CHAPTER 12
EARLY SPRING 6243 BCE

Eini sat on the floor near the fire-pit for warmth. Most of the night was still ahead of her, but she had slept a little during the day, and she had gone to sleep when the sun set. Outside the hut nothing was different tonight from any other night; if anything, the night seemed clearer than it had been recently. The night seemed safe.

Dismiss it, Eini told herself. *Live your day; do your work.*

But she knew it was not easy. She knew she could not dismiss it. Her mind was filled with thoughts of Assa, now grown, and of the daughter who had lived only a year, and of the new life she was feeling inside herself now.

Last year had been bad, or it seemed so to her as she thought about it now. So it seemed to Ceneta too. Not all; the early part of the year was happy. Yes, the year had started well. But her dream in middle summer, a terrible dream that, as always, told her nothing, came and went. She spent the rest of summer and the early fall telling everyone to be careful, be careful.

"Of course, of course," people told her.

She said this most strongly to Sntodi, since the dream had seemed to have something to do with him.

"I'm always careful Eini." Sntodi had said, dismissing any thought of real danger.

And that was true. As much as it was possible for him, Sntodi was careful. So after half a moon, Eini dismissed her premonition too. Who could know what the dream really meant? She almost forgot it.

Then her dream thing happened.

Eini knew what it was like to be in the forest when Perkunos came like that. She remembered such a day when she had been in the forest years ago, when she had run through the forest in a storm. But when Eini had been there in the storm, she had seen a fox—and she knew which places were better and which were worse.

In their storm, the hunters had seen no foxes, or none they told about.

They did not know which places were good and which were danger. If she had been with him in that storm, she would have taken him, taken all of them to safety. As she had when she was in the storm so many years ago, she could have taken them path by path to a place where no split trees would fall on them. And she understood at last that *only* she could find such places. Only her.

Her darkest dreams had left Eini then, after that stormy day, and had not returned until now. But Eini did not dismiss them anymore, even if there was nothing for her to do that she could see yet. After the storm, when Sntodi was injured, Eini finally understood—and accepted at last, that her sense did matter, and that the responsibility for heeding it was hers. She could not leave this to others anymore, even if there had been others who believed her, and there were none of those except Sntodi, Seneks and Welo.

And at twenty-nine winters of age, she was no longer a child. She had long been an adult; she was nearing the time when she would be considered an elder of the Téuta.

She took her cloak against the cold of early spring, and coverings for her feet against all the remaining patches of ice on the ground. Then she set out across the village.

Eini had become a more solitary thing after Sntodi's injury, after he seemed to withdraw from life. She found it possible to sleep during the day now, sometimes, but the nights were difficult; it was at night that she felt her difference most. Assa was a man now, fourteen winters, and was often away from her. Seneks did sometimes visit her still. And Welo, too, sometimes took time to speak with her when they saw each other. But much of the time she and Ceneta were alone. Ceneta was still young, and young men wanted her with them. Eini too, had only 29 winters, and many men sought her even with her burn scars. But although Ceneta sometimes was playful with the men who came to her, she did not intend to leave Eini's hut. And even with Sntodi injured, Eini had no interest in new men. Those who came to her for that were pushed away.

So now Eini's dreams were her closest and most constant companions.

She longed for clarity. Always the future was wrapped in fog and fog and fog. Some visions were good and others frightening, but most often the shapes meant little and seemed to have no purpose. They were just there.

It unsettled her, and at night—when the shapes stood out more clearly—it unsettled her most. So in the night, since nothing held her at home, she avoided dreams by staying awake and walking. Often, as tonight, she went far beyond the village. She was a woman, and not the largest or strongest, so it was likely foolish to wander the forest in darkness. But she was safer than most because of what she could see. The paths she chose were always safe.

This night she was not sure.

The walk took her farther than she intended because she was lost in thought, trying to understand her shapeless fears. The moon had progressed across a third of the sky when she looked around to see where she was.

Eini could smell the snow and old, wet leaves, and here, away from the trees, the cold wind chilled her face. Her village was well behind her. Ahead of her, the mountain rose into the dark. She reached a small clearing where the ground was too rocky for trees to grow, and below her, visible in the moonlight, was a valley; she knew that because when she looked in that direction she saw the tops of trees below her. Eini's back rested against a range of rocks higher than her head, and the rocks were cold against her back.

The future she saw here tonight held no hazards for her, but she was troubled, anyway. When she looked down into the valley below, she felt dread nestled there, tucking itself into the folds of the earth. Dread, even though the breeze-filled valley, with its treetops bending gently under the moon, looked to her eyes like simple beauty in the night.

Eini sat and held her knees, resting her chin on them as she watched and thought. What could she do alone, and with a new life inside her? Nothing. She thought about Seneks, about asking him for advice, but she didn't want to bother the old shaman so early, so far before dawn.

Beauty and beauty below her, and also dread, and here she knew that she feared losing the future, losing Sntodi and Assa—Assa!!—and Ceneta and everyone. *Maybe this is only the fright from the storm last fall,* she thought. *They came so close. All their living future was nearly taken away from them. And from me! I am just still frightened from that.*

But I am frightened, and I can do nothing. I need help.
I can't find help.

And then she thought: *why do I always look to those older than me for help? Maybe I should look to the young for that. Maybe I should have always been looking toward the young. The future is more theirs than mine.*

An owl flying low among the open rocks startled her, nearly silent until it was just overhead, and then her heart rate lifted at the unexpected flutter of wings so close. Then in a blink it was gone into the dark among the trees.

CHAPTER 13

Eini came to Welo before dawn and shook his shoulder, the easiest part of him to find in the dark hut since he slept on his side with his knees bent. The woman, still in the full vigor of life but since Sntodi's injury a woman with the feel of great age, shook him softly, and whispered. She wanted Welo to wake, and the others to sleep.

"Welo, come with me. I want you to see something."

Welo rolled a little onto his back, then back again to his sleeping position. To stay warm in the cold of the night, he slipped under his covering cloak. It took him a moment to recognize that Eini was really there, that she had come breathlessly to break his sleep. He had not seen her around the village in weeks. She rarely spoke to him even in the day, and now she came to wake him before dawn. What in the world did this woman want him for with such sudden urgency? Why did she drag him out in the frozen night?

But he understood why it was to him she came. She came because he too was strange. He sensed things that others could not, sensed behind rocks, or hills or forests, with a sense that others did not have, or had only dimly. He was not so different, in a way, from this woman who said she could feel misty fragments through the wall that hid the future from everyone else. Welo could sense through physical walls, and Eini through the wall of time. He might have thought her ability was a result of experience or age, but Eini was not yet thirty winters, and no one else had this, even those much older. For Eini alone, the wall that held back the flood of the future had worn thin, letting her sense what was behind it.

What did she want tonight? She had not yet said what it was, but Welo knew. Yes, he knew. She wanted him to use his strangeness to help her understand something her own strangeness had shown her. Who else would even hear her? The strange came to the strange.

So, against all his need for warmth and rest, Welo rolled to the edge of his sleep-bench, wrapped his cloak around his shoulders, and rose to go with her.

Welo liked to see distant places, and when he could, he often walked far from the village, sleeping in the open. On those walks, he woke with the first dim light. But when he stayed among the Téuta, Welo often slept deeply and woke late—while the cliffs were still in shadow, yet after the rising sun had already brightened the eastern hills to show their color. This was true particularly in the winter or the early spring, and spring had just arrived. Eini had come to him long before dawn, though, so the village was very dark. The other huts around them when they emerged were only blacker patches in the dark. Only a few had doorways dimly lit by hearth-fires within. The air was cold enough that their breath made clouds in front of them.

Welo looked at Eini, asking without words what troubled her, since everything in the Téuta was peaceful.

"Not here. Come with me." Eini walked away with more energy and speed than he would have expected so early in the morning from a woman who seemed old—It was odd, in this dark morning, to remember that she had only twenty-nine winters—but she behaved as though she had been awake for hours. Maybe she had.

Eini walked without speaking out past the last huts and down the river. After a time she turned off to climb the banks up into the forest, and she kept walking, with no sign of tiring and still saying nothing. Welo easily matched her speed, and didn't mind the quiet. He simply enjoyed the night woods as they walked. But when the distance became puzzling to him, he asked her where they were going and why.

"Where are we going, Eini?"

"To the place you need to see."

"This is a longer walk than I expected."

"Hah! A long walk. When I was young I was lazy like you. Now I don't sleep, so I walk."

Eini knew that Welo was anything but lazy, particularly for walking, but on this night she was impatient.

"Why do I need to see this place?"

Eini stopped quickly. Welo almost collided with her.

"You need to see because when I'm there I feel worried. Today I'm worried there, only today, not other times. Maybe you can tell me why it worries me."

"Today—so you have been there already this morning? And then came to get me?" Welo looked around him; the night was only now beginning to lighten a little, and dawn was still not here. These two, Welo and Eini, had walked far outside the village while even the dawn goddess was still asleep.

"Yes. I often walk when I wake early in the night. Now come. It is not far."

But they walked again far longer than Welo expected, into the hills and up them to where the rocks were tall, sometimes taller than the trees. He could see not only the surrounding mountain, but sometimes other mountains through the trees. Dawn had come at last and shown her face, had painted the far mountains as though they were spring flowers, and had gone again, and the sun was well over the distant horizon by the time they reached Eini's destination.

Eini, at last, stopped and turned to him, and gestured at the place around her.

"What is wrong here, Welo? Can you use your sense to see anything wrong?"

There was a rocky ledge above them to the east, and below them to the south was a valley. From where he stood, he could see the tops of the trees that grew there. A short way down the slope was a channel half as deep as Welo was tall with water running at the bottom, one of the many streamlets that spilled into the Téuta's river. This stream must enter the river well below the place where the Téuta village stood, though.

Welo looked at Eini. She was foolish to walk alone here in the dark, Welo thought, without a weapon against predators, and he also had no weapon this morning since he didn't expect to be so far outside the Téuta, but there was nothing he could see that would make her more wary of this place than any other. He closed his eyes to concentrate on his other senses.

He could find no predators anywhere near them. Higher on the mountain, some deer drank at the stream. Spring was old enough that the water ran freely, and the ice was gone from the water's surface. He sensed birds. Things that dig their way along the forest floor under the leaves. But nothing threatened them here.

Eini rocked from one foot to the other watching him. And there *was* something here. Frowning in thought, he cast his senses farther, listened farther, and his strangest sense that was his alone finally did find something that was unusual. In the valley full of a mist that only Welo could sense, something moved that he could not identify. Something was rising from the ground beneath the mist—small, cloudlike puffs, though not real clouds, since he couldn't see them with his eyes. They reminded him of the spray that leaps up when a waterfall strikes a rock and leaps to the air. These things moved strangely. The thing that looked to Welo like mist filling the valley flowed slowly downhill, like a pale river. But these little bursts didn't follow that flow. Once they lifted from the ground, they drifted about on their own, wandering in no clear direction, sometimes even moving against the mist's slow descent. Perhaps it was only the shifting valley breezes carrying them.

He had seen things like this before and had wondered if they were warning him about something, as an omen, but Welo was not an expert on omens. Because he was not a shaman, he could not ask the gods about them. But he could sense these things, and they did give a nervous edge to his mood.

He looked around himself again, carefully, far into the distance. There was no danger. No predators, no people outside the village at this time of day except himself and Eini beside him. He now, having seen these phantoms in the valley, understood Eini's worry. There was no real danger at all, yet around him—especially in the trees below—Welo felt a need to be aware, wary, careful. To stay alert. He told all of this to Eini.

"They come from the earth?"

"Yes, like weeds from the earth, but also maybe they come from higher on the mountain. From farther up. And once they come from the ground they move, and drift. And finally they flow down the slopes, as water does, as the mists do."

"They come down from higher on the mountain?"

"Maybe," Welo said, after thought. "Maybe they just come from the ground."

Eini paused in thought. She didn't want to ask Welo, had no right to ask, for what she wanted him to do. *What are these things?* she wondered. *They have dread in them. Like my dreams. Do these things come from whatever is hiding in my dreams?*

"I think you should find them, Welo. Follow them and find where they come from. We should find out what they are. And I can't walk far enough to chase them now, and anyway, I can't sense the things you sense, I only sense that there is trouble or danger, that they might bring a future that we will not want."

Eini paused again, and since Welo said nothing to that.

"Welo, you are the only one who can sense them. You are the only one who can find where they live."

"I don't know, Eini. I don't mind walking in the mountains, maybe after summer is over, after harvest. After cleaning the grain, when the work slows for the winter. But I don't know that I would find anything. And if I did find anything, what could I do about it?"

"I don't know."

After that, Eini had nothing left to say. She simply turned and walked back along the path they had used to get there, and Welo followed.

They walked back to the Téuta together in silence, each thinking their own thoughts. And until they arrived at the Téutas' river, until they turned and walked upstream toward their home, Welo continued to think about what he had sensed. But the river and the widening day seemed to wash all the wariness away. By the time they arrived at the village, Eini walked without worry, and Welo had nearly forgotten all that he had seen so early in the day.

It was well past dawn. He had work to do.

A moon later, Welo remembered his walk with Eini, and, having nothing to do for the afternoon, he returned to the place Eini had shown him. The things he had sensed, the omens that had frightened Eini in the dark, had vanished. Nothing showed in the valley but peace. He only felt peace, and nothing else.

PART II

Welo

CHAPTER 14
AUTUMN 6243 BCE

The wall of the dead was still in shadow. Beyond the shade of the cliffs, the clean light of the sun stretched wide on an early cloudless autumn morning, bright and alive across all the village that wasn't nestled close against the cliffs. The sun fell across the huts and the hills, and the people were chatting and moving all around him; they gathered into knots in eager, lively conversation. Then the knots unraveled, and new knots formed with new people. They wandered everywhere, clumping together here and flowing freely there, like dry autumn leaves in a swirling stream. Welo sensed them. All around him, the people felt the sun's heat on their skin and were glad of it on a morning well past the end of summer.

Festival day had arrived cool and cloudless, with no hint of the many rains that would come in a moon or two. Welo liked that too, though. He liked the summer sun, and liked the rains in spring and fall, and the cold that came after.

But for now he watched the wall. He watched the shadows moving as the morning grew. Many mornings and many evenings he did this, watching the wall, waiting for the dead that the wall was there for to awaken for day or to settle back to night. Because against all the chattering of the shamans, against the knowledge that they must have, he felt the dead were there. Most of the village felt this, no matter what the shamans said. To Welo, his mother was there within the wall or behind it, and his father, and all the ancestors through the generations before them, a great deep-woven sheltering cloak of ancestors warming and protecting the Téuta—all of this was dozing there until the sun reached the southern face of the cliffs to wake them.

The Téuta around him was a redolent tumult, a morning fresh and woven through with the scents of cooking mutton and venison and pork, and of thyme and onion, of bread and boiling or baking roots, lentils and peas and other things to eat, and also the sounds of bargaining for trades, singing in the distance, children laughing, running, playing at whatever they had invented for a day when the adults were distracted by social babble and some, even so early in the morning, by barley beer. Closer there were floating bits of softer chatter among the younger adults as they teased and tempted each other in the way that young people do. Later, Welo knew from past years, there might be a few fights as the beer took different directions. But above everything, it was festival time. Even the fights were brief and good natured.

The Téuta had again reached the end of the grain harvest, and all the year's crop was clean and stored. And they had also reached the cool, pleasant time of the year after summer and before the winter cold, when people in the Téuta often had time to do as they pleased. Welo sat at some distance from the tumult, perched on a stack of mud bricks beside the hut he stayed in when he wasn't off among the mountains. The hut was becoming crowded, so a second hut was being prepared next to it.

Welo waited for the sun to travel far enough to light the cliffs from the south. There was no reason, he had been told, to believe that the Téuta's many ancestors were any more alert at that time than at any other; the shamans didn't claim that or believe it, and Welo had endured many lectures from them when he was a child bold enough to ask about it. The ancestors lived in the *land* of the dead, not in the *wall* of the dead along the cliff face. But to Welo it seemed right that when the bright sun reached the carvings etched deep into the rocks there, when the white and dusty rose of the rock of that great and ancient work first dazzled each day, the ancestors must feel that and waken to it. The truly great among them were placed near the cliffs, where spaces were made for them there. And, Welo thought, even though the shamans claimed the ancestors lived in some dark and distant land that only shamans could visit, and they could visit only after long ritual and fasting, it was easier to believe the dead ancestors lived in that wall, which everyone could see.

This was also true: in spite of their lectures, every shaman Welo had ever met sat near the carvings when they wanted to speak to the dead. The gods they could speak to anywhere that was quiet enough, anywhere with enough solitude. But to speak to the dead, they went to the beauty of the cliff, as though the carvings there were a channel that guided their voices into the land that held the ancestors.

Welo considered all of this lazily as he observed the festival. He was glad of the warmth of the sun, the social ferment around him, and glad of the cliffs with their carvings for the ancestors too, glad of the slow motion of the light that would (for Welo) soon wake both the carvings and the ancestors. Those things happened every summer day, though. Mostly Welo was glad of the festival, of the noise of it, the food smells, all the joy in it.

He was also glad he was not at its center today. With only nineteen winters behind him, he should be down among the young, teasing and tempting with all the rest. Many lifelong friends or mates were made first at festival time. But the young women there had never seemed to take an interest in him. Some older women did, when he found them in quiet places, sometimes even lonely places, and he had sometimes taken pleasure with those. But most of the younger women thought that he was too tall, so tall he had to bend down to reach them, and also that he was too thin, too bony, and too strange. They, and everyone, called on him for his strength when they needed that, but at social gatherings he felt that others stood a little more distant from him than from each other.

But more than that, crowded places had always made him uncomfortable because of his extra sense that no one else seemed to have. When he paid attention to it in a crowd—and it was hard to ignore — he felt as though he were being pressed hard from many directions. He liked to watch from the outside. He liked people. The people were a pleasure to him, but he liked them only a few at a time. When there were too many too close to him, the discomfort was greater than the pleasure. Crowds filled his senses too full.

So maybe, he thought, *it is not that they stand more distant from me. Maybe I stand more distant from them.*

Restlessness seeped into Welo as he watched the swirling crowd. It often happened at the fall festival. The month before was all work, for the entire village, and Welo tried to do his part in that. When the community work was done, Welo wanted some time alone, and he wanted movement. After the grain harvest, he was loose, with no strong responsibilities in the Téuta.

To Welo, after harvest was done, fall was time for a walk across the world, to places he had not been before. Most of the Téuta spent their lives here among the huts, or in the fields above on the plateau, or ventured only as far from the village as they needed to go to hunt. Welo had learned that there was much more to the world than that.

The sun moved, the shadows moved across the ground; the shadow of the hut he sat beside moved slowly around, at first very long and to the side, and then slowly shortening and shifting more toward the village, toward the cliffs. Welo felt the moment coming. He waited, watching. When it began, the sudden flickers of light on the face of the cliffs, on every tiny roughness in the rock, stark as the sun pushed shadows down and toward the west, almost hurt his eyes to watch. The flickers were so bright after the long morning of shadow on the cliff face. While Welo watched, the small rough places sucked their shadows back into the rock.

Then, finally, when all the easy, accidental shadows had been swallowed by the rocks that made them, the light was full on the cliffs. The carvings were outlined with dark shade in their depths, and white and rose on their faces.

Surely the dead must feel this brilliance. His mind might tell him otherwise, but his mind was not all there was in him. If this cliff is like a channel that helps shamans to cast their thoughts to the dead land, then the stunning brilliance, the eye-dazzling brightness of this display must reach there too. And if that were true, the dead must now be awake. Awake and listening to the festival, listening to the joy of the Téuta.

The day moved on. Eyes adjusted to the new light, to the grandeur of the cliff carvings. The festival continued as it always did. But now it was not just a festival of the living. The dead too, now awakened by the sun, must be watching them, moving among them. The dead too, on this day, were celebrating.

Or so Welo felt. And so he meant to keep feeling, even if his mind and all the shamans in the world argued against it.

CHAPTER 15

Food was everywhere after the harvest, and sheep and goats had been culled for this. Hunters had brought deer, and wild pigs as well. The wild pigs were huge; two or three of good size would feed half the Téuta. And at the festival, beer was in every cup—except his. Welo rarely drank much beer. It dulled his senses, which disturbed him. When he drank too much beer, he could not tell where he was in the world, or where anything else was. That frightened him. He didn't like it. Welo left beer mostly to others.

Joy, though, is contagious. The tipsiness of the others around him, even just after midday, was enough to raise his mood, which was already high as the mountains. He had spent dawn watching the sunlight creep down the canyon from the east. Red first, like fruit or bright stones sometimes, red that colored the walls of the canyon and hid its truth behind the beauty of dawn, the shy, slow beauty of Hewsos, the goddess who was born fresh each day. Later, as it strengthened, the sun cast a brightness, lighting the wall of the dead, which always gave him its own kind of joy. The sun in the full day gave everything its true color, whatever that was. One rock at a time, the highest first, then down, until by late morning the sun was high and the water in the river played with it.

Here. The river in this place played gently in the sun. Welo had sometimes walked far up the river, and far down it as well. There were places higher on the mountain where the river rushed over rocks and through narrow places, with a thunder that might have been play for a river but was far from play for anything that was caught in it.

Where did the river start or end? Those two things Welo had never seen. Maybe it had no start or end.

It must have a start, Welo thought. *It always flows down the mountain, and the mountain does have a top. But maybe it has no end. Maybe the world goes on forever with the river running through it.*

Towards the end of the day, Seneks found him. The old man came to him to speak, and he looked troubled. Welo wondered about the mood he sensed in his friend. Seneks was an unusual friend for a man like Welo. Welo was very tall; Seneks was not. Welo wandered far from the Téuta when he could and the mood was in him for that, but Seneks rarely strayed very far from the wall of ancestors or the seclusion of the shaman's temple, and only to gather medicines. Welo was young, only nineteen winters. Seneks was an old shaman, possibly sixty or more winters.

One thing they did have in common was that they were both solitary by preference. Both enjoyed quiet. Welo kept to himself because of his extra sense, and Seneks was not a shaman with high prestige among the shamans, not well regarded even in his own ranks, largely because he was terse with those he thought too proud. Pride, even arrogance, was a common attitude among the shamans. They talked to gods.

But despite his testiness with the other shamans, Seneks was generally happy, with a hidden humor and a smile that not everyone saw because it was less in his mouth than in his eyes and in the creases there. But today he was troubled. It was a look that, to Welo, did not fit well on the old man.

"What has happened, Seneks, that makes you seem so worried? Why at the festival, where you should be glad?"

There was a long pause before Seneks replied. Before he did, he took a deep breath and let it out. Welo understood. Seneks wanted to talk about something that he should not talk about to Welo. He wanted to talk about shaman things. Things that Welo was not supposed to know.

But finally he spoke.

"Behind the temple is an opening into the cliffs, a cave, not too large, but enough. It's why the temple is where it is. Many shamans, many generations, are buried there in that cave."

"I know. I can sense it."

"Yes, I thought you might. Maybe you can come close to the cliffs later, or tomorrow. I want to know if there's anything you can tell me about the cave that I can't see for myself."

Seneks waited for several minutes, watching the festival with Welo. Then he stood and left without speaking again.

CHAPTER 16

The next morning, Welo walked to the cliff and studied the ground along its base, starting at the Wall of the Dead and looking far in each direction. He looked with his eyes, and with his other senses. He sensed nothing out of place.

Seneks is being foolish, he thought. *Give him a day and he will forget his interest in whatever he thinks has changed about the cliff.*

Even as he thought it, Welo knew that was not true; Seneks would not forget it. The cliffs mattered in ways no shaman would openly share with others. And Welo never spoke about his sense to anyone but Seneks, and sometimes with Eini, and not often with them. The Téuta people thought his sense was a quirk or a fantasy, and the shamans seemed to think it was a threat to them. Only Seneks would talk to him about it. Eini never did, really, although she had come to him in the spring to explore something. She simply knew he was different, just as she knew her own difference—one that troubled her more than his did. Hers had warned her of coming trouble, and the Téuta already believed they had all the trouble they needed.

After nineteen years of crumbling weather—of winters always, always colder and summers drier—everything was shifting. Game moved on. Crops failed. Now and then, the ground gave a tiny tremble.

The mountains, in every direction, were dotted with patches of desperation: the remnants of villages too small to survive where they were, yet too large—or too fixed—to move.

Violence, once far away, had come closer. People so hungry they had forgotten honor, resorted to violence and to theft. And even within the Téuta there were those who took first for themselves and left little for others. There were also raiders, who sometimes came in the night to the Téuta. They scavenged what they could and killed if they had to in order to take what they wanted. Then they left, disappearing into the forest. They had become adept at leaving few traces to follow.

The weather had corrupted these people. What had corrupted the weather? No one knew.

More than once Welo, sensing something moving in the world around the village, had given the Téuta warning of approaching raiders, so that the Téuta were ready when they came. Those who lived by raiding had learned by hard experience not to steal from the Téuta. At least they learned not to raid the Téuta first, and not in the day. Instead they raided others first, smaller villages. And those villages that survived the raids became even more desperate.

Something else was bothering Welo. Eini had shown him something in the spring that had disappeared, but he still thought about it through the summer. In the hills, among the trees, there had been things moving in the foggy world of his extra sense that seemed to herd together, like fish. One day in the summer, Welo had gone to see them again, but they were gone. Still, he wondered about them. And in the days after festival he had found time to walk in the world, as was his habit late in the year.

They were back. The moving things in the cloudiness along the valley floor had been there again, at the same place that Eini had shown him in spring, but now a little stronger than they had been. Welo had returned to the Téuta troubled, wondering what to do about them.

After his return from the mountain, Welo had not wanted to tell anyone what he had sensed. The things in the high valley were bad luck, bad omens, or so Eini said. He thought something bad might happen but had no idea how he could prepare for it. How anyone could prepare for it. Welo had waited nine days before he relented and went to look for Seneks. Because he did know something that others didn't, and it bothered him. He had sensed something no one else could. But it was not in the village; it was outside, in a valley half a day's walk away. Besides Eini and Welo, no one but Seneks would care about these invisible things that seemed so far away from the village.

He found the old man near the carved cliff wall where he went to talk to the ancestors of the Téuta.

"Seneks!"

"Welo, yes, I hear you. I'm not as deaf as that yet. What is it?"

"I need to talk to you."

"You *are* talking to me. But you aren't saying anything."

"Yes. Should I come back another time?"

"No, now is fine. I'm resting, and a little bored. What do you need?"

"You remember on festival day we talked about sensing things, about whether I could sense something that might help us. I don't like to talk about sensing things, but you were right to ask."

"Yes? There is something different about them? The ancestor's wall, or the cliffs around them?"

"No, nothing at the cliffs here. I did look, Seneks, I looked but found nothing different there than any other time. But I have sensed something that I don't understand. I don't know that it is anything important."

"You sensed something? Where, if not here?" Seneks looked around as though a vision would appear in the air.

"I'll show you if I need to, if you think it's important. But you will have to walk half a day to get there, and half a day back."

Seneks sat back, watching Welo.

"Nothing at all was different about the cliffs? Look again as we sit. You sense nothing inside the cave behind the temple? Did you use your sense to find differences in there?"

Welo closed his eyes and frowned, concentrating.

"There might be a change. I try not to intrude there, Seneks, so I might be remembering wrong. There seems to be something missing, I think. Maybe something that isn't there. But that's all."

"Yes. Something missing."

It took some time for Seneks to come to his decision. This was not something he should talk about with Welo, since Welo was not a shaman. *But,* Seneks thought to himself, *Welo can sense it anyway.*

So Seneks spoke, but softly, so he could not be overheard, although no one was near.

"Inside the cave are—were—two pillars of rock, natural pillars, from the ground to the top of the cave. They have been there forever, as long as the earth, maybe. As long as any shaman remembers, as long as there are stories about the Téuta. Just before the festival—two days before we talked—one of them was found on the cave floor, tumbled down. We, the shamans, have tried all we know how to do, and no one can find out why the pillar fell. It must mean something, but we don't know what it means."

Welo stood, paced, leaned against the cliffs with his eyes closed, again concentrating. Then he walked back to Seneks. He looked at the old man, sensed his nervousness, sensed a little fear.

"No one knows you have told me this."

"No. Even I didn't know I would tell you—but no, they don't know, and we should not tell them. There would be trouble if they knew."

"Trouble for you."

"Yes."

"Why did you tell me then? Maybe you should not have told me."

"I know you can sense it anyway. And I think it is important, and I think no shaman can understand it. I thought maybe you could help. I think so again now, after you remembered the something that you sensed that bothered you. I would like to go to wherever it is, to see if there is anything there that I can understand. That a shaman can understand."

Half a moon later Welo came again to watch the troubled valley, this time with Seneks, and that was the fourth time he had seen these things in all of his life. The fourth time—and the third within a single year.

CHAPTER 17

It was a long, slow walk for the old man, and Seneks had been fasting. For Seneks, it was much more than half a day's walk. They started before dawn and arrived late on a cool evening. Welo had never made camp here, in the beauty of this place above the valley of mists, but he had seen that there were large rock faces on two sides for shelter, and in the spring he had noticed a small stream not far below where they could get water, and also fish. Welo made a fire in a pit and a place to sleep, which was simply smoothed ground covered with brush near the rocks. He put hide over the brush, for both of them, and they lay down covered with their cloaks.

"It is quite satisfying, isn't it, to sleep here in the open? It has been many years since I did this," Seneks said, breaking many minutes of silence. "Many years. I was a young man then. I had forgotten this."

"Yes," Welo said. "It is peaceful."

"Your sense tells you when there are cats or wolves? Bears?"

"Yes."

"And are there?"

"None near. Bears on the other side of the valley. Many deer, and many rabbits. There are pigs, but not close. I sense no danger that will bother us."

"But we must wait for morning light," Seneks said, "to see your—whatever they are?"

"What? Oh, no. I doubt if you can see them with your eyes. I can't. But with my other sense, the dark makes no difference. They are there now, in the valley. Many of them."

"You have told me this before, but I don't understand. You sense these things in the dark?"

"Do you hear things in the dark? Feel the heat from the fire in the dark, with your eyes closed? Yes, I sense them in the dark."

For a few moments, Seneks was quiet, lying with his hands behind his head. Then he said, "Describe it to me, this sense of yours."

"How can you describe a sense to someone who doesn't have it? I don't know," Welo said. "You are a shaman. How would you describe what it feels like to talk to a god, or to the dead? Or how it feels to enter a trance that lets you do such things?"

"It feels hungry."

"What? What does that mean, it feels hungry? Is the trance like a predator stalking you? It might be!" But Welo laughed gently when he said that; he was teasing. "No," he continued, "I know what you mean, I think. To enter a trance you must fast, so *you* are hungry. But I don't mean what it feels like to get there. I mean once you are in the trance, talking to the dead, do you feel your hunger then?"

"No," Seneks replied. "I have thought about this before. Many times. The hunger stays with the body we leave behind us. We are not hungry when we are out of our body."

"So, talking to the dead, that probably just feels like talking, I would guess. But when they talk to you, what do you hear? It's not like hearing me when I speak? You have told me in the past that it *isn't* like that, but you have never told me what it *is* like."

"No, it isn't like ordinary speaking. Not when you speak to the dead, or to the gods. What it *is* like is a secret, or so the shamans think, although I have never understood why. But this, the changing earth, matters enough. So, I will tell you what it is like, if you don't tell others about what we say here."

"I would never tell others what we say between us. Why would I?"

"So." Welo felt Seneks nod in the dark. "What is it like to speak to gods? How do I say it? It's like-" He paused, searching for the right words, then said, "It's like hearing your bones speak to you. Or ring. No," he corrected himself. "Sing," Seneks said. "It is like hearing your bones sing to you. No sound, but still, that's what it's like. Like having your bones sing a meaning to the air. No, not the air. The air is for the body you leave behind you, not bones, because those are *in* the body you leave. But there is something that seems like your insides, like you have bones where your trance takes you. And speaking to the dead, or to gods, is like having these things that feel like bones sing out their meaning into all that is around you when you leave your body."

Seneks stopped, thinking about what he had just said. Then he continued."You're right, it's hard to describe it to someone who has never done it. We say we speak, to the dead or the gods, that's the word we use because there isn't any better word for what we do. But speak is wrong too. It's not like that, really."

He was quiet again then, staring into the valley below them, thinking, remembering what it was to 'speak' to the gods until Welo broke his reverie.

"It is the same?" Welo asked. "For the dead as for the gods? Are the dead like gods, then?"

"No," Seneks shook his head slowly. "No. Not the same. The dead speak in a murmur. It's hard to hear them. Others are better at that than I am, but all of us find it hard. Or most of us. Only a few hear them clearly."

Welo smiled at the strange ideas Seneks used to describe a sense few had.

"Do you *see* the gods?" He asked. "Is there anything like that?"

"No," Seneks said. Then added, "maybe a little. But mostly, no. When we speak with the dead it is as though we are in darkness, except in a place where nothing like light has ever been, so it isn't really dark, it's just there. In that place it doesn't really make sense to ask if we see them. We feel them, and what they want to say enters us somehow, and we understand. That's all."

"And the gods are in this same place with no light? The gods live with the dead?"

"No, Welo," Seneks said. "Don't speak nonsense. The dead are in their place, and each god is in the place that belongs to them. The place that is proper to them. We speak to gods, or I do, only one at a time, and when I do I feel almost like I am inside the god. The gods can be loud, and sometimes frightening. If you talk to Perkunos, it is as though your bones are singing in a smashing storm and thundering rain. If you talk to Hewsos, it is dawn. To Dhegm, it is the earth. Different gods are different."

"But they don't speak aloud, in words?"

"No," Seneks shook his head again. "Not now," he said. "I have heard that long ago there were people, not even shamans, who spoke to gods they saw and heard. Maybe those were just stories. That was in Saurig's time, when the Téuta was new. Maybe gods can speak aloud if they want, when that is important to them. But to us, to the shamans now, it is as I told you."

Both were silent for enough time for the sun to move down the sky to the rim of the world. Then Welo spoke the words he knew Seneks was waiting to hear.

"Maybe, Seneks, what I sense is the something around you, the not-air that you spoke about before. I don't know. My sense is neither hearing nor seeing, but it is much more like seeing, and I never see or hear gods or the dead. For me it isn't like ringing bones, or leaving my body, or anything as wonderful as that. Really, it isn't at all wonderful. It just is. It's just a way to know what is here, in this world, like any other sense. I think, mostly, I sense things that anyone might see with eyes if the things were close enough and not hidden. I sense a tree, or a fox in the brush, not gods."

"So," Seneks asked, "if it is not like bone-songs, then what is it like?"

"As I say, more like seeing than hearing, but maybe also like feeling. Like now, without turning, we both know the fire has waned and needs to be replenished. We don't have to look at it to know that. We just know, because we feel how it feels."

"What does a fox in the brush seem like in your sense?"

Welo thought for a moment. Then he stood, went down to the stream and walked four or five paces along the bank. Welo put his hand deep into the cold water and stirred the mud at the bottom. Then he walked back.

"See that boulder at the stream's edge?" He asked. "Get closer if you want to. Watch it, and imagine that you couldn't see the rock, but rather how the water moves around it. Because you see the water around it, and see a hole in the water, you know the rock is there. It's like that."

As Welo spoke, a thin flute of the mud he had stirred up flowed around the rock, curling and twisting in the current. As they watched, more mud struck the rock, flowed around it, making strange, elegant shapes in the current below the rock.

"What I sense," Welo said, "is like the mud in the stream. I don't have to see the rock to know it's there. I sense the looping and curling mud around it. But with a fox, or any living thing—and also with things that give heat—the shapes move differently. They move with more energy than the others. That's the best I can do to show you what I sense."

Both men thought about what had been said. They listened to the small noises in the forest around them and watched the stars move above.

"What do you sense in the dark valley, then," Seneks asked at last, "that we have come so far to watch? Is it like the rock, or the fox?"

"I...am not sure," Welo said. "Maybe like the rock, if it were jumping out of the water. Maybe a little like the fox. But maybe that's because living things are warm, or something. Like I said before, heat changes how things move. I don't know. What I sense in the valley moves—not just with the breeze, and not all at once. But you're right: it feels more like the rock. So maybe...I don't know. There's nothing there that you see? As a shaman?"

"I see nothing here but a pleasant stream, and a warm fire now that we have built it," Senek said. "I see mountains above us, and I know there is a valley below, although I can't really see it anymore since the night has closed around us. What of you?"

Welo took a long time to answer. What he sensed in the valley was simple, but he thought it might be part of all the change that had happened during his life, which was not simple.

Welo spent the evening explaining what was in the valley, what he hoped it might be, and what he feared it was. Some of what Welo said was known to Seneks already; it was the story of much of his life. But some of it, Seneks did not know.

At the end, Seneks walked to the rocks above them, asking Welo to leave him alone, not to watch what he did, but to guard that no one and nothing disturbed him. He had been fasting for three days, drinking only water. He filled a bowl with something from his pouch. Then he took an ember from the fire and lit whatever it was until it smoked. Seneks inhaled the smoke and closed his eyes. Welo didn't watch, but he couldn't turn off all of his senses. Seneks seemed to be singing to himself. Then he went quiet, and lay on his side, and was limp.

This was shaman stuff. Welo felt that just being there was an intrusion, and a violation of some code he didn't understand. He did not want to sense it, so he tried to ignore it. He turned his back, and closed his eyes, and covered his ears. But his other sense could not be covered. Nothing that he knew about could block it, except beer.

Finally, Welo walked to his sleeping space, the soft bed he had made. He lay down, safe knowing that anything that disturbed the peace would wake him, so he slept. Welo slept without dreams, as he usually did. The peaceful dark rose around him, closing over him like a blanket. Nothing came near that might disturb him. An owl, some field mice and rabbits, harmless snakes and lizards and insects of all kinds that moved in the night were of no concern to him.

Welo did not wake in the night. But before the sun was up he did rouse, and he heard, in his almost sleep, Seneks' old voice singing with unexpected richness.

It was a song of thanks to the dawn goddess, and to Dhegm, the earth, and to the sky for bringing the day. Shaman stuff, but very beautiful. Welo knew the songs. They were not secret. Sometimes the shamans sang them for the whole Téuta to hear. Sometimes when the shamans let them, or called to them, the Téuta sang the songs with them to welcome the day. The singing soothed Welo. Full sleep recaptured him, and he stayed longer on his bed than was his custom when he was away from the village.

CHAPTER 18

When Welo woke, the sun was well up, and Seneks was seated by the fire, feeding it new wood. He had either been up for some time or had not slept.

"So," Welo asked, "you found them? You know what they are?"

"No. Whatever is there is something that shaman trances can't find."

Seneks paused. A crease sat between his eyes as he stared into the fire he was rousing. He was keeping busy.

"But the valley felt wrong, and still feels wrong," Seneks said. "I don't know how or why, but it felt the way you said, like a worry, or a danger. It made me afraid. Still, I have to admit, I found nothing real. No gods, no dead. I don't know what you are sensing, Welo. But I believe you sense something, and sense it far better than I can even with fasting and trance."

Welo didn't look at Seneks. He watched with other senses but didn't speak; he just rose from his bed and readied himself for the day. That was fine. They knew each other well. Messages passed between them with the simplest motions, or the lack of motions, whether they spoke aloud or not.

The valley below them showed its beauty. Trees covered the floor except where the stream curved back and forth along its length. The sun was low but rising, and the air clear. The two sat, waiting for the full sun to reach and warm them. Welo finally returned to the topic at hand.

"You sense nothing there," he said. "But I sense something. With my eyes I see what you see, the clear valley, the green, the flowing river. But my other sense is alert here, more than alert. It's like the heat from a great fire when your back is turned to it. And with that sense, the valley seems to be filled with a kind of cloud."

"That is unusual?" Seneks asked. "I mean, have you seen that before here?"

"Yes. Less than now, but yes, I have. The cloudiness I always see, like the mud flowing in the river. But the cloud is not what disturbs me. Often it seems that whatever it is I am sensing has settled into the low areas. But here, now, I see something else. I don't know how to describe it. There are patches in the cloud that move. They seem at first to be no more than denser bits, but as I watch them, they seem to move on their own, against the currents around them. They seem to start far beneath the cloud, as though the earth were spitting them out, hard, so they rise to the surface and bloom like flowers there. And then they dive deeper, appear and disappear, constantly moving. Some seem to be chasing others. When they collide, sometimes they repel each other. Sometimes they don't, and instead seem to join together."

Then Welo said what really bothered him.

"They seem like fish swimming in a still place in the river. Sometimes many in the same direction, but sometimes one or more move away in a different direction. They seem almost like things that choose where to move. Like living things."

Seneks frowned hard at that. He sat thinking about it as the sun rose high above them. Without speaking, they had decided to stay another night to better understand the place. They chatted while preparing a stew of grain and dried mutton Welo had brought with him. Finally, Welo asked what had been most on his mind.

"These are not gods, are they? Or the dead?"

"I don't think they are anything like that," Seneks said. "At least, nothing like the gods seem to me. I don't see them. If they are tiny gods, they are someone else's gods."

"Someone else's gods? Are there other gods than the ones we know?"

"I don't know, Welo. All the Téuta act as though our own gods are all there are, all that matter. God of shining skies, or of storms, or goddess of the earth. They surely are the biggest, and the most important. But strange things sometimes happen. Maybe there are smaller gods who make mischief. Maybe they know us, or maybe they don't. But if there are strange gods, I think it's best to leave them alone. Best not to get their attention."

Welo thought about that for some time. It was an odd idea, but also one that seemed natural to him.

Then Seneks said, "Don't tell anyone else about this. Particularly a shaman. Don't talk about this to anyone else."

"Even shamans? Why?"

"Shamans more than anyone." Seneks turned to him, his face serious. "Welo, you are already a worry to them. They would not understand this, and they would resent that you can sense something that is hidden from them. Shamans, most of us, are proud that we can see more than others, and guard that special difference jealously. But I can't see the thing you describe. Even when I fast, when I drink the mushroom tea that I brought with me and inhale the flower smoke, even then I don't see them."

"I sense them," Welo said. "Still, now I sense them, but they are leaving. I've been feeling them move all day. They seem to move with their own purpose, but they flow down from the valley to the ground below, following the streams and the river. New ones seem to come from the ground, but some are also drifting down from higher up, from higher ground. But less now than last night."

"Where do they come from?" Seneks asked. "Those that come down from the higher places? Can you sense that?"

"Where does the river come from? I have never seen the start of it. Or the end of it. Has anyone ever travelled so far, to see that? I don't know where the things come from. I see them here, and haven't looked anywhere else. I don't want to see them," Welo said. "They mean trouble."

Seneks nodded. "I am troubled by them too. But I don't know what to do about them. Just leave them, Welo. Leave them. They are a danger, I think. Hide from them so they don't notice us."

But Welo couldn't just leave them. They bothered him. To Seneks it seemed they were only a troubling curiosity. To Welo, in part because Eini said so, but also because of how they felt to him, they were an omen that meant disaster, somewhere, to someone. To something. Something that mattered.

Eini had been right in the spring. He could follow them, find them. No one else could do that. And now, with summer gone and deep winter still a moon or two away, now was a good time to walk in the mountains. It was the time of year he liked to walk.

Maybe he would leave them alone once he found them, as Seneks said. But he might decide to find them first. Find where they came from, if he could do that in his autumn walk.

CHAPTER 19

The next morning, Welo kept Seneks company on his return trip to his temple, the proper place for an old shaman. But because he could not just leave his troubling visions, Welo did not return to his own hut. Instead, he set out alone to discover what he could, walking back along the path he had trod so often in recent weeks.

Welo planned to stay in a shelter he knew, one he had stayed in often. It was not directly on the path to the valley where he and Seneks had spent the night, but it was not far off the path to that. He liked this shelter, with the forest around him. It was beautiful at any time of year, especially in the morning. But Welo liked the autumn, the colors, and the sense that winter was coming, and with it, rest was coming, and the quick young sense that there was time for one last adventure before the year was over.

And this year it was not just adventure. This year there was purpose, if he had time enough to do it. He wanted to find where the river began. To find where the things that troubled him came from, the things that seemed to foretell trouble for the Téuta. If there were time. He meant to be home at the Téuta and in a warm shelter long before deep winter came.

The day had been bright and cloudless, but as Welo walked, thin clouds began to drift from the west. *The sunset will be full of color,* he thought. When it came, it was as he had predicted: beautiful as only a goddess can be, and wide and peaceful. Stopping, Welo took time to build a small fire and a shelter of fallen branches to sleep in. *Tomorrow early,* he thought, *it might rain.*

Instead, it rained overnight, waking him almost before he was truly asleep, and he was glad of his shelter, of his small fire, and of his fur cloak. As tall as he was, he had to draw his knees up to bring his feet under the edge of his cloak so he could go back to sleep.

When he woke, Welo finished his journey to the place where he had seen the strange motion in the mists . It did not take long to arrive. Morning was still only half over when he looked down into the valley.

Below him, he saw a place of great beauty, filled with trees, the sun gleaming on branches still wet from the overnight rains. He saw birds above and below in the trees and heard them squabbling and chattering to each other. With his other sense, he was aware of many things that were hidden from his eyes and ears: frogs in the pools along the stream, a rabbit hiding in the thorns nearby, beetles scurrying to their dinners, voles and mice huddling under the tree roots, the strange mistiness around decaying leaves and logs, and everywhere the long wind of his sense. Farther away, the bigger animals, more wary of humans, moved silently. But Welo could sense them. They felt like disturbances in clouds, and they trailed clouds behind them as they padded and crept across the valley floor.

Closing his eyes to observe more keenly so he would not be distracted by the tumult of visible nature, Welo perceived below him a valley boiling and tumbling in fog like a cauldron of thin, turbulent cloud. In that cloud he felt still denser places that slowly moved, a restlessness that seemed to spit out of the ground, zigging and zagging always down the slopes. There were too many to follow when he tried to see them at once, so many that they made Welo, who was so strong and so tall, feel powerless.

They were slower, and there were fewer of them than there had been when he sat here with Seneks only a few days earlier. Welo thought again of how he had explained that these things moved on their own, and that Eini had said that they meant no good to the Téuta village, and might be a warning or an omen. And he remembered how Seneks had warned him that the shamans could not even know they were there, so they were powerless to stop them.

Welo knew he had no power over them either. There was no purpose in following these things. Whatever they would do, he could not stop it. So why search for them?

Maybe it was alright. Maybe Eini was wrong. Because Seneks could not see them even in a deep shaman-trance, he didn't think they were an omen. And he didn't really think they were a warning, either. Seneks had said that they might be tiny gods of some kind, but if so, they were gods that would not speak to him. Maybe they were gods that didn't know the Téuta at all and didn't care about the village. Seneks had admitted that he thought they might be dangerous, but only as a running child is a danger to pottery. These gods, if that's what they were, might damage the Téuta simply because they were not aware of it. Welo had worried. But so far his worry had come to nothing. Nothing had happened in the village. So he would walk for the joy he always got from walking and forget these things. They would cluster and puff, and he would let them. So far, they were no bother to anyone. Let them be.

Since nothing in the Téuta needed his help, and these things were harmless so far and even if they were not he could do nothing about them, he decided to follow his other curiosity, to find where the river starts.

Welo could have turned back to the Téuta, as he had often after a night out in the forest. Instead, he turned the other way, following the small stream that flowed past this place. He walked upstream, up into the mountains.

He thought he would be away from the village for many days, perhaps a moon, or even two moons. After that, the cold would drive him home, if nothing else did. For now though, the cool air was refreshing. And he expected a warmer night. The wind was turning, coming from the south, so it would bring warm air up from the valley by evening.

Welo gathered his things and set out.

The warm breeze came and went. Air rising from the valley turned to mist in the mountain forest. The sun had passed its highest place, and there was a stream just below him. The world seemed quiet and soft when wrapped in fog. All the sounds of the forest were there, but fog brightened them. The creak of trees in the slow breeze was commonplace, but here, now, the sound seemed more distant, more secret, and more clear. The murmur of insects flying nearby, the rustle small things in the leaves on the forest floor, all of it came to Welo with clarity and softness, with a sense of quiet and isolation. Enclosed in fog, Welo felt alone in this high world. Welo chose to stop, to enjoy the peace of the late afternoon, he built a shelter against a tree, covering it first with a woven grass mat he carried with him, then with leaves. He built a small fire and placed his soft deerskin pot filled with water from the stream over it to make a stew of grain and dried venison. Then with his eyes closed, he watched, and ate, and almost dozed.

But the day was not over yet. Above everything, above the trees and the mist, the sun still shone, so fog did not have sole ownership of the day. Streaks of misted light found their way through the high branches above him, giving him quick glimpses of movement among the leaves, and sometimes movement farther away as animals lived their lives here in their forest-home. Glimmers of awareness of things outside himself reminded him to be alert. To remember that, as peaceful as the misted forest felt, there were still dangers in the world.

Welo again closed his eyes and rested, relishing the breeze and the cool of the late day.

But he could not quite relax. *Why am I so worried in this place? There is nothing here to worry me.*

With his eyes still closed, Welo felt the long, high forest. After a time, he sensed motion in it. A fox trotting by twenty paces away stopped and sniffed the air, smelling Welo's fire and the stew, then continued on its way. There were deer in the distance, and in another direction, even farther away, wolves. Then, Welo became aware that there was something else moving that he did not immediately understand. It was not the tiny gods, and it was not close. But it was not so far away that he could ignore it.

A group of what seemed like men, a large group, perhaps thirty of them, moved away from him, up the mountain, hidden in the fog. Behind them, also distant but far closer, was another much smaller group of six or seven men. They moved slowly and carefully, and with purpose, as though searching for something.

The second group, Welo decided, was following the first, but hiding from them. *The first group is far ahead, alert but confident and well concealed in the mist,* Welo thought, *while the second is hunting them.*

Welo packed his things and continued his walk, this time moving with the two groups, trying to understand what they were doing.

CHAPTER 20

The day was nearly over. Welo could have gone on, but the two groups he followed had stopped for the night, and he was curious. The first group, the large one, had stopped first to make camp. The second also stopped, seeming to wander in the forest. They seemed to have lost the trail they followed for now.

Following these people was no longer really idle. Welo had, he realized, decided to watch them, the chasers and the chased, rather than follow the river.

He made his camp for the night in a place he had never stopped before. He could tell that someone else had been here a few moons ago. Maybe longer than that. A set of branches leaned against a large rock with a protruding edge that provided some shelter, but they were not neatly stacked. Wind and weather had moved them and blown some to the ground. Near the makeshift shelter there were signs of a fire in just the place Welo would have chosen. The old fire pit was barely visible now. Whoever had used this place had, Welo decided, used it long ago. The evening was cooling quickly, so Welo built his fire first. His camp was small; his fire was small; he did not need more. He arranged and straightened the ring of stones carefully to contain the fire.

The larger group was some distance away, and almost directly upwind. There was little chance that they would detect his tiny camp. The smaller group, the hunters, were closer than the first group, but still distant. Smoke and the smell of smoke could travel. But since both groups were upwind of him, or nearly so, Welo did not think either of them would notice his small fire.

He was wrong. The small group moved generally toward him. Then they backtracked, looking for the larger group. Then they turned again, and Welo realized that this band of men who hunted men were now walking in his direction. It took only a few moments for Welo to understand that they were moving not just in his direction, but toward him, seeking him. There seemed to be no reason for that, but it was clear: they were walking directly to him.

They seemed now to be hunting *him*.

Welo quickly threw dirt over his fire. Gathering his things, he moved quickly to a hidden place higher in the rocks. He wanted to be close enough to sense who they were, although he thought he already knew, while staying far enough away to escape if they seemed hostile.

Watching from the safety of his hiding place Welo knew his other sense was enough for him to follow their actions even though they could not see him and he could not always see them with his eyes. Still, he was troubled. This was a lesson to him. He had been fooled by his arrogant confidence in his safety in the open world because of his sense.

As night deepened, and the small group kept coming toward him. They should have stopped. They should have made their own camp because it was so late and they had spent this long day following a difficult trail. But they kept coming toward him.

When the strangers finally reached his camp, they seemed to know that someone had been there recently. That did not surprise Welo. The fire was still warm, and the shelter was fresh and well repaired. Wandering around the little camp, the men talked with each other. Two of them made wide, slashing gestures as though they were upset, even distraught. A third paced, and seemed to try to soothe them, pointing repeatedly at something on the ground. Welo waited and watched. When the others had settled a little, the man who soothed the others called out. Welo could hear him, but he was too far away to understand what the man was saying, until he turned and faced Welo almost directly. Then Welo realized he was speaking Téuta. The man spoke as one of the forest people, peaceful people. He spoke as friends to the Téuta would speak to them. Still, every one of the group carried a spear and a knife. Four of the men were armed with bows and carried quivers filled with many arrows. All were armed with scowls, and draped in fierce anger.

"Téuta," the man who seemed to be their leader called, "come out. We do not harm Téuta, only the others. But we have lost them. Come. Speak. Have you seen others?"

He repeated this several times, yet Welo hesitated. He thought he knew this man a little. He came to the village during festivals to give gifts in the spring and receive them in the fall. Even so, Welo sensed that the men around him were dangerous, and full of strong emotion. But it was also true that Welo had spoken to the forest people when they came to the festivals, perhaps to the very man who called out, and had found them friendly.

Finally, hesitantly but steadily, Welo went down to them. Silent and watchful, he approached the camp. The group was still pacing back and forth like wolves sniffing the ground to find their prey when he stepped from the forest and called to them.

At the sound of his voice, the three with spears turned and pointed them toward Welo. The man who seemed to be their leader turned to them quickly, his hands outstretched, his voice calm. After a few moments the spears were lowered. The men who held them did not relax, though. Welo knew the spears could come up again, quickly.

The man who had calmed them turned to Welo and spoke. His words were fairly clear, although the sentences were laced with forest people talk. Still, Welo could understand their meaning well enough.

"You are at Téuta festival sometime," the forest man said.

"I think I remember you," Welo replied. "You remember me?"

"Yes. You are tall. Very tall. I remember you."

The man walked to him and pointed at the ground, then squatted and looked at Welo with expectation. Welo looked toward the group of others, then back to the speaker before he squatted, facing him. For a moment neither spoke, then Welo said, "My name is Welo."

"Yes, Welo, yes, I remember that. I am Newir."

The forest-people name sounded odd to Welo's Téuta ear. For a moment no one said anything. Then one of the others questioned Newir, who nodded and spoke again.

"Have you seen others?" He asked.

"You hunt for other men?"

"Yes."

"Why do you hunt them?" Welo asked. He knew forest people, but he did not know those they hunted. This looked like a deep trouble to him, so he was careful.

"They attacked our dwellings while we were away," Newir said. "They left many dead, children and old. And they take women and some girl children, some few things too. But we don't want things they took."

Welo sat and thought for a moment.

"You hunt them to get your women?"

"Yes. And girls, child girls."

Welo realized that the other group, the group ahead, must be one of the violent ones who could not live in the colder weather, and who attacked to take what they wanted. In the past, they had attacked the Teuta and had taken sheep. In the Téuta too, there were sometimes dead from those attacks, although as far as Welo knew the raiders had not taken women and did not seem to mean to kill. They were just hungry. If they had asked, the Téuta might have fed them. But they had not asked. They had come with no warning, and they had brought violence with them.

It was hard after all the time spent diverting attention from his extra sense, after so much hiding and pretending among the Téuta that his knowledge came only from better hearing or vision, to admit to Newir that he could tell where the raiding people were. But these were not Téuta, these were forest people. Maybe their reaction would be different. So Welo decided to help them. He pointed to where his sense told him the other group was settled for the night, nestled in fog, thinking they were safely hidden. But neither the fog nor the forest could hide them from Welo.

"They are there," he said. "It will take until early morning to get to where they sleep. They are far enough away that for the first part you don't need to be quiet. You can get there well before dawn."

Then Welo described how to find the others, while Newir stared hard at him.

"You know where they sleep tonight." Newir said this as a statement, not as a question.

"Yes."

"How? Did you follow them?"

Welo sighed and shook his head.

"No, Newir. I can sense them. I sense them now, while we sit here to talk. I'm sorry, I know it sounds strange. Everyone says it is strange. Still, it's true. They are where I said."

The mood between them had tensed. Although they could not understand what Welo said, the spear carriers could tell that Newir was distressed. The spears rose a little. "Through the trees, even with the fog," Newir said, looking closely at Welo. "You sense they are there in that direction."

"Yes."

Newir frowned hard and turned to look at the others. Then he talked, barely whispering, speaking in Teuta almost as though he hoped the others could not understand him.

"I do believe you," Newir murmured. "But still I think you are a good man, who is trying to help us."

"But it is strange to you."

"Strange? Yes. But we know of this. Don't say this again, Welo, don't let these know you have this. This is a child's story among us, a story to frighten children."

Newir paused as if deciding something. Then he said, "We have seen this before, not among those still living, but in the past. A woman had this, it is told, and used it, was cruel. Bad. Many ancestors ago, this happened, but there are many among us who still are frightened by this. They would not trust you if they knew. I don't know-" Newir paused, thinking. Then he said, "I don't know how I will explain it, but I will think of something to tell them, some reason I know how to guide them to the place."

Welo stood, nodded, and then sat again.

"How did you know?" He asked, "that I am Téuta?"

"Your fire," Newir said. "The way you made the stones around your fire. We have seen that among the Téuta, and it is not how we do it."

Welo nodded again. He had made this fire-pit the way his father had shown him long ago. A long habit, done now without thought.

"I could come with you," he offered, "To help you find them."

"No. I don't know if we could keep your secret with you helping to guide us. We will find them. They killed and took our people. We will find them, have no doubt of it. And once we are close, we will need no extra sense to guide us."

Newir stood, and so did Welo. "Thank you. I will remember," Newir said.

After that, Newir spoke to the others, and all of them disappeared into the forest with so little noise they might have been mice on the forest floor. It was as though the night took them. Within only a few breaths, if he used only his eyes and ears, Welo would not have been able to know they were near, or had ever been near.

When he was alone again, Welo rebuilt his fire and his shelter, and spent hours sensing them and everything else around him. He slept lightly that night, alert even in his sleep.

⫟⫟ ⫩ ⊦⊼⫟

Fog rose and spread overnight. By morning it covered much of the mountain. Dawn was muted, a distant hint of dusty color in the mist. Welo packed his camp, doused his fire, and sat thinking about the night before. If the attack on the forest people's village was the trouble, the omen of the tiny gods, then he had no strong reason to return to the Téuta village. And this could be. The forest people were friends to the village, and the village was a friend to the forest people. There were young men from the Téuta who had gone with the forest people for adventure when they travelled south to the plains for the winter, and sometimes forest people found mates among the Téuta. Many people known to Welo might have relatives among those killed in the raids.

My path is to the forest village, or to follow the forest men, to see what has happened among them, Welo thought. *Maybe to their village first, to see if there are injured that I can help.*

CHAPTER 21

Welo's first thought was to get Seneks, whose knowledge of healing was so much greater than his own, to help those injured among the forest people. But he knew that with injuries, sometimes time is more important than skill. So, he set out in what he thought was the right direction, chewing a bit of dried meat as he walked. He could not really tell exactly where the village was. The things that came up from the earth, whatever they were, clustered between him and the place he sought, cluttering and confusing his sense. In what he thought was the right direction, there was chaos. He headed toward that, hoping all would be clearer when he got closer.

It was Welo's good fortune that he was diverted from that slow journey. He meant the forest people no harm, only good. But the men who had remained with the forest camp to defend against any fresh raids wouldn't have known his intention, and they might have assumed the worst.

By mid-morning, Welo became aware of a group behind him and to his right side, moving through the forest in a line that would cross his path. From their numbers and direction, he thought they were probably the forest men he had met the night before, although he couldn't be certain. If so, they had added new people. There were several children, and at least one of this group was badly hurt. They moved slowly and stopped frequently. Welo turned toward them and approached with care. This could be his new friends, or it could be the raiders. He had no good way of distinguishing between them until he could see them with his eyes. Still, he turned toward them.

On his way to intercept them, a long and careful walk, Welo paused when he recognized useful things around him he might need for healing. He gathered honey, and small herbs and roots that could help with pain or keep a wound from festering too badly.

As time passed, and they gradually drew closer, Welo became increasingly certain that he knew this group. He knew them, and he wanted to help them. Again, he thought that Seneks would have known better methods, but Welo would do his best with what he had gathered. Finding them took longer than he hoped. The day was waning when he was finally close enough to see them. Rather than risk rushing up to the group, Welo turned away, walked until he was well ahead of them, then dropped his spear and bow and sat on the path to wait.

ᛏᛁᛏ ᚹ ᚻ

The sun was leaving the sky, and the Kujoté stopped to make camp before they reached him.

I should have expected that, Welo thought. *I was foolish to walk so far ahead of them. They have wounded. They will need to rest.*

He started to rise, intending to walk to them, but he sensed that two of the group had moved toward him. Welo realized that they knew he was here, although he did not know how they knew. He thought he had been nearly silent. As the two Kujoté men approached, Welo again sat and placed his weapons on the ground. The two men paused just hidden in the trees, watching him. Then Newir, his friend from the previous night, stepped forward.

"Welo," he said.

"Newir. It's good to see that it is you." Welo bent his head in respect. Newir sat and bent his head to Welo.

"You are waiting here for us?"

"Yes. You have injured, I think, from your movements. I think you found the people you were looking for. Did you find your people? Get them back?"

"Yes, all. But one of them dead. And two others who need help I can't give them."

"I have learned something of healing from a friend," Welo said. "Maybe I can help."

Newir tipped his head, a shadow of a smile crossing his face.

"What is your friend's name?"

"His name? He is called Seneks. He is a shaman in the Téuta. He is a good healer," Welo said. "Very good. I am not him, but..."

He stopped, because now Newir's smile showed itself. And now, too, the second Kujoté man stepped into view, apparently reassured by hearing the word 'Seneks'.

He really is a great healer, Welo thought. *Seneks can heal distrust with only his name.*

The second man spoke, in Kujoté, and Newir translated.

"We know Seneks. He has been friend to us for all of my life, helping us sometimes when we are sick or hurt. I myself, have had some use of his knowledge. When I was a child, I fell from a tree, and Seneks healed me. Come, then," he said, getting to his feet. "If you have any part of Seneks' skills, we would welcome your help."

Gathering his spear and knife, Welo stood, and together they joined the third man and walked back to the camp.

Welo found the group somber and tired, but most of them were well. Only two were badly injured, one man and one woman. A second woman was dead. Welo went first to the dead woman, to be certain. Her wound was deep, but did not bleed anymore. Any blood within it had been spilled and spent and was gone.

He turned to Newir.

"She died last night?"

"Yes. She died fighting hard along with us, but with no weapon. The man she fought with took her for some value he thought was in her, but when she fought back he forgot her value. He cut her without thinking."

"You carry her back to the Kujoté."

"She *fought* to be with Kujoté. We would not leave her there with them, even dead among their dead, we would not leave her."

Newir paused for a long time. He sat down next to the dead woman and looked at her before he spoke again.

"She has a young child," he said. "A girl child, still alive in the Kujoté camp who deserves to know this. To see that she is not taken by those others. To know that she is not with them. And to know what her mother has done. To know how fierce she was when that was needed."

Welo nodded without speaking. Then he moved to the other injured, treating and binding their wounds as well as he could. He would have liked to have had willow bark, but he did not. He asked Newir if he could find any, but willow had become scarcer over his life, in the cooling, drying years, so Welo did not wait for it, or expect it. Instead, he used strips of cloth dipped in a mixture of water and ash from the fire to keep infection away. Welo was finishing with the last bandages when he saw that Newir and some other of the Kujoté had gone out to the forest to cut willow bark. Thanking them, Welo used it to make a tea to ease pain. He gave it first to the wounded, and then to the others as well, most of whom also had small cuts or scrapes.

As he worked, Welo thought about the woman who had been killed.

The Kujoté have no wall of the dead, no big monument like that for them. So maybe they have no way to speak to them. I don't know. But they do know their dead. They value them, and they know them.

Thinking that, and watching as they shared their meal with him, Welo decided that he liked them. He felt pride in them. He knew this would be the first of many meals they would share throughout his life.

He knew it and was glad of it.

⊓ ⬤ ⊢⊣

In the morning the group rose, made some breakfast, and got underway. Welo offered to pull the travois holding the dead woman, but the Kujoté declined his help with that task. But they did allow him to carry some provisions and other things in his pack, to carry the things that those who did pull the travois might have otherwise carried. Welo understood. The dead woman was theirs to carry. They knew him now to be a friend, but their dead belonged to the Kujoté, and he was Téuta.

They approached the Kujoté camp at midday. When they entered the camp, they were greeted. They had been watched already for some time, so the people knew who was coming. Seneks was already there, busy with patients. Welo had known before—everyone knew—that Seneks sometimes visited the camp, particularly in the spring when the Kujoté returned from the lowlands. But this was not spring. Seneks had heard about the raid and come at once because the Kujoté had sent a runner for him.

What was more surprising, mystifying if Welo thought about it, was that Eini was also there. Why, Welo wondered, would she come? She had no special skills as a healer, and as far as Welo knew, she had never before come to the Kujoté. She could not speak their language well, and seemed to have no task, no purpose. So, why was she here?

For the time being, Welo and Seneks and a healer from the Kujoté camp were too busy to ask her about it. Even those who had no physical injuries needed something, some comfort that Seneks could offer with a tea of some kind.

Evening came, and for the second time Welo ate with the Kujoté, this time with all of them. Eini and Seneks ate too, and the three Téuta were assured that they were welcome to sleep in the camp, although shelters were scarce. The raiders had destroyed most of them. For Welo, this was not a discomfort. He was used to sleeping in the open.

The dead woman's daughter, a girl of no more than six winters, sat next to Welo. She was very close, nearly touching him. Welo was not sure why she would choose to do this. Perhaps she had seen that he and Newir were friendly, that he seemed to be easily accepted. Or maybe it was because he was not Kujoté, and she wanted someone who would not talk to her very much. Maybe she wanted to be left alone with her thoughts instead of being comforted. Or maybe it was because Welo was so tall that he made her feel safe after the terror of the raids. Once, when he rose to get something, and returned to sit a step farther away from her, the girl got up and moved close to him again.

Welo could understand the depth of her loss. It is hard to lose a mother, even in a traveling village like this where, he was observing, all the women were mothers to any child near them. Welo had lost his own mother when he was five winters old, and he remembered. He watched the girl, the memory of that time very strong in him. The girl did not watch him back. She did not look at him. She stared at the fire silently, but had nothing to say. She didn't seem to want his company; she just wanted to be near him.

What can I do for her? Welo thought. *There's nothing to do. I can't comfort her. There is nothing I can say, and even if I had something to say to soothe this pain, I could not say it, because I don't speak her language well enough to say it to her.*

Bewildered by the situation, he simply put a hand on her shoulder. To his great surprise, she responded by leaning against him, with an arm around his back, nestling into the great length of him. Welo looked over at Newir, who seemed sad, but also surprised and a little amused, grateful for whatever comfort the girl could find in this closeness to a tall, quiet stranger. She leaned against Welo for a long time, watching as the fire waned. And then her eyes closed, and she slipped down to put her head in his lap. In a short moment her breathing slowed, and she slept.

Welo, still out of his depth, not sure what to do but reluctant to shift her, looked over at Newir. Shaking his head and smiling, the older man brought a soft skin and rolled it up for Welo to put under his head. They needed no language to understand each other now. Welo accepted the rolled skin and lay back on the ground, staying as still as he could while the girl used his leg as a pillow. One of the Kujoté women came over to sleep close on the other side of the girl. And Eini too, slept only a few feet away.

Newir brought another skin to put over the girl for warmth, and Welo used his cloak to cover himself as far as it would reach. Much of the early night passed before he could sleep, because the lower part of his legs were cold, because the night was somber and his memories of the day pestered him, and because he had to remain as he was, facing the stars, and the leg the girl lay on had to remain still. Welo was not used to sleeping on his back. But to Welo keeping his leg still for the girl seemed important beyond any other thing he had to do right then.

In the night, he might become thirsty or hungry. And other things might make him want to rise in the night. And, too, he wanted to talk to Eini, to find out why she was here. But moving might wake this fragile girl and return her to her grief. That he would not do.

CHAPTER 22

Welo woke lying on his side. He was warm all over, and realized after a groggy moment that the girl was gone and that she, or someone, had put her covers over him when she left. His second realization was that Eini was already awake, sitting up, and staring at him no more than a step away. The air was redolent with the smell of fresh venison and boiled roots and grains. The others had been up long enough to cook and eat.

Eini waited until his eyes were open enough to see her before she spoke.

"What are you doing, Welo?"

"Waking up. Hungry."

"But then, after that? I mean, what do you plan to do now, after you and Seneks have helped the Kujoté?"

"I don't know," Welo said. "Maybe keep walking for a while."

Eini looked pleased at that response.

"Ok," she said. "I'll get you something to eat."

Eini brought him a crock filled with something that smelled very, very good. She watched while he ate, then took it to wash in a nearby small stream.

Welo was standing when she returned. He was looking for the child who had slept so close to him, who had clung to him the day before. He saw her across the camp with several of the village women. They were gathered around something on the ground. After a moment, Welo realized it was the child's mother, the dead woman. They were grieving together in some way that was practiced among the Kujoté as they prepared her for her long journey after death.

The girl had apparently forgotten about Welo.

That is good, he thought. *Whatever I did for her was good, even though I didn't know what it was. And now it is best that she finds what she needs within her own people.*

But he watched the girl, wondering what her life would be now, and remembering how it was for him when his mother died. Welo was so absorbed in thinking about the girl that Eini's voice close beside him made him start.

"She will be alright, Welo. The women will care for her now."

He turned to look at her.

"I know," he said. "But I am sad about what has happened here. All of it, not just the girl." Then, after a pause, he added, "But I admit, mostly I am sad for the girl. Because she has lost a mother, and because she came to me for comfort. And because for a long time she will *not* be completely alright."

Eini, whose mother still lived, agreed with him, but she seemed to have something else on her mind.

"Where will you walk?"

"I don't know. I started to follow those things you showed me. But I don't know. This, what happened here, maybe this is the danger those things were warning about? This raid on the Kujoté?"

"Maybe," Eini said.

"And" Welo added, "I'm concerned about the Téuta. Maybe I should go back with you and Seneks."

"No! You should not." Welo was surprised by Eini's vehemence. "You should not!" She said again, starting to walk away, then turning back, obviously upset at the thought of Welo returning to the village.

"Why does this matter to you, Eini?" And then, remembering that her being in the Kujoté village had been a surprise, "And why are you here? What happened that Seneks brought you with him?"

"Welo, you must go. I don't care about the things, whatever they are. I don't think they matter now. You must go for your walk in the world. Out there, not in the Téuta. I came here with Seneks to tell you that."

Welo stared at her. "Why? Why don't you want me home in the Téuta, Eini? Is there something there? Has something happened?"

Eini sighed, obviously agitated. She seemed reluctant to answer. Then finally she walked to him, took his wrist and pulled him toward the trees. Halfway there, he stopped her.

"Where are we going, Eini? What has you so upset?"

"I am not upset if you walk. Come with me. I want to show you something. You must walk, away from the Téuta. There is something out there we need. I don't know where, or what. I can't really explain it. I just know."

Eini paused, watching the trees.

"Assa is grown now," she said, finally. "But I have another child that will come in the spring. And I am getting older. But you are young. You are strong, and you can walk where there is no danger. So you should do it. I don't think you believe me, so I want to talk to you in a place where there is something for you to see."

"Well...Eini, this is strange, what you are doing. It is strange." Welo stood still, resisting her tugs, but she would not relent.

Welo would have continued his resistance until she explained her urgency, but Seneks had noticed what was happening and came to stand with them. After a moment watching Eini in this contest of tug and resist, he sided with her. He said nothing, but he pressed Welo with a hand on his back. When Welo eventually relented, when he moved to walk with Eini, Seneks chose to walk with them.

"Will we go far?" Welo asked. "Will this take a long time?"

"No, not long. And not very far, but more than a few steps."

"And it's important to you?"

"It's important to everyone."

Welo looked at her. She was serious; everything about her showed that she was serious.

"Ok," Welo said finally. "Let me tell Newir we are going."

But Eini, ignoring him, continued to pull him along.

They went on in silence, Eini ahead, Welo following with Seneks, until they felt utterly alone in the forest. They walked steadily uphill until Welo wondered if Eini really knew where she was going. Did she know the forest this far from the Téuta?

Eini did know. When she finally stopped, they stood high on a hillside, next to an immense fallen tree. The trunk lay on its side and had deteriorated enough so that it lay flat on the ground with some even beneath the ground. Welo still had to look up to see the top of the fallen trunk. A tree that, when it had been standing, was wider than Welo was tall. Standing beside it, looking up and also along the great length of it along the ground, Welo raised his hand and placed it against the bulk of it.

"This is what you want to show me?"

Eini did not answer.

Finally, she said, "Welo, we have talked sometimes about my dreams. Stop, don't just turn away from me, everyone does that. I don't want you to do that. You and Seneks are the only people in all the Téuta who even sometimes listen. And now, I need you to listen to me."

Welo, who had not turned away at all, stood watching her. Something in her determination made him listen with care.

"Sometimes we have talked," Eini said, "or maybe just I have talked, about these big things that seem frightening, big monstrous things that seem to move toward me in my dreams. Toward us, I think. Toward all of the Téuta."

"Yes, I remember. But you don't know what they are. Right?"

"I don't know what they are. But they are bad things. I am more sure all the time," Eini said, "that they are bad. And you know that in the forest sometimes I do see bad things, but I find paths in the forest to stay away from them. I find good paths."

"Yes, I have seen you do that."

"Well, there has not ever been a good path to avoid these biggest, farthest dream-things. I have been afraid of them, afraid of what they have meant for the Téuta. Or maybe just for me. I don't know. Maybe what they are is only me going to Dhegm. Only me becoming dead, and going to her. But that would not really be a bad thing, would it? To be with Dhegm. Why would that frighten me? Why does it frighten anyone?"

Welo didn't know what to say to that, so he said nothing, but watched her. She had not finished.

"That's why I wanted to show you this tree."

"I don't understand this, Eini."

Eini walked back and forth, no longer looking at Welo. Seneks, standing to the side to watch, was silent, only an audience to this talk.

"When I was young," Eini went on, "I could see this tree. Not from the Téuta village, not from the huts down near the river. But if you went up to the plateau, or to the rocks across the river, you could see it. It was the tallest tree in the forest. It was a giant among the trees. It rose above the tops of the other trees as though they were just a field of grasses, and this was the only tree in all the world. But in a storm a long time ago, maybe fifteen years, you were too young to remember, it fell. We didn't notice at first. It was a long time before I noticed, before I was up on the plateau where I should have seen it, and it was gone. But it mattered to me. It was long after it was missing that I came to the forest to look for it. I loved this tree when it stood for us to see from the plateau. So I looked until I found it."

"Yes? I'm still a little lost, Eini."

"It's one tree, Welo." She looked at him. "It makes me sad that it is gone. I loved it. But it is only one tree. Look around. The forest is still here, still beautiful. Other trees will grow as tall as this one was. Maybe a long time from now. But it will happen. It is sad, but not frightening that this tree fell. But if all the trees in the forest fall? What would that be like? Would that make you afraid?"

"Yeeesss" Welo was still not sure what she was trying to say. "OK," he said. "But..."

"So if this big thing stumbling toward me from so far away, stumbling toward me in the night, if that is my own death, it might frighten me but it would not frighten anyone else, even if they believed in it. It might make them sad, but it would not frighten them."

Welo was quiet, watching her.

"And it does frighten me," Eini said. "And it does not frighten anyone else."

Welo stayed quiet. He could see that Eini still had more to say.

"But I think it doesn't frighten them because they don't believe in my dreams."

Welo leaned against the fallen tree and waited.

"So maybe it isn't just me. Maybe it is the whole Téuta that will die. If one tree dies, it is still ok if all the forest is still alive. Like that. When I die, when we all each one dies, you and me and all the trees and the birds and the foxes, then, each of us dies one by one, but the forest goes on. The Téuta goes on. But if all the Téuta dies, there will be an emptiness in the mountains. All would be gone, Assa, Sntodi. You. Seneks." Eini paused for a moment, lost in the emotion of that thought. "There would be an emptiness on Dhegm's earth," she continued when she could. "Maybe this thing will take the future from us, or the past. Without the future we would have nothing. Without the past we would *be* nothing. But until now I have seen no good path that avoids the thing that is coming."

Finally, Welo spoke.

"And now, you see a path?"

"Now I see a *maybe* path, a maybe something. The path is not something for me to do. Maybe that's why it was so hard to find. The path is you, Welo," Eini said. "It's that you must go to the world, go walking in the world as you do. But this time you must keep walking until you find what we need. I don't know what it is. I don't know anything. And maybe it's all wrong. I don't know. I don't know," she said again, turning and beginning to pace, growing more agitated as she spoke. "I don't know. I am maybe foolish."

Uncertain of what to say or do, Welo and Seneks remained silent, watching her.

"This," Eini said. "You, walking, finding—it's just the only thing I have seen, ever, in the time since I first had this dream. The only thing that looks like a better path. Like hope. Or at least, a little like hope."

Welo looked at Eini, then at the forest, then back at Eini. He glanced also at Seneks, who was still watching, and still silent.

"This is crazy, Eini," he said, finally. "You don't know what I am supposed to find?"

"No," she said, stopping and looking at him. "I don't know. It might be anything. Maybe it is where the tiny gods come from, or where the river starts. Or maybe it is a rock or a shell, or flint or salt, or a bear made of water. I don't know."

"But I must walk until I find it."

"I don't know, really Welo. Yes," she said finally. "You must find it. That is what I feel."

Welo turned to Seneks, frustrated with Eini's vagueness.

"Seneks. What do you think? From your great age and wisdom, tell me what I need to do."

Seneks looked at the tree, and at Eini. He did not look at Welo, but he had a hint of a smile at the idea of his 'great wisdom'.

"From my great age and wisdom," Seneks replied, "I think you should walk. I believe Eini. I have learned to believe her. If she says that sending you to find things is good, then you should walk and find things. And keep finding things until you feel you should return. But," the older man's face grew serious, "be careful, Welo. I wouldn't want anyone else to do this. We have just come from strong proof that there is violence in these mountains. But I think you, who can sense the violent people far away, can be safer than any other."

For a long time, they were quiet. Then they all stood and walked back to the Kujoté.

The next morning, very early, Seneks and Eini went back to the Téuta.

And Welo went into the forest, with no destination, and without any knowledge of when he would return.

PART III

Akesh

CHAPTER 23
WINTER 6243 BCE

Welo walked upward, hoping to find where the river started in the high mountains. But there was no start, as far as he could tell, or there were many starts. Trickles became rills, which became streams, which tumbled together until they were creeks. He found several big enough to be small rivers. When they all spilled together, they made the river he meant to follow. He wondered if he should have followed the river downward to find its end instead of searching for its beginning.

He also found many other things before the cold set in. Welo came across several places where other people had made a camp. He found a new and abundant source of salt. He had found great deposits of flint and chert, and others of obsidian. At one, the obsidian had fractured and left almost vertical flat areas that reflected the sun just before it set in the west. When he stood in front of those closely during the day, he could see himself, a glimmer of his image trapped in the black rock. These were marvels, each in their own way, but none of them seemed to Welo to be what Eini needed.

He walked until he passed over the mountain, not at the very peak but near it, and began to make his way down the other side. He had never been this far from the Téuta village, and knew of no one other than the Kujoté who had. The forest people did travel far, but their travels were in the other direction, not over this mountain, but down it to the plains. He didn't think they had ever come this way.

On the far slopes of the mountain, Welo discovered different rivers, and learned that the world is big. Really big.

In a way, he had always known this, as everyone knows it. But things like that are both known and not really known. The greatness of the world is not felt. Here, Welo felt it. The world seemed bigger when he truly saw it, when he was in it far from home.

Welo continued down the far side of Téuta's mountain and into foreign places. To places where he thought no Téuta had ever been before him. And on that far mountainside, far away from the Téuta's slopes, Welo found two great ponds, or small lakes, where creeks flowed into wide basins on the mountain. The ponds were huge with fish. He ate well that night.

In the morning, Welo continued on, determined to find whatever Eini wanted him to find. But the signs were mounting that true winter was near. Cold was coming. At the end of the second day away from the lakes, he decided he would need solid shelter soon. The lakes seemed to be the best option for Welo to stay over the winter. They had been a plentiful source of food. There were craggy cliffs and ridges close to them where he might find caves to shelter in, and the cliffs, like the Téuta's cliffs, broke the wind. He returned to the lakes to prepare for winter.

After searching the area for a few days, Welo still had not found the deep caves he expected. He did not want to spend many weeks looking for caves that might not exist. But he found something that was almost a cave. He found a shallow, hollowed place in a mass of rock with a long overhang above it. It would be deep enough to keep him dry when rains came and warmer when it snowed.

He spent the following weeks working on his shelter, turning it into a place where he could survive the months of cold weather high on the mountain. There were trees not far away. He used branches from these, and the mud from the lake bottom, to create walls. He did not really build a proper fire-pit, but he hollowed out a depression in the floor where fires could stay dry, and made a smoke hole above it.

The mud did not dry completely before the first real snow, and his shelter froze on the outside. At first, Welo feared the ice would break his walls, but it did not. They stayed true and firm. The fire kept the interior of his little cavern dry and warm. That was enough. He could keep his shelter comfortable, as long as he could find wood or dung to burn.

He spent the winter there on the slopes, fishing and hunting, and surviving in his simple shelter. In the evenings he watched the sunsets, and in the morning the sunrises, over peaks he had never seen, across a wide pond very different from the river he was used to.

When Welo was not asleep, he explored. Even at night he walked the rocky shores of his lakes—*his* because there was no one else near. There were goats, wolves, and bears, but no people.

I have never been so alone, he thought in the evenings as he watched the stars and the dark mountains around him. *Never so far away and alone.* There were cliffs, which felt right, but there was no wall of ancestors to comfort him. No Seneks. No Eini.

In spite of that, he was, in those early days of deep winter, never really lonely in his mountain dwelling. He felt the solitude, but he also felt something else, something that calmed him, and that felt like a companion. He felt the presence of the earth, the gods he knew, and felt that although he was away from his people, the gods, his gods, lived with him on the mountain. He did sometimes see the things, what they had called stranger gods, that Eini had shown him so long ago in the valley near the Téuta. But here, without the cover of the ground mist of that distant valley, he could see that they were only puffs of something pushing up from under the earth. They were not gods. And in this wild place, with the stars above him and the moon's milky light at night, and the sun in the day both bright white on the surrounding snow, he was glad. He had no use for stranger gods.

And maybe that is what Eini needed. Maybe she just needed to know that.

Maybe that was it.

But that answer did not satisfy him. Welo did not feel that he should return with only that. Both Eini and Seneks had said to walk until he found something that mattered, something that was enough. They had said he should walk until he felt he should return. With just this, it did not yet feel right to return.

Winter became deep. Welo had to hammer holes in the ice on the pond to find fish, and he had to maintain the ice holes every day. Eventually even that did not suffice; no fish swam past his holes. He gave up on fish until spring. Food was not as easy to find here as it was during the summers at the Téuta, not nearly as easy as just after the harvest of the grains. Despite that, through early winter he was almost never starving. He had gathered salt, and he did salt some meat from a goat he had taken in the rocky ground high above the lake. Although in the winter cold he didn't need to salt the meat to keep it fresh. In the cold mountain winter it stayed fresh without that.

In the nights, sometimes, Welo watched the mountains through the doorway of his shelter, close enough to the fire behind him to stay warm but still aware of the chill of night in the mountains. He could never quite forget that. At those times he wondered what he was doing, spending a long winter so far from home. He spent many nights watching the stars and thinking about this. What could Eini need? What could she want, sending him out like this across the wild mountains with no direction, and no idea what he should find? He had seen what there was to see. As winter wore on, he became sure he would find nothing more that might help her.

"I am not the right one to find your path, Eini," he said out loud into the night. "I've been walking for a long time. I have crossed to the other side of our mountain. But I have found nothing. Nothing. Salt, I found that. But we have places to get that much closer to the Téuta. Flint. Goats with long hair. I have found these, but nothing that could help you, Eini."

When he spoke those words out loud, he realized that he had done little talking on his walk. His voice sounded strange to him. It felt strange in his throat. He spoke again, just to hear himself, and to feel it. But even as he relished the now unfamiliar sound, Welo knew he meant the words he said.

"I think I am done. Eini, I think it's time for me to be done. You must find someone better. Someone who can know what is needed. I am only Welo. I can't find this thing. I have tried, Eini. I have tried, but I don't know what to look for."

And on another night he told the stars: "In the spring I will return to the Téuta. I don't want to walk anymore in strange places. I want my home."

CHAPTER 24
WINTER/SPRING 6242 BCE

Winter deepened. On the high mountain, it was longer, colder, and more bitter than any Welo had known before. The game that had been so abundant disappeared. Even using all his senses, Welo struggled to find enough to eat as most of the smaller animals retreated under the earth and ice to wait for spring.

He had used his grain up quickly in early winter and consumed the roots he had found and stored in the first months. Welo had taken one of the high mountain goats in his first weeks at the lakes, when food seemed boundless, and he had thought he would have enough meat to get through the winter, but he had been wrong.

When his food was gone, he ate snow. He had arrows and new arrow heads; flint and chert were all around him at the lakes. Picking his way through the rocks beyond his shelter, looking, sensing, all around him, Welo hunted daily. But there were no goats, no deer that he could detect.

Still, he survived. There were days when he found little to eat; days, in truth, when he found nothing, and ate either scraps from days prior or, on a few days, nothing. Snow was all around him, though, and he kept his fire going, so he always had water. There was scrubby, woody brush here and there that pushed up through the snow around the lake, and early in the winter he had found two fallen trees of some size. He had to walk a fair distance to get to either of them, but like the scrub, they were fuel.

Welo had faith in his resilience. Some evenings, though, he wondered whether that faith was right, whether it was true even here, in this winter, at this lake.

At the end of an evening of great beauty when stars spread across all the clear sky, Welo sat just inside the door of his shelter wondering if winter would last forever. He wondered what it could be that Eini needed, that she had sent him to find, and what failing Eini in this task would mean. He thought about her waiting, and waiting, to use whatever it was to save the Téuta.

It became a rhythm for him. He hunted and scavenged in the morning, then prepared what food he found and warmed himself later in the day. Welo enjoyed all of it, but in that winter the evenings were the best of life. In the early night he watched this lonely world from the door of his shelter, his fire beside him. He *kept* watch with his other sense, to be sure there was no danger coming. But it was what he saw with eyes that made the time after eating enchanting. The distracting stars and the long hum of wind through the crags above him, the quiet tick and flicker of the fire, made a kind of trance inside him. The great song the wind sang echoed deep in his chest. He would sit all evening feeling this place, then sleep or try to sleep.

Sometimes at night, before he fell into dreams, Welo tried to stretch his sense as far as he could, trying to find game for the morning hunt.

One night he went to his bed still feeling the hum of the wind, and then, by habit as he lay to sleep, also stretching his other sense. His eyes closed to sleep. But with the fire behind and the night outside, and the long ice across the lake, snow in every crack, sleep would not come. He stretched his senses to find the goats. Where had they gone? He stretched, and stretched, to the limit of his sense.

His mind seemed to lift out of himself. On this night, with the great mountain around him, his solitude around him, the winter, the lake, the humming wind around him, his mind left him behind.

He shook his head to clear it as he came back to the world. He wondered what had just happened and, for a moment, whether he would be still in the world when tomorrow came? His thoughts seemed so meager. He left thinking behind and chose only to be with the mountain. He felt the mountain, and as he did, his mind left him again and seemed to ride out across the snow that covered the lake. His eyes closed. Without sight, his other sense grew and stretched. Stretching it as far as he could, he floated on it, sliding into the distance across the lake, and behind the visible rocks.

Beyond that, this sense had always become too diffuse to understand. But on this night, hungry and cold, with stars across the whole clear high-mountain sky, concentrating on one thing in the distance, one point where he thought he had discerned movement—with all of that, and his mind floating—Welo slid past his sense's end. Then he was not where he really was, not where his body was. He was only riding on the end of his sense, like a leaf tumbling on a river current, on and on.

His awareness of what was there seemed to take a new leap, as though he were sensing again from the end of his ability to sense, coming again to an end where he could not sense further, and then, concentrating on one point in that distant place, riding on again. Up the mountain to the very top, along the rivulets and trickles that made the rivers when they gathered, and then he felt the river around him as though he were a fish.

On that long sensory journey, he found the goats. They were down the mountain, far down where he thought he didn't have strength to go while the winter was so deep. Perhaps he could. If there were no other option, he would try.

But he also found smaller, burrowing things, cavy and rabbits and voles, and they were much closer. Some close enough that a moderate walk would find them, their burrows so shallow he might be able to pry them out.

Welo wondered again what was happening to his mind, whether this was all a fever, a dream, created by the cold, and by the solitude there. He wondered whether this thing that had happened in the night, his mind flowing like a river, was his journey to the land of the dead. If so, he had no fear of it. What he had felt was glad, and beautiful.

His fire waned, and morning came. To his surprise, he woke whole and alive. That day he spent finding rabbits. He took two of them and took them to his shelter at midday to simmer them until they were soft enough to eat. He ate well through that afternoon. Then he slept again, sated. The next morning he woke strong and alert, and went again to find rabbits or cavies. The goats would return when they returned. But now, with this new food source, Welo could wait for them.

Three days later, he remembered his long sense-journey. Remembered getting to the very end of his ability to sense anything, and then sliding past that end along a sense at the end of his sense, and then another at the end of that, as far as he had wanted to go that night. He had found the goats, and pigs, and bear, all beyond the usual range of his sense. How had he done that?

He closed his eyes again and tried to remember. He failed. He tried again. Failed again. Tried again—and suddenly the more distant sense came into focus for him. He felt as though he were in a turbulent river being carried by momentum across the world. He could see across the mountain, down and up, even, he imagined, almost to the Téuta itself. It made him dizzy to do this; in fact, he realized abruptly that it made him sick to do it. Welo rose, moved quickly, not running but not quite walking either, onto the sturdy surface of the lake, and emptied his stomach onto the ice.

Over the next days he kept trying. With practice came acceptance, until he could far-sense without sickness or dizziness, even without very much strain. It did take concentration, and after each effort he was tired. But that was a small price for so great an ability.

Sometimes, to escape his long solitude, Welo tried, on his sense journeys, to find the village itself, the Téuta. He tried to see Eini and Seneks. And sometimes he almost *felt* he could achieve it, although he did not really believe it. He was sure it was just a wish. The village was too far away for even with this new ability to find.

Yet, even if it was only a wish, Welo's solitude began to feel less lonely. And in the evenings as he watched the stars, he felt he was watching for all the Téuta, that all the Téuta people could watch through his eyes.

Snow was falling in the Téuta. The ground was white even where people had walked, because snow fell so fast it filled their footprints until they were only dips in the whiteness. All the hut-tops were clothed in white, with some gray near the smoke-holes. But with the snow still falling, even their gray rims were quickly covered.

Eini stood outside the door of her hut watching whiteness fall across her village. The sky, dark with cloud, and the snowflakes dotting her face as she looked up, was peace itself.

So why did her thoughts have Welo in them? Why did she suddenly wonder about him? He had been gone for six moons. People said he was probably dead, out in the deep winter. If he were dead, then Eini had caused his death by sending him. She would feel that burden for all her remaining life, if it were true. Since the day she left him at the Kujoté, she had felt a deep worry about him. One that only grew deeper as time and winter went on.

But suddenly, now, standing with the snow falling on her face, she was certain it was *not* true. He was alive somewhere. Somewhere cold, even colder than the Téuta. Welo was alive. He was happy. She did not know how she knew that, but she was sure of it. He had not found the thing she needed, but he was alive and safe for now. He was fed and warm, and nothing threatened him.

Eini's burden drifted away with the snow. She closed her eyes.

It had been her habit for all her life to dance when she felt light like this, and so she did. She heard the music of the snow, of the river, of the night. Eini turned and turned, her face still lifted toward the falling snow as she danced outside her hut. She danced with all the winter's weather. With night. She danced with the Téuta.

When she opened her eyes, both Ceneta and Sntodi were outside with her. They stood, each for their own separate reasons, entranced. Ceneta, after a time, joined her, and danced with Eini in the snow.

Sntodi then leaned against the hut, watching them both. Glad of them. Proud of their dancing. Grateful for the honor of seeing them, he alone and no one else.

⚘

When spring came, Welo remembered the winter days when he swore he would return to the Téuta, swore that Eini had chosen badly, and that he could not find what she needed. But he did not return to his great village. In the spring he thought, *they are depending on me. Eini is depending on me. If she is right, the Téuta is depending on this long walk. I will go on. Not forever. But for a little way, I will go on.*

He packed what he could carry and walked down the slopes and onto another mountain. It was not a *completely* strange one. It was the mountain just beyond the Téuta's mountain, and the Téuta could see its peak from the plateau above the village. Sometimes there were travelers who had come from this mountain who passed by the Téuta, particularly on festival days when many people came to trade things. Obsidian, of course. And curious long-haired skins of goats. Now, Welo knew where to get those. The same travelers also brought carvings and colorful cloths with curious weaving from a village across the mountains that was known for its excellence in those arts.

So Welo knew the mountain from a distance, having seen its peak. But he had never expected to be on it.

He kept moving up this new mountain. Spring had raised his mood again. He hoped he could find what Eini needed. In the warmer weather, with the new tips of green growth around him, he was exhilarated by this adventure so far from home. Climbing again toward a new mountain peak, making camp each night in a world new to him, Welo was glad of the weather, and of the world, and of all the gods that made them.

CHAPTER 25

SPRING 6242 BCE

Night turned above him, stars moved in their arcs across the sky, the wide moon traveling with them, making the world bright. Welo lay under his cloak to watch them after he ate his night meal. But he couldn't sleep. He was uneasy for no reason, or none he could sense. Something far away seemed to be moving, more distant than his ability to sense it unless he knew where to search for it. He was uncertain about what it meant. It could be benign, just another ordinary thing. But it felt angry. Or hungry. He did not know how he could know that, but Welo had often found it best to trust these feelings. He could sense things long before he was aware of sensing them.

He watched the moon until it had moved close to the horizon. Then finally he slept.

The morning was damp and cold on his face, and on the rocks beneath his hand. Fog had come down while he slept. It seemed to chill the world and choke the meager embers of his fire. Dawn, the siren, the amber goddess, was still hidden behind the mountains to the east. She threw fresh, bright beauty ahead of her over the high peaks. Welo stood, stretching. In the early light, the mist covered everything. The mountains to the northeast glowed with a bright but almost shapeless stain of gold and coral against the gray.

Welo's other sense, the one that had caused him both opportunity and trouble all of his life, could find the dawn but not the beauty of it. Dawn's beauty was for the eye. According to his other sense, today's dawn, like every day's, was simply a more turbulent spot on the edge of the world.

The fire was out and would be hard to start again on the wet ground. He was cold. His parka and hood kept some warmth inside it, but he knew he needed to warm himself. He could struggle to start the fire, or he could move. Since this place was no better than any other to him, he gathered his things and began to walk, chewing on a bit of dried salted goat meat from his pouch.

By mid-morning the fog was gone, and Welo felt the warmth of walking, and climbing, and also of the sun above him. He sent his other sense out far ahead to see what dangers or opportunities might be there. He had plenty of meat, some salted fish, and some spring greens with him. So he simply walked to find out what there was in the world this far from the Téuta.

There was a village ahead of him, he thought, perhaps two days of walking away, but one, of course, that he had never seen before. He thought it might be one he had heard about from travelers at the spring and fall festivals. Welo thought he remembered hearing that the village was friendly, that the villagers farmed and raised goats and were not hostile to strangers. He hoped that was true. He wondered if the new way of weaving he had heard about, or the different dyes this village used, might be the things he was supposed to bring back to Eini? He didn't know how weaving could save the Téuta from anything, but he didn't need to know. He just needed to find something, anything, that seemed different, that felt new, and right.

The afternoon's walk was easy and quick. The village was only half a day's walk away when Welo made camp. Tomorrow he would be there, and then he would see. There was no rush. He would get there. As he prepared a small fire, well hidden among the rocks, Welo wondered what these people were like, what their customs were, what their language was. If it was like the speech of the Téuta, he would be able to talk to them. But probably it was not. He would know tomorrow. It had been many moons since he had seen any other human, and Welo had to dampen his eagerness and his anticipation to get to sleep.

When he woke in the early morning, the moon was long down. He was uneasy again, and that puzzled him. The dark didn't bother him. He liked it; the dark held no fear for him. His sense told him there were no predators near him. He had come far enough down the mountain that the clouds were above him now; there was no fog to dampen his fire or his mood. He shook his head to clear it, stood and stretched, slapping his cold legs to make them warm again. His fire was nearly out. There was dry wood nearby. He could start it again. But he didn't need it, and he was eager to meet these new people, these weavers.

Welo covered the fire to douse it, packed, and walked for a time toward the first ledge on the way down to the village. From that high vantage point, he might be able to see the village with his eyes.

His other sense, though, was now telling him why he had been feeling such unease. He could sense little puffs that he thought were humans moving toward the village, with care, with stealth. Why would they do that? He could think of no good reason, but one, at least, that was not good.

He must have sensed this before, when he woke, an hour ago, but it didn't register. Then, he had been aware of uncertainty, of uneasiness, but not danger to the people of this village.

Welo also sensed that the village was alive in its morning, with people working in fields, in the streets, and in their huts without any awareness of what was coming toward them. Welo began to move faster. There was nothing he could do to warn them. He was much too far away for that. He felt urgency saturating the late-morning light, soaking the air and tumbling down the rocks toward the people below.

When he reached the ledge, he still could not see the village. The trees were thick along the slopes. But although he could see none of what was happening with his eyes, he saw all of it with his other sense. He could do nothing. He was strong, and tall; he frightened many of the Téuta with his size. But he was only one man. And even if he were a hundred men, he was much too far from the village. Everything would be over by the time he made his way down the cliffs, then the slopes, then through the trees to finally reach them.

Still, he hurried. He watched his feet, or his hands on the rocks as he descended, and when he was not climbing down, he watched the village below. Soon he saw smoke, a great deal of smoke, rising from the village. Something there was burning.

It was afternoon before Welo approached his destination. He didn't need to see what had happened. He didn't want to see. Even sensing it from a distance disturbed him to his bones. But he had to enter the village. There might be something he could do for anyone or anything that was left. It was safe enough for him. The raiders were gone. They had left the burning, ruined village long ago, when morning was still young, heading south, down the mountain. And while the dead were everywhere on the ground and in the remains of the huts, there were three people still living that Welo could sense in the area near him.

Although they seemed, in the distance and to his sightless sense, to be unharmed, they were not moving much.

The village was clustered around an open area with a large stone marking its center and pits for fire in several places around it. Welo threaded his way between the huts. Reaching the center stone, he felt stillness flowing through this place that was florid with slaughter. Why did it seem so still? There was noise. The sound of spent fires cooling, and fires still burning, and now and then the crumble of a wall where burning timbers had left it without support.

But it wasn't living noise. There were no birds, no nearby animals in the forests, no sounds of the lives of people. No talking, no bickering, no grumbling or laughter.

The three living that he sensed here were quiet. They were hiding, and fearful and silent in the wide, wooded mountain day. They lived still, and now closer to them he still thought they were unharmed.

But their village was dead, and nothing could revive it. This village, perhaps the one whose crafts had been admired among the forest people, whose weaving and colors had been admired even among the Téuta, had been removed forever from the world.

CHAPTER 26

Welo walked from hut to hut, and through the spaces between them, counting the dead.

He nodded. Now he had seen it. It was time to find the three who had hidden well enough to escape the raiders. He could find them; it wasn't possible for living animals or living people anywhere near him to hide from Welo.

He walked first toward a house on the edge of the village because the smallest and closest of the survivors was there. It was a child, a girl, curled under a musty goatskin, which was itself under a refuse heap. Welo called to her, but (wisely, he thought) she said nothing. She was alive and well, but she didn't know who he was. After a few moments, he reached under the ragged skin that covered her, and tugged her arm gently, making what he hoped were comforting sounds, shushing and soothing, and crouching to seem smaller and less frightening. The girl knew she had been found, so she emerged, seeming both panicked and resigned. She came from her hiding hole certain that horror would greet her. She appeared to have about seven or eight winters, although through the fear and dirt it was hard to tell.

"Calm, calm, I'm not one of them, I won't hurt you, I won't harm you..."

Although she still stared at him with huge eyes, terrified eyes, she heard the tone of his voice and wanted to trust him. But the events of the morning had killed her trust in anything, and she did not understand the words he used. Welo patted the ground, showing that she should sit with him. *She wants to run but doesn't know where to go,* he thought. She looked for something in the woods but didn't find it. After a few moments she did not sit but squatted near him, still staring at him with her eyes huge and frightened.

One of the two in the woods was moving toward them, as quickly as possible without making too much noise. A woman, he thought. As he watched, she emerged tentatively from the edge of the forest. She was an older adult, not a true elder, but instead a woman near to forty winters. He thought she might still be attractive if she were not sweating with fear and covered in soot. Then he chastised himself for having such thoughts amid this field of carnage, when these people were in terrible shock.

Welo reached toward the child's shoulder, but she flinched away. He dropped his hand, then lifted it again and pointed to the woman who had just emerged from her hidden place among the trees. The child hesitated, but finally turned to see. One glance was enough. She was up and off before he could blink, running hard toward the woman. When she got there, she threw her arms around the adult she knew, clinging hard, burying her face against a familiar waist. From their appearance, the child and the woman did not seem to be related, but they clearly knew each other well. They weren't running away. But they weren't coming closer either. They saw that there was only one of him, and that dressed differently from those who had come with the dawn. But they were wary.

The third survivor was hiding deeper in the forest. She was not moving at all, and seemed unaware of them. Welo found her to collect all of them together. He stood—the woman and child were visibly more frightened when he stood, not least Welo thought, because he was so tall. But when he walked past them, they spoke quickly to him, clearly asking him not to go, not to leave them alone again. Welo did not understand the language, but he understood the meaning. He motioned that they should stay where they were. But when he walked into the trees, they followed him, distantly, as timid and quiet as shadows. While they were apparently afraid of him, they were obviously more afraid of being alone in the village with all the dead.

Welo walked quickly through the trees. His trembling followers had to nearly run to keep up with his long legs, but even running they made little noise.

The last survivor was in a gap under the twisted roots of a tree with many trunks. When he rounded the tangle of roots, she was there. She looked to be almost thirty years, perhaps a little less, Eini's age. A woman ten winters older than he was, stared into the distance. She seemed to be so shocked at what had happened that she didn't know he was there, knew nothing was there. But what struck him the most, struck him into such awe that at first he could not speak, was her beauty. She was the most beautiful woman he had ever seen in all his life.

Until she turned. He spoke to her, something simple like "I am not one of them" or "Don't be afraid". He didn't remember later what it was he said. But she turned, and he saw that the side he had seen first was stunning in its beauty—he had himself been stunned by it—but the other side of her face was disfigured badly by scars. Not new. Not from the events today. Not even recent. They seemed to be burn scars, very, very old and healed for many years. Scars that would never leave her.

Her eyes, her face, followed him as Welo walked to her and squatted on his heels. She showed no fear. Life had given her so much pain already that there was nothing left for her to fear. When he reached to touch her scarred face, she barely moved.

Welo's two shadows came tentatively around the tree, looked to see who was there, and startled a little when they saw. Not with surprise, but with relief, if anything at all could be read in their faces.

"Akesh," the older woman said, with what seemed like hope and respect, and happiness for one she knew and liked, but one with ambiguous status, all in the same breath. Welo looked from the two behind him to this woman.

"Akesh? What does that mean, Akesh?"

The seated woman frowned for a moment, then understood. She put her hand on her chest and said "Akesh."

Welo still sat, seeming puzzled.

The woman again put her hand on her chest, said "Akesh". After a brief pause, she pointed at the older woman. "Senne," she said. She pointed at the younger girl and said, "Nedeh". Then she pointed to him.

Oh, he thought. Names.

"Welo," he said, and pointed at himself.

Then he wondered what he could say to them, what he could do. Using all his senses, he scanned the world around them and saw little danger remaining nearby. The raiders had taken what they wanted. They had taken all that they thought was worth searching for and killed or burned the rest. They were far away now, to the south. Why hadn't they taken these three? Nedeh had hidden herself well, and she was so young they might have just killed her if they had found her. Senne was too old to be worth the time it would take to find her in the forest. And Akesh was beautiful on one side, but scarred on the other. She might have frightened them when they looked at her. Or maybe they didn't know that she was here. Maybe she ran soon enough that they did not see her.

Welo squatted near Akesh, and seeing him the other two also squatted, but tentatively and they kept their distance. From watching them, he thought that of the three Akesh, no matter how ambiguous her status in the village, was the one the others would follow. They treated her strangely, it seemed to him, but they seemed to look to her for decisions they could not make for themselves. About what to do now, and where to go. About him, and whether he was a danger or a defense from danger, or both, or neither.

Welo looked at the two huddled together to his left, the old one and the young one, and then at Akesh. He looked back through the trees toward the village, and back at Akesh.

"How do you honor your dead?"

Akesh stared at him, understanding nothing of what he had said. He pointed back to the village and stood.

"There are many dead there," he said. "What do we do with them? We shouldn't leave them like that. Wolves will come."

He hesitated for a moment, then began to walk back to the village and gestured for them to follow. As he walked away, he sensed Akesh slowly standing and following him. The other two stood then, and followed Akesh, staying close to her, all of them staying back, wary of him. Watching him.

If this was the village he thought it might be, it was a village that had welcomed strangers, he had heard; they had seen strangers before, and embraced a tradition of hosting them, and trading with them. This was a village known for its weaving, and for the colors of its cloth. Usually, for them, strangers were good.

But Welo had arrived just after strangers who were *not* good had come from nowhere to destroy all they knew. He was, to them, a mystery. A coincidence. Fearsome, and possibly dangerous, but also possibly the only safety or hope left for them on earth.

CHAPTER 27

In the village, the three women stayed close together, Akesh walking through the streets, dazed by what she was seeing. The other two stayed within a pace of her. Akesh seemed to be walking about randomly, and Welo noticed that all were still keeping their distance from him. He understood and was patient. Through half the afternoon he waited before he walked to Akesh to ask his question again, pointing to the bodies in the street. And at last she understood him. She pointed to the smoking thatch, and with gestures made him understand that the bodies should be burned. The practice was familiar to him, even though the Téuta buried their dead, choosing to lay them to rest in the right places. The revered they buried near the wall of the dead, loved ones under their huts, or if that was not possible, as close to the Téuta as they could. The Téuta wanted their dead to stay with them, to stay home and not forget the place they had lived in, or the people they had known there. But Akesh said that this village practiced the same rituals Welo had heard the forest people did for their dead.

As she looked around the ruined village, Welo could see that Akesh was struggling to control her grief and bewilderment. Then acceptance of the truth came to her, and that too, showed grim in her sooty face.

She crouched by one man who had obviously been important to her, trying to straighten him and lay his arms across his chest. The other women saw, and they also began to put the dead in order —all of them, those in the street and those in the huts, those that had been dragged to the edge of the forest and killed there.

As he watched them set about their grim task, Welo saw that he had been right about Akesh. She had taken control of herself, and the others then knew that even in tragedy they must do what must be done. Akesh was not just alive now. She was living. Numb, slow, drowned in grief, but, despite the surrounding horror, she was living through her actions.

It seemed wrong to Welo to do what they were doing for their friends and relatives, but it was their custom and these were their dead, and he could help them. For several days, with instructions from Akesh, Welo dug a long trench for them, using a digging stick he made from wide antlers that he found in one of the huts. In this trench they piled wood from the forest, and thatch that had not burned. Then they laid the dead across the long pyre, and they lit the flame.

The pyre burned all afternoon and late into the night. When it had subsided, Welo and Akesh began to push the dirt back over the pit, but Akesh pushed him aside. Yes. Again, their dead, their task. Welo walked to what he hoped was a respectful distance and watched as these three women buried the ashes of their friends and lovers, their parents and children and teachers, of everyone they had ever known.

Almost. Almost everyone. There were, he thought, some young women of the right age who had been taken away with the raiders. He did not want to think about that. The three women working to bury their village, he thought, were also trying hard not to think about it.

Welo saw quickly that once the fires had died and the trench was filled with dirt, there was no reason to stay here. There was nothing for him, and nothing for them. And he could not leave them here. Nor would they want to wander forever through the mountains with him, searching for something not even Eini could name. These women needed a place to be—and Welo thought he knew where that place might be. He decided then and there that they should come with him back to the Téuta.

So, his journey had to end in failure. He had found nothing for Eini. But here were three women who needed help, and for now they seemed more urgent than Eini's task. He could perhaps come back next year to find what Eini needed.

The women were reluctant to leave their village, the place where they had lived through the whole of their lives, the village where everyone they knew—almost everyone—was now burned and buried. The village where their ancestors had, in their time, been buried with fire. Welo thought he knew what that meant. He would hate to leave the Téuta for good. But now, what was left to keep them here? Nothing. Welo waited for them to know that.

For sixteen days Welo and the women stayed at the village, doing the work needed to provide for the dead. In the days after the fires had all subsided, Welo noticed that Akesh came to sit near him, not close, but close enough that if they had spoken the same language, they could have talked. Senne and Nedeh sat farther away, doing whatever they chose for each moment, but clearly waiting for Akesh to decide what was next.

Welo needed no common language to understand that Akesh knew what he knew, and that she too, was waiting—not for the other women to decide, but for them to be ready to accept this truth, to accept that the life they had known was gone and that they would have to travel to find another.

One day, the women seemed to be sorting through the ruins looking for something. Welo had no idea what it was, but it seemed important to them.

And always, the three women watched the woods around them with fear. Welo tried to reassure them; he could sense no other humans anywhere close. There were wolves some distance away, but for the first five or six days the fires still smoldering from thatch roofs fallen into the huts kept them far away, and after that they seemed to have an interest in something else.

Through all of this time Akesh watched Welo closely. After the first few days she seemed to trust him to be peaceful, and to trust him to know where danger was. She could not have understood how he knew, but she saw that he did, and so even in the grip of her grief she was calmer. That seemed to settle the other two as well. The way the girl and the older woman treated Akesh, and their attitude toward her, was confusing to Welo. They seemed to feel some distance from her, yet they followed where she led like baby ducks following their mother.

Senne and Nedeh watched Akesh with clear concern. They watched as though they expected her to do things that she wouldn't, or couldn't, do. As though they were afraid that her grief would end her, and they would then be lost. No matter what her status was in the village, Akesh was who they looked to, and by the third or fourth day the other women saw that she survived, and would survive, and they took solace in the poise she showed in doing all that had to be done.

There were still pots of wild grain in the village that had survived the fires. Perhaps the raiders had taken all they could carry and simply left these, or perhaps they never found them, since they were buried in huts that had been burnt. The grain, like everything else in the village was covered with ash, but to Welo and the women, hungry from their work, it tasted fine. On their third day in the village, Welo went hunting and brought back a small red deer. He made a stew with the venison and some of the grain, and with some roots he had found in the forest around them; to these things he added water and some young wild onion, still too green but good in spite of that. The three women were astonished that this strange, tall, bony man could cook something that tasted as good as that. They tried, at first, to push him away from the cooking pot, thinking that cooking would be their task. But Akesh, watching him closely, spoke to the others and then they all sat to witness this strange thing.

At first, when Welo spoke, the older woman, Senne, could not understand him at all. But Akesh, who was a good mimic, and Nedeh who was simply young and curious, learned new words from him. Welo also learned words from them, discovering that although their language sounded very different, once he understood it, it was in fact similar to that used by the Téuta and the forest people. It was not long before Welo and Akesh could communicate, and eventually she told him a little about that terrible day, the day her village died.

"They came like wolves," she said, "wild things with no mercy."

The raiders, she told him, came not as one or two, but as twenty.

They were tall and vigorous, and fell on their chosen victims suddenly. They picked the strong men first, killing them before the village knew the raiders were there. They killed the men, all of them, and the boys, and took the women they wanted. Not that there were many, only those ready to make children. So even girls too young and old women were killed.

Who were they, these men who came so abruptly, who had never come near the village before? These strangers with their violence? Welo asked. And Akesh answered that they were unknown people who came from emptiness and returned to it when they left.

The child often listened to them quietly, patiently, since they were adults. But sometimes she would say something to Akesh after Welo spoke, seeming to translate some difficult phrase for her. *The child understands even better than Akesh does*, Welo thought, after the first few times this happened. *In a moon or two, she will speak Téuta as well as I do.*

Over time, Welo noticed that Senne and Nedeh spoke little, but sometimes when they did they called Akesh by that name, and sometimes by another. Sometimes they used the name Eksi when they spoke to her. Welo asked Akesh about it, but she would not discuss it and would not answer him if he called her Eksi. She answered him only when he called her Akesh.

One day, Nedeh, hearing him try to call Akesh by her other name, came to him when she saw he was alone to explain.

"It is special name," she said. "Friend name. Or child say that name sometimes. She is name Akesh, except for special friend."

Ah, Welo thought. *A name used 'for special,' and I am not special in that way. Of course not. I am a stranger still to these women.*

He didn't call her Eksi again after that.

On the sixteenth day, the women reluctantly accepted that their village existed no longer, and that they would have to return with Welo to wherever it was he came from if they wanted to survive. His strength, his size, his skills, and his strange ability to know where there was danger and where there was none, all had value too high to ignore. He seemed safe. They had learned over sixteen days to trust him.

Finally, Akesh came to him. She stood while he sat and said words he couldn't completely understand. But he understood their meaning. It was time to go.

So on the seventeenth day, early in the morning, they walked together into the woods, and up the rocks, back along the way Welo had come.

CHAPTER 28
SPRING/EARLY SUMMER 6242 BCE

To return to the Téuta they first had to climb up a slope full of steep rock faces with few handholds. Welo thought he would have to help the child, but Nedeh was a wonderful climber. Akesh also could climb without much help. It was Senne, the older woman, who slowed them, sometimes needing a strong hand to help her over the top of a steep rock. By the time they reached the top, she climbed well enough, and they made good progress. They talked little during this first day of the journey. The climbing was hard enough without wasting breath. When they finally reached the top, the path traversing the plateau was easier. By the end of the afternoon, they reached the place where Welo had camped on the night before the raid.

As they ate and then prepared for sleep, Welo noticed, as he had before, that Akesh helped the others first, not only the child but the older woman too, and then made her own bed ready. She slept quickly, tired after her long day of walking and climbing. When they were sure Akesh was well asleep, Senne woke the child, and they both moved closer to where Akesh lay. They had learned to trust Welo, but Akesh—Eksi to these women—Eksi they had known all their lives. She was their village to them.

Welo was an odd man from a distant town, the Téuta, that until he arrived had been only a legend. It seemed impossible to them that the story of the big Téuta was true, and that a man from that place was with them. Friendly, seemingly peaceful and safe, and a protection in a dangerous world, but he was still the strangest of strangers. When they slept, they wanted to be close to their own.

It had taken Welo more than half a year of walking, a period of sometimes aimless traveling, and a stopover in the winter, to reach this little village. He had traveled alone, rising early and moving all day on strong, tireless legs. But it had been a quest, not a journey. Now Welo thought that if he were alone, it would take him only a moon, or perhaps two, to return to the Téuta.

But he was no longer alone. He had three companions; one a child who walked with energy in the mornings but tired as the day wore on, and another who was slow not only because of her age, but because something had injured her early in her life. Senne walked with a slight limp. One of her legs was weaker than the other, so sometimes Welo had to help her over obstacles. But worse, all of his charges were still shocked and grieving.

Often both Senne and Akesh seemed to be slow to rise, slow to start out, and to tire long before the day was done. The trip back did have one big advantage, though. While the three women were walking across mountains they had never seen before, Welo knew his way well. After half a year of traveling through them, these mountains were familiar to him. He knew which path they needed to take to return to the Téuta.

Now and then, Akesh would wander away, climbing higher into the trees to look at plants. She was never out of Welo's sight, though, his sight with eyes, or the eyes of the two other women. Each time Akesh did this, they stopped and watched her and waited for her to return to them. Akesh always asked Welo whether it was safe before she ventured away. Even when he reassured her that it was, she looked anxiously at the surrounding forest, and frequently glanced back to make sure she could still see the others. Senne and Nedeh stayed always close to Welo, always fearful even though he tried to tell them, too, that there was no danger anywhere near.

Welo had been puzzled at first at the frequency of Akesh's excursions, but he waited for her each time. The women seem to see it as natural, as ordinary.

Then he understood. Akesh knew healing. Not always the same healing he knew, but close enough that he recognized what she was doing. He had watched Seneks gather these same plants often enough to know that she was not only looking for food but also for medicines.

The women had no notion of where they were going. They followed Welo, since that was all they could do. Nedeh, the child, clung to the older woman, to Senne, as though she were life—and Senne followed Akesh, and Akesh followed Welo. But often she seemed to follow him only because he moved, and because she was still so deep in mourning that she had no energy left for deciding on her own. Both Senne and Nedeh watched Akesh from the depths of their own grief.

Day after day Akesh followed Welo with no thought, and the others followed with thoughts only of Akesh.

None of them seemed to think about what Welo was leading them toward, didn't think about what the rest of their lives would be. They seemed to feel no interest in that. Whatever happened to them would happen. It might not be a happy future for them. But they—particularly, most importantly, Akesh—had no happiness, no memory or hope of it, left in her. The young one watched Akesh as though she herself could not rise from her grief until Akesh rose first, and the older because she had watched Akesh grow.

And both acted as though gladness could happen only when Akesh gave it to them.

Days moved into days, and the trip became a routine they all understood. It was the natural routine, the only possible routine. None of them imagined or bothered to imagine any other. Talking became more frequent. The women learned more Téuta words, and Welo learned the words they used. Gradually, speech could happen between them.

Grief, however deep, can't last forever in the living. The first smile came in the evening, after a hard day of climbing down toward lower ground. Welo knew there was another climb ahead of them. He was planning their route as he walked, but the women still lived only in each moment. They did not really care how far they had come or how far they had left to go. They were simply moving through a long world without past or future. But he noticed that each day Akesh walked a little closer behind him and gradually began to walk almost beside him.

Each day Welo chose a camp site, sometimes one he had used before while traveling, and prepared a meal for them. Then one day, Akesh took the grain and meat from him, and set to work preparing their dinner. She had cut some plants and put them into the water with the meat and grain. Welo watched her and wondered what she was putting into their food, and Akesh, who understood fear, showed him what she held. He took her hand and pulled it to his face and recognized it quickly. She held herbs and garlic she had gathered along the way. It was a combination of herbs a little different than he had ever smelled before, and the smell alone made him hungry.

While she worked, she hummed a little, very quietly, lonely, sad notes lost in the night while Akesh was lost in her own thoughts. Her hum, quiet as it was, had a strange power in it. It was new to him, this humming, this power in humming. When Akesh hummed, Welo wanted to listen.

The water with onions and garlic and herbs began to boil. Soon it gave a fragrance that made Welo move closer to the fire, nearer to Akesh, and the shy ghost of a smile played over her face. Nedeh watched her and exchanged glances with Senne. They also drew closer, the good smell coming from the cooking pot reminding them of quiet and safety, of food as had been cooked at home, of eating in their village. Soon, spectral smiles played inside them too. Not on their faces yet. But Welo could see it in them. Sadness was still deep, a sadness that never seemed to leave them, intense now even with, or perhaps because of, this new comforting memory of home. They remembered the food, but also families now all dead. Grief and homesickness wrestled with glad memory, and now, finally, also with the sense that home was not fully lost to them. However far they went away from it, the home they knew was carried within them.

Akesh's ghostly new smile seemed to Welo to give the other two permission to smile with her, and a hope, feeble and small, began, at last, to rise in them.

That night Akesh slept a little closer to Welo, and Senne and Nedeh, as always, slept close to her.

CHAPTER 29
SUMMER 6242 BCE

Through the days that followed, Akesh cooked their dinners most nights, sometimes with flavors that Welo did not know. During the days the group was happy to see her stray, looking for onions and garlic and roots, and their progress slowed a little. The evenings were still not happy ones, but they were less heavy with grief than they had been. Often, Akesh simply watched the sky after dinner, but she also sang quietly to herself. To Welo, the songs seemed wild, unordered, and lonely. But they were not completely separated from life as she had been when he found her. Senne and Nedeh knew these songs, and sometimes they also sang. They also still watched Akesh, and seemed to be waiting for something.

One evening Akesh began to sway, then dance as she sang. But she stopped very soon and simply watched the sliver moon, sitting a little apart where the light from the fire was less and the stars were clear across the sky. Welo closed his eyes, sensing where everyone was, and sensing around them for danger. There was none that he could find. There were wolves, but very far away, and deer and mountain pigs, which were no danger to them. From what he could sense, he and Akesh and Senne and Nedeh were the only people on this mountainside. The Téuta and the forest people were not here. They were on the next mountain. Their small group was alone.

Welo had laid back, resting after the evening meal, when he heard the clear, bright notes of a flute. His eyes opened. Akesh was playing a bone flute that had been darkened and charred in the fires. She must have carried it in her pouch all this way without touching it. She played wonderfully. The tune was one that Welo had never heard. His heart, all the hearts that heard her music, were quieter to listen.

Senne and Nedeh held each other's hands. Watching Akesh, they seemed to have more hope. When Akesh finally finished and sat, a small voice called out, "Eksi." And Akesh took Nedeh to her lap and held her.

Welo watched and thought, *How good for her, for the young one, to have a name so intimate to call out, to be allowed to call out, and to then have a lap produced for her to rest in. How good to have a lap that can give her comfort.*

Seeing that, Welo felt sharply exactly what he was here. He saw their small group, the only remnants of their village, and knew he was not one of them. He didn't mind. It was natural. He knew then that he could lead them to a new home, but he could not heal them. They had to heal themselves with things like this, the familiar food, the music, Akesh taking Nedeh to her lap. Welo had never seen her do that before, and, strangely, it comforted him to see it.

The next day the walking was easier, and the mood was lighter. Akesh moved with a fluid grace Welo had not seen before, and the other two moved as though the string that bound them to her had been weakened; they strayed far from her sometimes. But still, it seemed they were waiting for something. Akesh had revealed her secret flute and the beauty she brought from it. What else were they expecting from her? Whatever it was, Welo was sure he wanted it to arrive.

In the evening, they made camp near an outcropping of rock above a ravine cut by a small stream. Akesh brought water from the stream in the large skin they used as a cooking pot. She threw in a small amount of grain, since their supplies were low, and some garlic she had found along the way. Then she turned to Welo and asked, "Is there danger near?"

"Nothing near," he replied. "It is safe."

"Nothing?" Akesh asked.

"Nothing."

Satisfied with his answer, she walked into the evening woods, out of sight, to forage. Soon she returned with onions and roots that could be eaten if cut small and cooked well. She borrowed Welo's knife to cut them. Welo offered her some of the dried red deer he carried, and she cut that into smaller pieces and put it into the pot, too.

She said nothing to anyone, but stood then, while their dinner was heating, walked to the stream and took her clothes off to wash them, and to wash herself. The other two saw what she was doing and eagerly joined her. They were tired of being dirty. Akesh first, and then the others, drank deeply from the mountain water, and savored the cold it brought.

When they had finished bathing and spread their wet clothes on the sun-hot rocks, the women lay on the shore to dry. Welo watched them, smiling quietly to himself. They had followed him because he was all there was. They had trusted him enough for that because they had no other choice, and they had stayed close. But he had always been a stranger before, distant and unknown. Tonight, at last, they trusted him enough for this.

When the women had dressed and had returned to camp, their clothes still damp but drying quickly near the fire, Welo took his turn in the stream. The water felt fresh and lifted his mood.

CHAPTER 30

Dinner was finished. The night had come over them. Stars scattered above, the great white path arching down the sky above their heads. The fire was low, slowly turning to embers. Welo decided it was time to sleep, and he began to prepare to do that. Then Akesh asked him again, "Is there danger here?"

"No."

"People?" She asked. "Are there any people here, anywhere near us?"

"No," Welo said. "I can sense no one near, Akesh. Why are you nervous about this?"

The night was silent for a long moment, as Akesh stood watching the sky. There was something she seemed reluctant to tell him.

But finally she said, "I want to sing."

"Then sing. You have been singing for many days."

"That was singing for myself," she said. "And for Senne and Nedeh." She glanced at him and away again. "And for you. Maybe. But now I want to sing for the world and for the sky." She raised her hand far above her head, to the sky but including all of existence in the gesture. "For all of this I want to sing."

Welo was puzzled by this response. It made no sense to him. Singing is singing. What difference does it make who you are singing to? He was terse when he answered, not unkind but brief.

"Still, there is no one anywhere close. Sing if you wish to sing."

Akesh walked a few steps away from the fire so she was half hidden in the shadows. She stood, one side dark and the other shimmering slightly in the firelight. She was swaying, eyes closed. Just this gesture was curious. There was a sense of imminence. Welo watched her as she swayed, interested, then fascinated, then almost mesmerized. He could barely think of anything else, but he did spare a moment to look at the other two, the older woman and the child, who seemed to be holding their breaths, waiting. They held each other very close and watched Akesh. They were tense, sad, afraid and lovely. It made Welo smile to see them.

The silence continued, broken only by the rustle of wind and the hoot of a distant owl.

Akesh began to hum, and Welo's interest ebbed a little. He had heard her hum before. He turned to tend the fire.

Akesh sang softly as on any other night. Then her song rose, and her voice rose. Her singing seemed to rise above the peaks, above the mountain, soaring and growing until her song matched the size and the depth of the nature all around her.

Akesh sang to the trees, to the forest, and to anything in it. All the creatures in the forest seemed to listen, to pause all else they were doing to hear her. The owl was quiet now. Insects stilled. No mouse disturbed the forest floor. Even the wind was quiet. Everything paused to hear Akesh. Her voice pricked the dark and made it lighter; it was a sensory grace in the firelight. At this, Welo twisted to look at her; he had not heard her sing with so much heart before.

Akesh's eyes were still half closed, but they opened as she sang. Welo glanced again at Senne and Nedeh and saw that this was still not what they waited for, but he saw also that they thought the wait was nearly over. They were full of anxiety and sat close together as they watched.

And then finally and abruptly Akesh's voice became wide and big. The change shocked him with its suddenness. Until this moment, her songs had been as light as butterflies compared to this. But this was different. It was as though she had not really been singing until now.

But now, at last, she sang full, open, wide to all the earth, wide to the stars and the sky, and to the sky's sliver moon which had already crossed half of it. Welo turned completely to stare at her because her voice had filled the night almost beyond what it could hold. It was not so much loud as it was big in its heart, in the heart she gave to it.

No, he thought. *It is more than big. It is much more than that. This that I am hearing is vast, as the dome of stars is vast. Now her song dominates the night. Now her song absorbs it. Now her song is the night.*

When Akesh began, her song had been like a trickle down the rocks. Then, when she sang aloud, it was like a stream. Now, she released herself to the world. Her song came like a flood, wild and raw, strong, like a flood that pushed trees ahead of it, frothing against the shores, that pushed rocks ahead of it crashing them against each other, breaking and lifting them, and lifting or breaking everything in its path.

The song pushed images into Welo's thoughts, strange images that seemed to come from nothing. He imagined a great, black-clouded and deadly winter storm. Of course he imagined that, with singing as big as this. But then he imagined a buck and a doe mating in the forest, then the same buck running, and proud-antlered, strong, an invincible buck disdainful of danger, running, running and in the end foundering under a hunter's spear. He imagined wolf pups playing in the hills on a warm spring day. He imagined deep snow collapsing along a rocky slope. He imagined a tree that was short, twisted, thick, and very old, growing from a crack in a cliff, bending in the untamed winds on a mountain top but clinging forever to life. And he remembered the opposite, Eini's fallen tree that had been so grand and mighty before it fell to the ground.

Now Welo understood why Akesh had worried about people on the mountain hearing her. Anyone on this mountain, high or low, anyone on any mountain would hear this, and know it to be their song, their heart.

Akesh sang of all the pain she had seen in her life. It was the sound of deep and terrible anguish, of her recent pain, of the death of her village, yes, but also of pain long past. She sang the pain of the fire that had scarred her as a child, of rejection for her scarred ugliness on one side of her face, and greed for her beauty on the other, and of all her losses and pleasures in all her life, and as she did, tears stood on her scarred and beautiful face. All the water she had taken in the stream came out to flow down her face as she sang. But she sang also of resilience. She sang her acceptance. She sang of her turbulent, frightening strength within her grief.

Nothing good or bad in all her life was overlooked, and she took all of it within her and sang it. Welo looked at the other two women, whose silent faces were also wet with tears now, so full of grief, but also, finally, full of solace and release. Their heartache, their desolation for their lost village swept over them in the flood of Akesh's song, but the song lifted it all like a great rock and broke it. They felt it, their grief, and they held it fiercely close and yet released it, and it hurt, it *hurt* to let it go, as though some vital part of them was being torn out of their bodies. Senne had her arm around Nedeh, holding the grieving child tight against the curve of her breast, and both watched Akesh, as all the earth had to be watching her. When the song became too big for her, Nedeh buried her young face into Senne, crying hard and silent because she would make no sound that might compete with Akesh.

Welo sat down hard on the ground. Akesh both consumed and terrified him. He realized then that he also had tears on his face; he realized this because when he sat, wetness dropped from his chin onto his hand and startled him.

The song Akesh sang had no intellectual meaning for Welo. She sang in the language of her village, with words that were still strange to him. But her voice told him of all the grief in the long history of the Dhegm's world, the sorrows and loss and wretchedness. But it spoke also of all joy and forgiveness everywhere. Akesh's song told all who heard it that grief was here and would always be here, but that joy too was here even when you could not find it, beauty was here even when it hid from you, and that even now after everything, after everything, after all and everything it was alright, it was alright, it was alright, it was now and forever and always, alright.

Dhegm the goddess sang through Akesh. It had to be that. Nothing else could explain the power of this song that proclaimed and held and vanquished all loss.

This is what Senne and Nedeh have been waiting for as they watched

Akesh through all the days since the death of their village, Welo thought, and he understood them. Hearing Akesh sing this way made Welo understand everything.

Welo had no sense of how long Akesh sang for them. It hardly mattered. The fire had waned when at last she stopped, and he rose like a ghost to fetch wood for it, moving without thought to do what was habit.

When Welo returned to the fire, Akesh herself had dropped to the ground, spent. The other two women huddled with her, holding her to keep her warm. Welo walked to her and lifted her in his long, strong, strange and bony arms where she draped like a soft and well-worked pelt. He listened to her breathing as he carried her and held her close. Then he put her in a place good for her to sleep. He covered her with her cloak and put his own over her too. He did not care if he slept cold that night. He cared only that Akesh was warm and safe. The two other women, who would not leave her, were with Akesh under these coverings, still sharing their heat with her. She had given all of herself and was empty.

Welo lay down to sleep some distance from them. He didn't want to intrude on so private a moment for these women whose village had been taken from them with a sudden and terrible violence. And he was exhausted from her song. He too needed some moments alone.

But Akesh was not truly asleep, it seemed. She was not empty after all. Welo slept until much later in the night, she woke him. For the first time in their long walk from her village, she came to him and lay close against him. Senne and Nedeh followed and lay behind her, bringing the skins to cover this precious treasure and keep her warm. And Welo knew she was as she had been in the stream, wild and alive and wearing nothing. No, not nothing. This time she wore hunger. She held him hard, climbing eagerly under his clothing to find his skin, turning him, kissing his back, neck, chest with her wild and yearning mouth. And he turned to her and held her tight against the surrounding dark.

Death, and the danger of death, sometimes has this effect, he thought; *sometimes it raises the need to create new life to keep the earth vibrant with it.*

He complied with her need. He complied in part because it was his need too, and had been for many days. But it was not only because of that. It was because he knew in long bones that after this night he would do anything at all that Akesh asked of him. Anything she needed she would have, if he could give it.

His exhaustion was gone. That was good, because the need that was in Akesh lasted much of the rest of the night. Welo realized that the other two women were watching, and that they were very close. Not to him. He was just part of nature, a thing there for Akesh, something to meet her need but that for now had no other importance. They were moving to be close to *her*. Senne and Nedeh, and Welo too, and, Welo felt, everyone everywhere, needed to be near Akesh.

Their ruined village had been known only for its weaving and the colors of its cloth. They must have worked hard to hide the secret songs of Akesh through which she gave the strength of the earth to those who listened.

Their village had been raided for things of such small value. What the raiders should have wanted, what those crazed, violent and broken men should have taken, the only thing that might really have been able to push their splintering desperation away, was Akesh.

Welo was very glad they had not found her.

⚶ ⚶ ⚶

When morning came, they packed the camp and walked. The three women seemed lighter, less pressed by grief, but otherwise no different than they had been before.

For days and days, they walked, down the mountain where Akesh sang and up another, and over the top of that one. The women, as before, simply walked wherever Welo took them.

But Welo moved with more focus. The women saw it as he walked. He seemed to be moving toward some specific place, some specific thing, which came as a surprise to them, because they had forgotten that any place existed other than walking with Welo through a world they had never seen. Soon they knew they would discover what his focus was. That could wait until it happened.

The little trickles along the rocks they had used for drinking and cooking turned into cascades when it rained. On the afternoon of a day when Welo had wakened them early and walked so quickly that they had to hurry to keep up, they came to a larger fall of water with a pool below deep enough to bathe in.

The women were smiling and excited by this, and even though the weather was cool, the sun was still high above them. In almost no time, the three had dropped their clothes by the water and were under the falls, washing and playing, far more carefree than they had been at the smaller stream before Akesh sang. They drank their fill here too.

Then their long walk continued.

At the end of the next day, the group arrived at the top of a high cliff. Below them, was a vision familiar to Welo but astonishing to the others. Below them was a town many, many times larger than their own had been. It was many times larger than any the women had ever imagined.

On the last part of this long journey Akesh did not sing at all. She did not approach Welo in the night again, nor did the other women. They had, it seemed, been sated, and had forgotten all of that. It seemed to Welo that they had almost forgotten him, except that they still stayed close and followed him for safety.

But there was one thing Akesh knew quickly, long before there were signs of it, and it was a thing she could not forget. Her brief yearning, her need to create new life, had been satisfied. Deep and secret inside her, Akesh knew she was growing something wonderful. Inside her was a child—a daughter, as she would later discover, although she did not yet know that.

CHAPTER 31
AUTUMN 6242-EARLY SUMMER 6241 BCE

The trip down from the cliff would take time, so, deciding to spend the night, the group made camp. A small spring Welo knew well and had used often was set back a hundred long paces from the cliff edge. It was not big enough for them to wash themselves, but it provided plenty of fresh water that they could drink.

In the morning they walked along a game trail down toward the river, then upstream toward the Téuta. When they rounded the last rocks and the village came into sight, Welo was not surprised to find a group of people waiting for them. A shaman, not Seneks, stood waiting for them, and an elder who often came to speak with strangers because she had lived with the forest people and knew their language, as well as others who were simply curious.

Men armed with spears and bows stood on either side of the group. The Téuta intended a peaceful greeting to whoever came, but they had learned that it was wise to be prepared for anything.

Eini sat on a stone looking down the river. She had found her way there in the early morning, having seen some phantom future coming. She had not, at first, known what that future would be, or whether it was a thing to make her afraid or happy. As the morning passed, happy seemed more likely, although she did not understand why.

Seeing her there sitting on the rock, a few others who had less doubt about her visions came to her to ask what she was looking at.

"I am waiting," Eini told them. "Someone will come."

"Who will come?"

"I don't know yet. Some are not Téuta, though."

"Raiders?"

"I don't think so." Eini replied. "I don't see that. I can't be sure."

Those few ran off to tell others, who in turn told more people, and some began to gather to wait, including the elder who spoke the forest people's language, and the shaman, and some with weapons in case it was raiders who came. They had to wait until late morning, so they were restless, and a few thought it was a waste of time to be there. Some turned and left, muttering that it was only one of Eini's foolish visions, while others glanced toward her with growing doubt. Through it all, Eini sat quietly, never turning her head, never seeming to notice even that they were there.

Before anyone even came into sight, Eini whispered to herself so the others could not hear, "Welo? Who else could it be? What does he have?"

And then they came, Welo with three women who dressed strangely in colorful cloths. One was old; one a child. These two followed a third, who walked beside Welo, upright and confident, but exhausted. This third woman walked as though she was the world, and the world was crushing her with trouble.

Since he had been gone nearly a full year, many had believed that Welo was dead, frozen in the winter mountains. But because he was so strangely tall and had so odd a structure that his bones seemed almost too big for him, they had recognized him in the distance soon after the group had rounded the last corner of rock. A murmur ran among them: "Welo is back, and who has he brought with him?"

As the group approached it became clear that the woman walking beside Welo, the one the world was crushing, was scarred badly from a fire long ago. Some of those waiting found her scars disturbing. Some wondered if she was a bad omen. Many glanced at the shaman to see what his response was. But he seemed not to even notice the scars. A few also glanced at Eini, who was smiling wide for once, directly at the scarred woman.

Eini stood then, not waiting as she should have for the shaman or the elder to move, and walked toward Welo. She was the first to greet them out loud.

"Welo," she said, "it is good to see you again. Who are these women?"

Welo explained the ruined village and that these three were all that remained of it. He introduced them properly, Senne first as the eldest, then Akesh, then Nedeh, the child. He explained that Senne still had difficulty with Téuta speech and might not understand everything they said to her.

Eini greeted them one by one, and paused at the child who spoke quickly and easily. Then she turned to Akesh and faced her as though she were the summer sun. She looked closely at the scars on half of this stranger's face.

Akesh watched Eini with a puzzled smile. She realized that while all the others were nervous of her, this woman meant to be friendly, and in fact thought Akesh was important somehow. Akesh was used to both reactions, and thought the others would come to her with time, and that the men would come when they could forget her scars. But Eini's approach so close, and her seeming instant and openly happy acceptance was new to Akesh. It almost seemed as if Eini did not really see her face or body, did not even see the scars, but saw something else instead. Eini's first words dispelled the first notion. She might see something else as well, but she was aware of Akesh's scars.

"May I touch them?" She asked.

Akesh was startled at such an intimate request as the first meaningful words between them. For the first time in many years, she felt shame about her scars; they had been with her for so long that she almost forgot them sometimes. But Eini was a stranger, and clearly

Welo's friend, a close friend. And Eini had never seen Akesh's scars before.

Akesh's expression alerted Eini to the wariness Akesh felt, and to her hint of shame about the scars. So Eini lifted the right sleeve of her parka, showing Akesh her own burn scars, which spread like a great web across her arm from near her shoulder to her wrist.

Startled, Akesh looked at Eini's scars, and she started to stretch her hand toward Eini's arm, then paused, not sure what she was supposed to do. Eini stepped closer, took Akesh's hand and placed it on her own arm, on her own scars.

After that, Akesh was still lost and nervous about the rest of the strangers surrounding her. But she had no objection to being touched by Eini, who, at least in this one thing, was her sister. As the others watched, amazed and curious, Eini placed a hand softly on the scarred side of Akesh's face, smiling with obvious happiness.

The moment lasted some time before Eini dropped her hand and looked down toward Akesh's belly.

"You are two," she said, "and I am glad of both of you. Your child and you will save the Téuta. Or your child's child, or some future child that comes from you. I know it. I don't know how. But I know."

To herself Eini thought, as she watched this scarred stranger in the Téuta, *I thought you were only a childhood dream. But you are real, and you are here. And the thing that shambles toward us in the night is still coming, and it still makes me afraid. But now—now this stumbling night-mare is also afraid. It fears you, Akesh. It fears you and your children, all of your children, forever. Why? I don't know. I don't care. It doesn't matter why. You are what Welo went to find, and now that you are here, it fears you.*

ᚻᛏ ᛰ ᚻᛏ

Word that Welo had returned, and with visitors, had seeped toward the closest huts, and from them to those beyond, and from those to others. The people came out, at first to see Welo because of the rumors that he had gone to chase stranger gods. No one knew where the rumors came from, or whether they were true, but the gossip had started soon after Welo left nearly a year before. They regarded Welo with some nervousness. Who could know what their own gods would think of someone who boldly chased other gods, stranger gods that did not know the Téuta?

But the people quickly turned their attention to the women. They knew Welo and were accustomed to his returning after long walks in the forest. These oddly dressed women were new to them. People stood in the day to watch as Eini led Akesh to her own hut, welcoming her there, and as Nedeh and Senne followed. Since Assa had moved off to live his own life, Eini's hut had room for these three.

Senne and Akesh and Nedeh understood even before they crouched to enter that this was home to them, that Eini welcomed them there. The hut—all the huts they saw here—were differently built than those they were used to. In spite of that, they felt as though they knew it, almost as though they had already lived here.

And now it was a hut filled with women, with Eini and Akesh and Senne and Nedeh and Ceneta too, who still lived there. Quiet Sntodi was the only man.

Left standing where Eini had greeted them, Welo felt abruptly alone. But he had fulfilled his responsibility to the survivors, and also, it seemed, to Eini. He had nothing left to do. So, after a hesitation, he walked to his old place, the hut where he had lived a year ago. There he was welcomed home in the usual way. When he went inside, though, the others who lived there remained outside to watch and wonder at the newcomers. They, and all the Téuta, watched until Akesh, Senne, and Nedeh disappeared inside Eini's hut.

The moons came and went, and the women new to Téuta learned to wear clothing that others expected, but they also taught the Téuta women how to weave the cloths their village had been known for, how to shift the loom weights and tie the warp as their village had. But they had arrived in the Téuta too late in the year to gather the insects they used to make their dye, the vibrant red that had made their weaving famous across the mountains.

Through the winter Akesh grew until, by spring, her child was making itself known to all around her.

No one doubted who or where the father was. Only Welo had been with her when this child was created, and Welo would not leave Akesh for more than a day at a time. It was as though he were tied to her with a great leather rope. He could escape for a day or two, when that was necessary. But when that happened, he returned as soon as he found it possible.

Akesh chafed a little in this new life. She was not accustomed to living in so large a town. She was not accustomed to living *in* town at all. In her own village, she had not lived close to all the others. Her scarring bothered them. And of course, that was her good fortune in the end. She had lived alone, a little outside the town, and that had saved her when the raiders came.

To help her, to give her a place to get away, Welo built a small hut at the top of the cliffs near the place where she had first looked down to see the Téuta, a few steps from the spring there so she would always have water. It took time to get there, but Akesh went when her need for solitude was strong enough. Welo himself sometimes slept there alone, or with Akesh. He had learned the value of solitude while he walked for so long in the mountains.

Most of the time, though, Akesh stayed close to Eini in the hut in the village. There were those in the Téuta who reacted to her as her own villagers had. But after their first meeting, Eini did not seem even to notice her scarring. None of those who lived in that hut seemed bothered at all. And Welo, when he visited, was moved by a different knowledge of her.

In the hottest time of summer, Akesh's girl child was born. The baby was now her only child, but it was not her first. A girl had been born to Akesh when she was barely adult, but that one had not lived long, a half a moon or less. Her two others, both boys, were killed when the raiders came to her village. For this child, her labor was not long.

Akesh gave her new daughter a name that was common in her village, but in the Téuta made her seem exotic. The girl was called Belisse.

When he was allowed to see his daughter, Welo came. The hut with so many women had become well known, and it was also well known that only brave men should enter there. Strange Eini lived there, and

Akesh, who awed those who knew her, and frightened those who did not. But also, the old one, Senne, once she had recovered as much as she could from grieving and had become used to the Téuta, showed that she had a sharp and impish sense of humor when men came to visit. Once Senne began it, the teasing from these women was cheerful but merciless.

Many wondered how Sntodi could live with these women and their sense of humor. It was clear from many observations that he was not exempt from it. But he seemed to enjoy the teasing, and even sometimes returned it in kind.

Welo, too, when he came, was usually pestered and vexed by all the women except Akesh. Even his friend Eini, who seemed to gather confidence from living with the others, vexed and teased him. But when Welo first came to see Belisse, they relented. On that visit, they treated him softly, and only with kindness. And on that visit Akesh came to him to tell him she was glad he had found them in their ruined village, that she was glad of *him*, which was something she had never said to him. Perhaps it was something she had never said to anyone.

When she did that, she tried to turn her head to hide her scars so that only her beauty showed for him. But Welo had heard her sing. He had heard all of her out in the mountains, and seen all of her, and he did not want just half. He turned her face so he could see both sides, and then he held her very close.

Akesh buried her face in his chest and mumbled something long but quiet into his parka. He did not understand what she said and asked her to repeat it, which he thought she might have done, although he couldn't really tell. She was speaking in the language of her village, saying many words that he did not understand. He looked to Nedeh for help.

"What is she saying?"

Nedeh, watching them, had a smile big enough to show most of her teeth. She was very near laughter to see Akesh like this. Her response displayed a little of the hut's usual impishness. Nedeh teased Welo, telling him only the kernel of the truth, and no more.

"She says you may call her Eksi."

In the river of words that she poured into his parka, Akesh had said much more than that. But that was all Nedeh thought she needed to tell him. She left the rest for him to figure out.

Still smiling with mischief, Nedeh turned and walked away. She looked back once, smiling over her shoulder, her smile still teasing Welo, then turned away to help Eini and Senne care for the newest Téuta, the youngest Téuta, the one who was called Belisse.

Watching Nedeh as she ignored him to tend to the child, Welo experienced again a mix of emotions he had felt before in that hut and had never felt anywhere else. He was partly confused, partly curious, partly frustrated, and entirely happy with every part of that.

Sometimes joy spreads bright across the dawn, and sometimes it hides so deep you think it can never be found again, he thought. *And sometimes it just mumbles against your parka in a language you can't understand.*

PART IV

Prsedi

CHAPTER 32
EARLY SPRING 6235 BCE

*I*t is hungry, Welo thought. *A leopard eats when it can. But this leopard has not eaten today, and probably not yesterday.*

The leopard was a distance from him, on the far side of a deep ravine that separated them. He had noticed it because leopards were rare here, and it had taken him some time to recognize what his sense was showing him. But the signs of hunger were there; he had no doubt about it. He had no fear of the big cat either. It was too far away and there were too many barriers between them, to worry him. And it seemed to have another meal in its sights: it followed a doe and a fawn. Welo had the sense that this leopard had followed her prey for some time, waiting for the right chance to eat.

He turned his attention away from the leopard, more interested in his destination, his business on this side of the ravine. Winter had seemed to be colder and last longer each year through Welo's life so far, but the Téuta held their spring festival by the arrival of the spring moon, so cold or not the festival was approaching. Welo wanted to be sure the Kujoté were back from their summer home in the valley, and that they planned to be near when the festival came. The long friendship between the Téuta and the wanderers mattered to him, and to many others as well. But the changing weather made many things difficult. If the winters lasted too long, those who spent their summers in these high hills might choose to stay down in their winter homes instead.

Welo walked on toward the usual area for the Kujoté summer settlement. From the Téuta village, it was more than a day's walk away, but Welo knew the forest well and could move quickly through it. He expected to find them very soon in the late evening and looked forward to greeting old friends. By now, he was sure they were there, that they had come again. He smelled fire in the distance, very faint, but clearly there, so he walked now with purpose, with anticipation. But that didn't prevent him from observing everything around him, seeing all the life of the world. It didn't keep him from feeling the pleasure of an evening walk.

ꜩ ꝏ ꜩ

The leopard's paws were slow, careful, quiet. Her head was down as she crept through the sparse grasses. Hiding was hard for her here, but necessary. A doe and a fawn were eating from bushes, dark shapes, dark motions, in the shadows of rocks above them. The leopard's eyes easily saw them though, despite the dark, and their scent was strong in the air.

A quarter moon slid across the spring sky, the night dark and quiet. Wind whispered high in the trees, causing an occasional creak as the treetops bent, sometimes an owl in the distance, or the sound of lizards on the rocks; only those things sounded in the dark, and those sounds were useful. The night was quieter than the leopard would have wanted, but those hushed sounds, small as they were, helped her. She hid inside them.

There was a cliff nearby, just to her left. Beyond the cliff edge was a long drop. But the leopard was agile and strong and far enough away from the cliff that there was not much danger. She would be careful to stay well away from that. She could use it, in fact; the deer could not flee in that direction.

The cat paused with one paw lifted, still and invisible. She crouched and watched the silhouettes of the young doe and its fawn. They were almost close enough, but not quite. She wanted to be sure. Success depended on a sudden ambush from a short distance; otherwise, the deer would bound away too quickly. It was possible, also, that a stag was nearby to defend them if her attack was too slow. In that case, she might get the fawn, but the doe would escape. She wanted the doe. She wanted a meal tonight, and also tomorrow.

The deer looked skittish about something. Not about her. If they had scented her, they would have been gone. They would have leapt away through the grasses and into the forest, where the hunt would be useless. She would lose them in the trees, which was all to the deer's advantage. If the doe and fawn got to the trees, she would need to start again, watching and following, waiting for another chance.

Each inch was gained when the deer looked away. They ate bushes, often looking from side to side. The leopard crouched silently, and the doe, clearly aware that the night had danger in it but not aware of mortal danger so close, walked slowly toward her, stretching its neck for higher leaves. It was not quite close enough when something trembled in the ground. Both the doe and the fawn looked up, ready to bound away.

The leopard had no choice left. The doe would be gone if she delayed longer. But her senses told her it was time at last. The doe was just close enough, and she was ready, her legs already gathered under her. She leapt for the doe. If it ran toward the trees, it would come straight to her. If it turned away, it would be trapped by the cliff.

Her attack was perfect. Reflecting silver light across her coat almost more brightly than the moon that gave it, she was all beauty as she lifted into the air and flew like a lance toward the doe.

But the doe didn't move toward the trees, or toward the cliff. The doe moved in a direction the leopard could not have considered. It moved down. The fawn, with the quick acuity of the young, reacted almost instantly to the small tremble in the ground and ran hard away from the crumbling cliff toward the safety of the woods, but that hardly mattered. The doe was the target, and the leopard's teeth missed the doe by a hair's width as it fell away from her. The great cat reached with her paws, all of them in turn, paddling the air with clawed feet. But the doe was gone beneath her, and the fawn was long gone into the forest. Both were lost to her.

The leopard was philosophical about her miss, accepting it before she landed. Some days ended hungry. She had missed before, many times. It was simply the way life was. It was a misfortune, but the mountain was full of prey. She would find food elsewhere, a smaller meal if that was all she could find, and if not tonight then tomorrow.

But the doe and the cliff were both falling away beneath her. Softened by recent rains and weakened by ice expanding in all the rocky fissures over the winter, even the smallest tremor of the earth caused the edge to collapse. It cracked and tipped and fell.

When she left the ground, the leopard's landing was clear before her. But there was not much left to cling to when she came down again.

Cats are quick and supple, and so the leopard struck the crumbling ground with three feet, then one slipped off and she had her front feet only on the remaining cliff top. She scrambled to put all four feet on firmer ground, and almost did it; her claws were scraping the edge of the land, but she couldn't quite pull herself onto it. Down she went, rocks beneath her, rocks around her; she struck an outcropping and bounced. Then, always a cat, she righted herself in the air and struck hard against a ledge that remained. Her first landing was only two, and then three paws on the ledge, but the ledge held, and she held also, and then she was secure with all four feet under her.

Her fall had not injured her much. But a large rock came down just behind her, landing on her hind leg.

The pain was immediate and terrible. She ignored it. Her focus was on the doe spinning through the empty air below. The leopard watched as it tumbled, watched as its hooves pawed the emptiness, neck thrashing, eyes straining back and forth looking for a savior. But no savior came for the doe. It fell, and fell, until no air was left to fall through, and it split its body there, split its life out on the rocky ground far below.

There must have been sounds. A brief and muted doe-scream as it landed, the snap of bone and sinew, the tearing of skin and the blood raining on the ground. But at this distance, the leopard could not hear them.

The doe was too far, too far, and there was no quick path to get to it. She knew that by the time she got down the winding path to where it lay, scavengers would have left nothing much for her to eat. The cat's long patience, her silent hunt, the magnificence of her final ambush, her injury too, and the doe's death, had all been useless.

She issued a barking roar in the night, the sound of a frustrated leopard that has missed her prey.

She assessed the height of the rocks above her. The top was within easy reach for a healthy young cat. One strong leap, and she would be there. And perhaps the fawn was not too far away. As she drew herself into position to leap, though, her injured leg recoiled from the ground; each movement of her leg, even the smallest, hurt like embers burning in her marrow. Putting her hind paw on the ground felt like lightning striking her whole side. She stopped, looking again at the rocks above her, and at all the tumbled rock around her.

There was a path, a route to the top that required only smaller leaps. She took that, jumping off one hind leg, the other hanging like a rag that slapped the ground painfully each time she landed. Leap by leap she rose, and at last she found the level ground.

She was still hungry and would stay hungry for now. With her leg so damaged, she couldn't hunt again tonight. Tomorrow would come. Then she would see what she could do.

The leopard carefully walked into the trees to find a place to hide until her leg healed, or until she died. She was not sure which would happen first.

Through these events, the quarter-moon had barely moved. It continued, serene and cold, on its silent trip above the earth.

Instead of late evening, it was early night when Welo arrived, but he had been watched through the last of his walk and was expected. He was known and well liked there. Friends greeted him in their own language, and he responded in the same. He was fed with fresh meat and boiled root vegetables, and with ale—a great deal of ale. Welo and his friends spent much of the night in talk and laughter, until the ale overcame them, and they slept.

CHAPTER 33
SPRING 6235 BCE

Sun and sparse clouds, and air that was still very cool but not winter-cold; there were still patches of snow here and there, but much of the late winter's snow had melted away. It was a gleaming, shimmering spring day well before the festival. Prsedi, who still had only six years, ran laughing with her friends, and especially with Belisse, who was her favorite, and famous because of her mother, and with others of her age. She hid from them. She was found, tumbled with them, let them hide and found them, and ran, hiding again.

She was crouching beside some large rocks near the trees on the wide, sandy riverside field outside the village. She wanted to climb to the tops of the rocks, where she would be hard to see from the ground. Prsedi was a good climber, and knew she could climb these rocks, because she had done it many times. But even some of the older children, even Belisse who was good at everything, might have trouble climbing here, and no one thought it was fair for her to hide where they couldn't go.

So she was huddled on the ground, crouching and staying still, when she heard a chuffing coming from behind the rocks. She felt safer than she should have. Some part of her realized she should be wary. But she was young and playing with friends on a sunny day, and it was only a short run to her mother's hut. Prsedi imagined she could see through the open doorway, even from this distance. See her mother inside, working. Far bolder than she should have been, Prsedi peered around the rocks to see what was there. At first she saw nothing.

Then she saw something that was doing what she was doing: hiding in plain sight.

Then she saw what it was. She *recognized* what it was, what it must be from descriptions, although it was something new to her.

The leopard was only thirty steps from her, lying on the ground, panting, one hind leg stretched, trailing behind it on the ground. Leopards were rare, solitary, and silent. Prsedi had never seen one before. The Téuta's hunters, maybe, or the travelers who lived in the forest, had seen them. But leopards were not the predators that troubled the people here and tried to take their sheep. Wolves did that. The Téuta took care in the woods because of wolves or bears, or even pigs, not because of leopards.

Prsedi had no way to judge, nothing to compare it to, but to her this cat looked very thin.

Prsedi thought she was silent, but the great head turned toward the rocks toward Prsedi when she peeked around them, the great yellow eyes were staring at her. The leopard did not rise, did not chase her. It looked as though it did not want to rise. Its hind leg splayed out as still as the rocks beside her, as though it hurt to move it. To Prsedi, the leopard looked distracted and tired. It seemed to be waiting patiently. Perhaps for death, she thought, because it looked as though it had given up.

Thin or not, injured or not, Prsedi knew the cat was very dangerous. But it was also very beautiful. For a moment, she forgot herself, staring at it, and even eased forward a little to see better. She was entranced by the eyes, by their color and intensity, and by the sleek, supple glory of the animal.

But she was sad to see anything so badly injured. And also sad to see anything so hungry. Prsedi wasn't sure how long they looked at each other, neither one moving. Then she realized she had not hidden well or run, or anything. She was simply kneeling with one knee on the ground, almost completely in the open, with a hungry leopard thirty steps away.

Prsedi knew she should back away and find a grownup. But few of the people in the Téuta, and even fewer of the grownups, would accept this with calm. They would either fear the cat or worship it, and neither of those responses would help it. She paused, staring into those wonderful eyes. *I can't outrun a leopard anyway,* she thought. *So, there's no point in running.*

She was startled when the leopard let out a roar that was half bark, half chirp. It was not loud, but it was clearly a warning. Prsedi bent her head toward it to show respect before she eased slowly back behind the rocks.

She did go to Chermesh then, her mother, who was a grownup but a grownup who was kind to animals. Kind to everyone, really. Prsedi told her what she had seen.

"Injured, you think?" Her mother asked. "And hungry too?"

"Yes. Both. I don't think it felt very much hurt as long as it didn't move, and I don't really know if it was hungry right now. It didn't chase me. It looked very thin. Maybe that's just the way they look."

"Where, again?" Her mother asked, watching out the door of their hut. "Close?"

"Yes, pretty close. Just there, behind those rocks." Prsedi pointed to where she had knelt to watch the leopard. From here, the rocks looked distant and small, although they were in clear sight.

"Why is it here?" Chermesh asked, to herself really since Prsedi certainly didn't know the answer. "Maybe it came to the river in the night for water and just stopped there beside the rocks on its way back to the forest."

Prsedi was still concerned about the injured leopard, but also nervous now at the idea of leopards walking so close to her hut in the night. She said nothing, though.

"Best to leave it alone," Chermesh told her in a voice calm and quiet, a voice without fear as though this were an everyday conversation. But her mother also looked toward the spear that had leaned in the corner of the hut for a year without moving. Or without moving very often. They had used it sometimes to fish. But now they had a fish trap in the river that was often full. Chermesh went to get the spear and kept it close at hand.

Prsedi wanted to play again but was afraid of the leopard. She wondered aloud to Chermesh whether they needed to tell people not to go near the trees and rocks where the leopard had been. But Chermesh also was thinking hard about the cat, about what to do about it. She began to rise to go to get help. Then she stopped, and sat again, frowning.

Prsedi was quick to understand others, and she could tell what Chermesh was thinking. Her mother knew what would happen if they did tell people. There would be a debate, respect against fear. And in the end, fear would win, and the village would kill it. They would very respectfully kill it, but it would still be dead. Prsedi could almost see the thought pass across Chermesh's face. *In the end, that might be what is needed. If it is injured badly, that might be best.*

But Chermesh had always felt warmth toward animals and particularly injured animals. She stood and said, "Wait here. No, Come with me."

Prsedi saw that her mother had some plan to follow but also that she didn't want to leave her child alone with a dangerous cat so close.

Together they walked to the river, taking the old spear with them. They went to their fish trap to see what was in it. The river was not frozen now. Deep winter had passed, and for weeks the weather had been warm enough to thin the ice to nothing. But the water was still freezing. It hurt their arms to pull the fish trap up.

There was good luck. Two big fish and three small ones came up with the trap. Chermesh put the big fish into a sack and let the smaller ones go. Then she put the trap back, lifted the sack with one hand, and put the other around Prsedi's shoulders.

"Show me," she said.

Prsedi took Chermesh's empty hand and pulled her toward where the leopard had been. But Chermesh didn't want to be so close to it; she made Prsedi show her where to stand to see the place from a safer distance.

The leopard was gone when they arrived at a place where, Prsedi said, they should have seen it. Nothing was there where the leopard should have been. So they walked toward where it had lain earlier in the day. When they were nearly there, Prsedi said "stop", and she stood for a moment looking hard at the trees.

"It's there, in the trees, I think," Prsedi said. "It's watching us. It doesn't seem to want to leave, or come toward us, but I think it smells us, or maybe it smells the fish. It's sniffing the air."

"You can see it? I can't see it."

"No," Prsedi said, "Well, a little. I can't see it exactly. I just think it's there. Maybe I'm wrong, but I think it is there, watching us."

Chermesh slowly walked forward to where she could see that the leopard had been on the ground, where the grasses were crushed down a little. Then she tipped the bag up to drop the fish on the ground, where they flopped limply and then lay twitching, then still.

"Come away, Prsedi," Chermesh said, stretching out her hand. "We'll leave the fish and go."

They did, hoping the cat would find its dinner. Then Chermesh and Prsedi went to tell the others that a cat had been seen, but was gone, so people would be warned, and would take care when walking there.

When they went back the following day, carefully observing the spot from a distance before they approached, there was no leopard but also no fish. They left another fish and some scraps of meat, and the next day those were gone too, and there was still no leopard. The day after that, they returned with fish, but with less care since the leopard seemed never to be there when they arrived. It was probably far away in the forest. The meals they left had probably been taken by scavengers. So mother and daughter walked directly to the rocks where Prsedi had hidden when she first saw the leopard and looked with care around the edge.

The leopard was there in the field, exactly where Prsedi had first seen it. Chermesh stepped back, frightened, but then reasoned as Prsedi had, that it was pointless, since she couldn't run faster than a leopard. Still, she didn't want to get too close, so, slowly and gently, she threw three fish as close to the leopard as she could without disturbing it too much. At first it startled, lifting itself on its front legs, looking like it wanted to run away. If its hind legs had been healthy, it might have done that. But instead, it sniffed the air again. It stood. It walked—limped, its hind legs stiff and one of them very reluctant to touch the ground—to the closest of the fish.

When it got to the fish, it looked straight at Prsedi and sniffed the air again, seeming confused, trying to capture the scent of these odd humans who threw fish on the ground. Then it lay down next to the fish and began to eat.

Prsedi and Chermesh watched, knowing they should leave. But the beauty of this animal kept them fixed. For some reason, they weren't afraid while the leopard was having dinner that was not them. The cat glanced toward them as she ate, but didn't seem to want to approach them. Prsedi again, and now Chermesh, were captivated by the sleekness of the great cat, and by the grace of its movements even when it limped so badly, and by the beauty of its eyes.

The sun shone on the new grasses that were just coming up green from the ground, and on the rocks and trees, and it reflected in waves of gold and black on the soft, sleek, rippling coat of the leopard. Chermesh had to tug Prsedi's hand to remind her that, gold or not, shining or not, this was still a big, dangerous, injured cat, a solitary animal that liked its own company and no other, and that they should leave it to its small meal.

Every day for the next weeks, Prsedi and Chermesh rose early and, before breakfast, brought fish and other things for the cat. They could not provide enough food for a full-grown leopard, but it was something. The leopard must have been supplementing what they brought with small prey from the forest. Its injured leg would prevent it from hunting larger or faster animals, but there must have been enough smaller creatures it could catch. Some days the leopard was there, and some days it wasn't, but each day the fish they had brought the day before were gone.

Within a few days, they had a name for this beautiful thing. They called her Kata-Gosom. Once the leopard had a name, they felt friendship with her.

After the first week the leopard was sometimes waiting for them in the field. Prsedi would throw the fish, and twice the leopard caught the fish in the air, which delighted Prsedi. The leopard, after a stare, accepted her laughter and went on eating. Slowly the animal gained weight, and her leg seemed to hurt less as the days passed.

Then the cat did not appear for several days, and the fish remained where they left them. After five days, Prsedi and Chermesh were ready to believe the leopard was gone. That either it was dead, or it had healed enough to find its own food. But on the sixth day as they approached the field where they met her, they heard her chuff behind the rock. They continued carefully peeking around the rocks. The leopard was there, much closer than she had ever been before. She was standing ten steps from them. When she saw them, she sat, waiting, and chuffed several times.

They threw their fish to her. She sniffed the fish, chuffed at them again, picked up the two large fish, both in one bite, and ran with them back to the trees, strong, supple, her legs making a strange rhythm with three of them running fast and the fourth rarely touching the ground.

They didn't see her again. Prsedi thought that last trip was not from any need on the leopard's part. Watching her run, watching her healthy vigor, Prsedi thought the last visit was to thank them, and to say good-bye. That the leopard had returned only to tell them her need had passed.

CHAPTER 34
SUMMER 6233 BCE

Wind rose in the morning, whistling through the village and around the huts. Clouds moved across the morning sky, some high, which moved very slowly, and others lower, which ran across the sky as though they were being chased. But the higher clouds seemed darker. The Téuta watched, hoping for an increasingly rare midsummer rain to nourish the crops on the plateau. But by mid-day the clouds were scarcer, the winds smaller and the sun hotter, and all hope of rain had gone.

Eini had spent the morning working at home, stretching and tugging a newly cleaned deerskin to make it soft when it dried. But after the sun had passed its highest, the hut was hot inside, so she sat outside to talk. Belisse, eight winters old, sat with her. She knew that with only a little urging, Eini would tell again the stories of how the Téuta began. So did Akesh, who was nearby and had never heard these stories until she heard them from Eini.

Akesh had her own stories about the village she had lost so many years ago. That was still her home in some inner place, but it was a home that no longer existed. That sorrow would never leave her. Sometimes she did tell Belisse about it, but she knew her daughter was born Téuta and would live her life as Téuta. And knew also that she, Akesh, had become Téuta too. She liked the people, liked her hut full of women, and was glad to be in a place so large and so safe.

When Belisse had first arrived, Akesh stayed with her always, carried her always. She had lost two children when her old village fell and did not want to lose another. She needed no more tragedies in her life. Even when her restiveness and her need for solitude drove her to seek Welo, and to spend a day or two with him in the hut he had built for her at the clifftop, she held Belisse close always.

Akesh liked the clifftop. There she could see the village, cling to the village safety, a safety she felt more deeply with Welo near her. But in her clifftop hut, she did not have to interact with anyone else. She had learned to love the Téuta, to be happy in it, happy as part of it. Happy that her child, Belisse, would grow here, would be a woman here. But scarred Akesh was used to loneliness, used to long solitude in her birth-village, and she missed her loneliness when it was absent for too long.

As Belisse grew, and as Akesh learned the village, learned its ways and learned its people, her grip on her newest child relaxed. Akesh did sometimes need to leave the girl with Senne or Eini so she could care for someone else. Welo had introduced her to Seneks, and from that moment the two healers enjoyed each other's company through all the following years. They respected each other's knowledge, learned from each other, and often went together to provide help when people were sick or injured.

But in mid-summer there were few sniffles or coughs, and within the Téuta no injuries for weeks, so Akesh and Seneks had little to do. Akesh had time, for now, to listen to Eini's stories. Sometimes in her old home when she found learning such ancient stories to be a chore, or a distraction from more important things. But with Eini, it was a plea-sure, a relaxation. Eini made the stories interesting to anyone, even those who were not born Téuta. And Akesh and Belisse were both Téuta now, so the Téuta stories were the ones they needed to know.

Eini talked through much of the latter part of the day, and others noticed. Her telling of the old stories was well liked by the children, at least by the older ones, so when they saw her with a little audience in front of her, they came to listen. Belisse's friends, particularly Uébe and Prsedi, loved the stories. They came in the afternoon and were eventually joined by Chermesh, who actually came to find Prsedi, but when she saw Eini was storytelling, stayed to listen too. Nedeh came too from her hut some distance away, where she lived with the young man who had finally captured her favor. Nedeh had been the most gleefully vexing tease of all the women in the hut when she grew old enough for that, but she was also an attractive young woman with an exotic and enticing accent when she spoke, so she tempted the young men. Many of them came and endured her teasing. It was the young man who most gleefully teased her back who finally convinced her to leave this hut of women.

When evening came, the others went to their dinners. Eini, and Akesh too, helped prepare their evening meal. Senne had brought fish, and soon it was poached, and the women were eager to eat.

A stir outside the door interrupted them. A young man, a shaman, came to ask for Akesh to care for someone who was sick. The man had fallen as he walked and needed help.

"You are a shaman," Akesh said. "I recognize you. Doesn't Seneks care for the shamans? I will come," she added, "but..."

The young man hesitated, looking troubled.

"What is it?" Akesh asked, watching him.

"It is Seneks who is sick. We would have cared for him, but he asked for you."

Akesh sat up, alert.

"What has happened to him?"

"He says he has pain in his arm and back, and that it is difficult for him to breathe."

"He has fallen?" Already, she was getting to her feet. "Did something injure him, on his shoulders or back?"

"No." The young man said. "No. Nothing like that happened. He seemed fine, but suddenly he didn't want to stand up, and fell to his knees. He says he had this pain before. He says you will know, that you will understand this."

Akesh did understand, at least she understood that this was not a promising start for a man she knew had all the dignity of age, but that she had never thought was really old. But he *was* old. Very old. He had, the young shaman said, over seventy-three years.

When she heard that, Akesh moved quickly. She grabbed the sack she always kept ready with medicines, and particularly with leaves of willow and foxglove that she would use to make a tea for Seneks.

"Where is he?"

"Near the cliffs, just outside the shaman hut. Outside the old temple."

Akesh stopped abruptly and turned to look at the young man.

"Outside?"

"Because you cannot enter there. You are not a shaman."

Akesh clicked her tongue. She instructed the young man to return to the shaman temple at a run to ask them to boil water and wait for her. She told him that, assuming he could run much faster than she did. He did run very fast. But Akesh was not far behind.

When she arrived, Seneks was sitting up, drinking already a watery tea he had made from the same medicines she would have used. He seemed much better and said he felt better. Akesh sat with him in the warm evening. The old healer had known, of course, what he needed to do for himself. He had sent for her to be sure she knew what had happened, and what to expect, and even more than that, because he wanted her company. Welo, his closest friend, was visiting the Kujoté just then, or he might have sent for him. But Akesh was also a valued friend to him by then, and a talented healer as well.

One of the shamans brought them some thin mutton stew that those who stayed in the temple had been making for their dinner. The two friends sat outside in the warm evening, leaning against the wall, and talked until the darkness came and even until the moon rose over the eastern mountains, making the night light again. Then, since Seneks seemed well enough and had more tea available for the rest of the night, and since he slept inside the temple where she could not go, Akesh rose and walked back to Eini's hut. But she was troubled on her walk back. She had felt that Seneks was forever. He had never been sick before.

Only Eini was still awake when Akesh returned. She spoke softly to the healer as she entered the hut.

"Seneks is well, then? You have helped him?"

"Seneks is not well, but he will live," Akesh replied. "He will live for some time still. At least I don't think this will end him soon."

"You didn't cure his sickness?"

"I can't cure this sickness, Eini. Not really. He is old and his age is weary in him. I don't know of anyone who can cure that. Even Seneks himself can't, and he knows he can't. But he may be with us for some years still."

"Oh," Eini replied.

This was not the news she had expected. She sat thinking about it, then shook her head. This was an ordinary thing, a sickness of age. It was not one of the things that blundered about in her foggy dreams. But Seneks had been part of her life always, and a close part since she was ten winters. Along with everyone, all those who had used his knowledge of healing and those who knew they might need it in the future, Eini had never thought that there would be a time without Seneks.

But now she knew that at seventy-three winters in age, he might not be forever after all.

Akesh smiled at Eini in the waning light of the fire-pit.

"I should tell you that he had no need of me," she said. "He had treated himself perfectly by the time I arrived. He just needed company, I think. That is what I have been doing since I left you all to your fish, just talking with him."

"You ate something there?"

"Yes. Seneks had thought of that too, and he had asked for two portions of the food they had prepared. I would rather have had your fish!", and Akesh laughed with more noise than her talking made, but as quietly as she could. "He didn't need me for medicines, or to care for him. All of that he did for himself. But he did not want to be alone, and Welo is not nearby. I think he would have wanted you, Eini, but didn't have a good reason to call for you at the end of the day. With me, he can simply say he's sick. But go to see him tomorrow, if you can."

"If he had asked, I would have come. He knows that I think. He wanted you, Akesh."

Talk continued, in soft tones, for a short while after that. Akesh didn't want to sleep. Eventually, though, sleep did come to her.

Seneks did not die that night, nor the next night, nor through the fall or winter. He slowed a little, and when he was short on medicines, he sometimes asked Akesh and Welo and Eini to gather what he needed instead of going himself on the long walk through the forest.

CHAPTER 35
EARLY SPRING 6232 BCE

After winter had passed, but before spring was warm enough for most people to linger outdoors, Seneks was walking one morning beneath the cliffs, below the carvings of the Wall of the Dead. The ground trembled hard enough to spill baskets and topple poorly balanced pots. It was not enough to damage the huts. Tremors like that had happened before. There were far more of these trembles recently than when Seneks was young. But the Téuta still stood, and this tremor did no great harm to the village. A moment to right the pots, and all was well again.

But this trembling ground cracked some of the cliff-rocks a little, cracked two of the carvings in the wall above him where rock had been carved away beneath them. One of those struck Seneks on the neck before he even looked up to see it. The next rock struck his head and knocked him over, knocking him to the ground. No one saw. He lay bewildered and dizzy on the ground.

After a few moments when he was not sure where he was, Seneks managed to stand. He managed, with one hand against the wall, to get back to the shaman's temple for help. There was no need for him to explain. He had blood on his head, and a gash on his neck. The young shamans at the temple who saw him when he entered washed and covered the wound, pressing a cloth against it.

Then they sent for Akesh.

There was no delay; they sent for her as soon as they saw blood on the old man, and she came on a run to help her friend. Eini, seeing Akesh's urgency, ran behind her, arriving only a moment later than Akesh did.

When Eini arrived, though, Akesh was already at work. She cleaned the wound again, and applied a plaster, and prepared a tea with foxglove and cedar leaves. As she cared for him, Akesh asked Eini to speak to him to help distract him.

"There is no need for that," Seneks said. "I'm alright, or I will be. You are a great healer, Akesh."

But his voice wavered and was weak.

Akesh and Eini both smiled at him. "What should we talk about, Seneks?" Eini asked. "The old stories?"

"You know I am always ready to talk about that with you. I need to make sure you get them right when you tell the children." Seneks smiled. Even now, with blood on his head, he teased her. "What have you told them lately? Yesterday?"

"Yesterday—I don't remember what stories I told yesterday. I remember one of children stayed after everyone else ran off to play. She started to leave but came back to ask something."

It took a moment for Seneks to respond. Eini wasn't sure he had heard. When he responded, though, his mind was still clear.

"What? What did she ask?"

"Well, I always tell them that the future is what we have, and the past what we are. This girl said that might be inside out. That maybe the *past* is what we have, and the *future* is what we are."

"She challenged you? A bold child, to challenge Eini!" Seneks was teasing again.

"Yes, I guess she was. Or no, maybe not quite—" Eini paused long enough that Akesh glanced up at her, and Seneks spoke with more seriousness.

"You shouldn't be angry with her for that, Eini. You were also a bold child. I remember. Bold even at our first meeting."

"No, I mean yes," Eini said, finally finding the thing she wanted to say about the girl. "I wasn't angry, maybe because I didn't think what she said was a challenge. I did not feel that from her. But if that was a challenge to me, then a moment later she challenged herself. She said, half to herself and half to me, that maybe her version was also inside out. That maybe what *we have* is the past, and what *we are* is the future. That sounds like it might mean the same as the thing she said first. But it doesn't really, does it?"

"It doesn't?" Once again, Seneks appeared distracted, and weak again. But what she had said obviously interested him, so Eini went on.

"No," she said. "The first way she said it means the past is something we keep. But the second means that everything we have, everything we are used to from the past, like the hut we live in, or the jar of grain against the wall, all of that is *from* the past, but it might also be *in* the past. We might not keep any of it. Maybe it means we might not *need* to keep any of it. But also, more, the first way she said it means that the future creates *us*, and the second means that *we* create the future."

"That's interesting. Which child said this?" Seneks asked.

"Prsedi."

"Ah. Yes." He nodded. "I know Prsedi. She is not stupid. And she runs. She runs like a wild person when she plays with her friends. She and Belisse are very close, I think. They are almost always together."

"Yes," Eini replied. "Yes, Belisse, Akesh's daughter. You know what I think about her. That she is a special thing, that she will help us some-time, maybe her or I don't know, something about her. I don't know. Like I never know. Only a feeling about something wandering in the fog. But to Prsedi she is just another girl to play with."

Eini and Seneks continued to talk, even though Akesh was finished with whatever she had been doing to the dressing on Seneks' head, so Seneks no longer needed distracting. Now, Akesh listened to their talk, sometimes joining them or asking questions. She was interested, or seemed to be. Her hand never left his shoulder, but it appeared that she almost forgot Seneks was injured.

Seneks was tiring. He was curious about one last thing, though, before he rested.

"Eini, you said you didn't think Prsedi was challenging you. What did you mean by that?"

"Oh," Eini said. "Well, she was smiling all the time, and sometimes she bent her head to show honor to me, very formal in some ways, even though she didn't feel formal. I never felt disrespect, or anything like that. It felt like it was just fun for her to talk to me like that. It felt like she was having fun, and she wanted me to have fun. It felt like when she suggests a game of climbing to the top, or hiding and finding to her friends. Like she was inviting me to play with her."

Seneks closed his eyes, then opened them again to laugh.

"She runs like a maniac, but I like Prsedi. But do you know what I think?" He asked. "I think that Seneks is the past and Prsedi and Belisse are the future." Teasing again, the women thought, teasing almost in his sleep.

Eini turned to look at him and laughed with him.

"Really?" She asked. "Are you saying that Seneks is what we have, and Belisse and Prsedi are what we are? Or the other way around? And what is Eini in this game?"

Seneks looked at her, still smiling but also thoughtful.

"Yes," he said. "Yes. What is Eini in this game? That is a question, isn't it?"

There was quiet for a moment, then Eini became serious.

"Seneks, I think Belisse and maybe Prsedi too, are part of a good path. Akesh is, of course. But not just her. Belisse too. And now I think maybe also Prsedi."

"The good path? From your old dream?"

"Yes. I don't know that, and I don't know what part, but it feels like that when I see her."

"You see? I told you that you would find the good path, Eini. And you have. And you are. All the time you are finding it. I said you would."

But as he spoke this, Senek's voice became very weak. His eyes closed then, and he rested.

Akesh watched Seneks' eyes close, and spoke then, to Eini, or to anyone who could move.

"Send for Welo," she said softly. "He deserves to be with Seneks now. And Seneks deserves for Welo to be here."

As a comfort for him, the others thought.

Akesh sent for more tea for Seneks. By the time the tea was ready for him to drink, though, he could not drink it. He tried, but could not.

Welo came. It had taken time to find him, and even though he hurried, it took time for him to come. And so, even hurrying with his long legs, hurrying as only Welo could, he arrived too late to comfort Seneks. By the time Welo arrived, Seneks was silent, and would forever be silent. When Welo finally came, Seneks was no longer there. His body was there. But inside it his good heart had stopped.

Others had seen Welo's quick pace toward the shamans' place. Eini's friend Chermesh had been at the river checking her trap, and she had seen Akesh and Eini earlier, hurrying toward the shaman hut before, and then saw Welo also going there. She wondered what had made those three hurry with such anxious haste. Chermesh stood and walked in that direction, both curious and concerned. Sensing that something was happening, others followed.

But there was no help anyone could give. Seneks was gone. One by one, subdued and a little uneasy at the meaning of what they saw, those still living who had other duties left again. Chermesh left to return to her daughter, and others returned to what they had been doing. They returned to tasks that had much less meaning than when they left them.

No one had ever thought very much about Seneks unless they were sick or hurt. They just always knew he was there, always available when they needed healing. He was a snappy, irascible old man, but that was not a change; he had been a snappy, irascible young man too, with little patience when others were slow to understand the things around them. When he died, though, when he was suddenly gone, the whole village thought hard about him. They were abruptly aware, with some surprise, of his importance in the Téuta, and of how long his importance had been overlooked.

The Téuta mourned him very deeply, to their great surprise. They felt lost without him. There were songs that were sung for the dead, to comfort them and help them on their journey, and the shamans around Seneks began to sing them. Word of this death spread quickly through the village, and soon there were few left inside the huts. Most of the Téuta were outside, also singing the songs for the dead.

One voice rose above the others, though. Few had ever heard Akesh sing very strongly, so her voice was surprising. Now she sang aloud for the village, and for her great friend, in songs that were not her own. In fact, she did not know all of them. But she was quick to learn them once she heard them. She sang simply, clearly, just joining in the Téuta grief, mourning Seneks in the Téuta way and supporting her adopted home. But she sang with such great clarity, such great love for Seneks, that all the village listened.

Just hearing these songs from her tore their grief from inside them and held it before them like a fire.

Late that night a few voices rose from Eini's hut, singing strange songs. The Téuta were hearing, in clear and wild and beautiful voices that filled a stunned and lonely night, the death songs of Akesh's now vanished village. Akesh and Senne and Nedeh sang in their own language, with their own grief. It was the last time those songs were sung. By anyone. It was the last time they were ever heard on the earth, and the Téuta that night were the last people ever to hear them. And in these songs, the Téuta were absorbed and somehow comforted.

But still, the Téuta had not heard Akesh truly sing.

In the morning, she went to the small hut on the cliff top. She stayed there grieving her friend Seneks for three days. And late on the third night her voice rose again to sing above the cliffs. Akesh sang a true song then. She sang to the sky and the earth, her voice falling on the village from above as the voices of wolves had on a night many years before, seeming to come from behind every hut, from beside every person who listened. The whole of Téuta heard it. In every hut, in every place, the people stopped. Most stepped outside to stand silently in the open air. They stood in the cold and listened to a song in a language none of them knew, one they did not need to know to understand. They all heard what the song meant, and they stood with tears on their faces. Akesh sang through the dark, until night was half gone, and all the Téuta heard what her voice told them.

Akesh rose in song to tell the Téuta that grief is always here, always ready to take us, that it can be deep, it can take root inside us, and it can hurt to let it go, but that joy also is here even when you can't find it, and beauty even when it hides. Grief will never leave completely; never ask for that, her song told them. But joy and beauty will stop hiding. They will come back, they will find you again and show themselves, if you let them.

Every one of the Téuta heard Akesh sing the song that was in her heart for her friend. From it, her entire village—her new village—drew all the strength of the earth. They thought in their deepest, most astounded hearts: *Akesh! Akesh! With Akesh to help us, what harm could ever defeat us? Nothing. Nothing,* they thought, *ever could.*

CHAPTER 36
SPRING 6231 BCE

Late on a hungry day, the leopard walked silently, almost invisible against the shadow-stippled ground, quiet as fog, moving down a thinly worn path, both sides thick with trees and brush, looking for prey. She didn't know this part of the forest well, but she knew she was on a game trail. Something must have made it. Because of her limp, she couldn't often catch fully grown deer, and she had seen no deer at all for several days. But this trail didn't smell of deer. It smelled of rodents and dogs, and pigs. The rodents would hide or burrow. The dogs, if they traveled in a pack, would overwhelm her, teeth on all sides of her. And big boars would be too dangerous for her. Even the sows could be deadly. But somewhere on this trail, she might find something easier than that. She might find young pigs still small enough for her to take. So she walked, moving like a leopard moves, like a mist moves among the trees.

She stopped and shrank down. Low to the ground, she moved slowly off the trail. She had smelled what she was looking for somewhere nearby.

She had learned through the years to keep her bad leg well up, off the ground when she hunted. If she let it drop, it might brush a leaf or a twig, making a sound that would warn everything alert enough to hear it.

Then she saw what she needed. She raised her head and nosed the air, but she scented no danger, no adults. She thought that strange; surely the sow would not leave them alone. She scented the air again and found the sow not far away, but not too close either. It was possible. With luck, it was possible.

The cat hesitated. How much luck could she expect? This was foolish, to snatch one of these piglets with the sow as near as that.

But she was very hungry.

ꛠ Ⳡ ꛯ

The gradual change in the weather, the thirty-one-year decline in temperatures was an abstraction to Prsedi at nine, but she knew that the day was colder than usual for the spring festival. She also knew that some of the Kujoté returning from the south would be there today. She liked to listen to their strange talk and even understood a little of it. She wore a felted vest and carried her woven parka behind her on her back.

As usual at festival time, the village center was crowded, and a few of the people were already well into their beer. She walked toward the long, high house, where she knew the forest people were talking with some from the Téuta. She knew it was strange and delicate talk. The forest people were different. They didn't trade for things, even though that was really why they came. Instead, they gave gifts. Prsedi knew that the gifts they gave now were partly to renew the friendship with the Téuta after their return from the southern lowlands where they spent the winter, and partly so that the Téuta would give them gifts of grain before they went south again many moons from now. These gifts of grain were more meager now than they had been in the past, both because of the cold and because the long, dry summer season made grain crops smaller. But the Kujoté were important friends. So far, the Téuta had always saved at least some grain to give to their friends when they left.

There was nothing in the high house that interested her, really. But it was where the forest people were, and there was nothing much else for a nine-year-old child to do on festival day except eat, and she did not want to eat. So Prsedi just kept walking in that direction. And as she passed the house, she saw a child her age, a Kujoté boy, sitting beside it waiting for something.

Prsedi walked to him and sat beside him quietly. The boy too sat quietly, watching her, then spoke. It was nearly impossible to follow his meaning; the language used by the Kujoté was so different. A few words seemed familiar, but even those seemed out of place where he used them, so Prsedi found his speech hard to understand. Still, they were two children of almost the same age. They both understood *that*, and gradually play began to happen. In a few moments, they ran through the streets, laughing and ignoring the grownups completely, running everywhere.

Somewhere Prsedi found her friend Belisse, and the three young people played happily on a cool, breezy, sunny day.

In the afternoon, with the sun halfway down the sky and many of the Téuta tired and filled with beer, Prsedi saw someone else running: a woman, a grownup, running hard, which was unusual even on festival day. It was a village woman, so Prsedi could understand her words, but her new friend could not. Even Prsedi couldn't understand everything the woman was trying to say, because she was upset or excited about something, and she too had filled herself with beer. At first, it was entertaining. The woman was looking for something or someone, but each person she encountered disappointed her. Some were too drunk. Some were haggling and didn't want to be disturbed. Some were dancing, or trying to dance, or were done with dancing and were trying to find some private place to be closer together than dancing allowed. Prsedi and her new friend laughed at first.

But soon Prsedi got the essence of what the woman was upset about. She stopped laughing then. With no transition from laughter, she became serious, which perplexed her new friend.

Turning to Belisse, her face full of concern, Prsedi said, "Get your father. Can you find him? Tell him to come." Then she explained where she was going.

Prsedi began to run back along the woman's path, back to the thing that had upset the woman, with her new friend running behind her. Even without language, he understood that they were no longer playing. But it didn't matter. She was his friend now, and he would help with whatever had troubled her so suddenly. Prsedi ran so hard, and with such desperation, that her new friend found it difficult to keep up with her. Prsedi had to run past her own hut; inside Chermesh was working and saw them as they passed.

Chermesh was used to Prsedi running, but something about how she ran alerted Chermesh that this was different, and so she followed at a slow jog. When Prsedi reached the field at the edge of the Téuta and kept running toward the rocks across the field, Chermesh was suddenly certain that she knew what Prsedi was running toward, and so increased her speed until she was closing the space between them. She could not catch Prsedi in time, though. Prsedi reached the rocks and peered around them.

Exactly where she expected it to be, a leopard lay on the ground. It was panting heavily, and the ground had blood on it, and smelled of blood. Her new friend also peered around, and started back, started to pull Prsedi back.

Chermesh caught up then and peered around the rocks with Prsedi.

"Oh...oh, Prsedi. Stand, wait, stand still, don't do anything."

The two women stood openly, watching the leopard so close in the field. Prsedi's new friend didn't know what was happening, but he didn't want to leave her either. Slowly, trembling a little, he came to stand next to them. He had once seen a leopard kill a deer on a long low meadow while he and his father sat high above on a bluff. They had been watching the deer when the leopard rose out of the grasses, as though appearing from nothing, and closed on the deer with astounding speed. He had known then why the forest people had such high reverence for leopards, talking about them in serious and quiet words, almost as though they were gods clothed in flesh. What he had watched with his father that day was one of the glories of the earth to him. But it had also been frightening to see death appear so suddenly, and with such speed.

The boy had never imagined being as close to one of these great creatures as the three of them were now. He had seen what a leopard can do and was afraid. But he stayed with Prsedi, who did not seem to fear the danger that was so near. *Why is she not afraid?* He wondered. *What kind of girl is this, who stands so close to such great danger but doesn't tremble? Does she not know what this is?*

"This animal is wounded, really wounded, Prsedi," Chermesh said. "We need to stay far away. It will be in pain. It doesn't look like it can move, but it got here, so maybe it can."

Prsedi almost never spoke harshly to anyone, certainly not to Chermesh. But she was frustrated. She turned to her mother and spoke quietly but intensely.

"'This animal', Chermesh?? This 'animal?' You know! You know who this animal *is!!*"

"Yes, I...I know Prsedi," Chermesh said. "Yes, I know. But she may not remember us after so many years. She might not think we are helping her now. It's been too long, and she is—look at her, Prsedi. She won't know who we are."

Prsedi knew there might be reason in that. But this leopard was not a stranger. Watching the leopard, she was sure, in spite of reason.

"She knows us, Chermesh." Prsedi fought to keep her tears from showing. "She remembers. She came here *because* she remembers. She came here for help. From *us*. Because she remembers that we are her friends."

She looked behind her and knew that the village was slow in the late festival afternoon, was distracted in the festival, by the beer, by the trade and by each other, but the rumors of this wounded cat were seeping out along the streets. The leopard had been their private secret three years before, but now everyone would know.

"Can we get something, some fish or something, for her to eat? There is so much blood. She is going to die, Chermesh. Please, let's find something for her. Before everyone comes to kill her."

Chermesh watched Prsedi's face and understood; she felt it too. The leopard did know them. It had not forgotten. Still, Chermesh hesitated, worried, but then...

"Stay, *do not* go near this leopard while I'm gone Prsedi. Promise."

"Ok."

"Promise me, Prsedi!"

"OK," Prsedi said. "I promise."

Chermesh turned and ran to do what her daughter wanted. She left them there, Prsedi and her friend. She wasn't leaving them alone with danger, though; by this time there were two men watching them. Welo, that strange, tall man, walking in great strides with his long legs, had arrived first, with a forest man just behind. And Belisse was there too now, standing with Welo some distance from the rocks.

Welo was large, but not armed. The forest man carried a spear. He had come here through the forest and would have to return through it to the wanderers' summer camp. After Chermesh left, the Kujoté boy saw Prsedi looking at the men, and tried to reassure her. He said many things she did not understand, but she got his meaning. He was telling her that the men would protect them. "Newir," he said, pointing at the Kujoté man. Then, after a slight hesitation, he pointed at himself. "Nemas."

Prsedi smiled at him briefly, since she was more concerned with the leopard than with names. But she gave hers back to him.

"Prsedi," she said, with her hand on her chest.

Welo had been standing five long steps away from Prsedi when he first looked around the corner. He had immediately become alert when he saw what was there. He looked again at Prsedi, who was standing openly in the easy sight of the leopard. Puzzled reactions were on his face. He did not understand why Prsedi was so deeply concerned here, or why she was not afraid, but he saw, without doubt, that both were true. Chermesh had been there and had left her daughter alone with the leopard—and having seen Chermesh running so hard for something, he knew that both of these, the child and the mother, felt safe here. They were not afraid; they were grieving for this wounded predator. It was on his face that the thing was beyond his understanding. What was not beyond his understanding was that he didn't really need to understand. He saw the truth in these two women. He knew very well who Chermesh was and respected her, and he had until this moment been aware of Prsedi as a village child, one of his daughter's young friends. Welo's initial instinct to assert his adulthood to draw Prsedi away stalled as he looked at her. He felt he should defer to her judgement, which perplexed him. She was a wise child, but still only a child. Maybe he paused because of the certainty she showed, because of her confidence as she faced the animal in front of her.

Welo saw more clearly with each moment that Chermesh and Prsedi were not frightened by the wounded leopard only steps away from them, but instead deeply concerned for her.

Welo had little connection to either of them beyond acquaintance, and perhaps a trace of friendship. He knew them through Akesh and Eini, but they had never been close. Still, for a single instant, Welo loved them both.

CHAPTER 37

Prsedi saw the two men, knew they were there, but she wasn't really worried about these two. She wasn't sure anyone in the Téuta, or in the Kujoté either, could understand this, but these two, she thought, were easier and better than most. The forest man was a forest man, like her new friend was a forest child. And this tall, quiet, awkward man, Welo, was almost a forest man too. He was Téuta but seemed to live almost always outside the town and often far away from it. Welo, she thought, lived in the world, and with the world.

The leopard had chuffed softly at Prsedi, appearing to accept her and the boy, but barked out a growl, a warning, whenever anyone else seemed even thought of coming nearer. The forest man looked hard at Prsedi, frowning, then at the leopard, then again at Prsedi. Welo wanted to move closer, to defend Prsedi, a Téuta child who stood far too close to danger, but the leopard wouldn't allow it.

Then the forest man took Welo's arm and tugged him back. They whispered together. The whispering, the quiet, were a kind of respect, Prsedi thought. For the day, and for the leopard. And for death, which was a part of every day in the wide world, but also, somehow, a special thing.

Then Chermesh was back with a small amount of dried mutton.

"It was all I could find, Prsedi."

Behind her, Prsedi heard a commotion in the village, and she glanced back, hating what the villagers would do and thinking she was helpless to prevent it. But it was lucky that this was late on festival day, and that so many had taken too much festival beer to care about the simple drama of a dying animal. Still, there were now a few adults running toward them. Two had weapons, a spear and a bow. The one with the bow was fitting an arrow even as he ran.

Prsedi watched the cat panting on the ground, with wounds too deep to ignore, too deep to repair. She turned to Chermesh, then turned around to the few others already here. Prsedi's eyes were dry, but there were tears in her voice.

"Everyone stay away from her! She's afraid! She's afraid," she said.

Welo wanted to comfort the girl, and her new forest-boy friend did as well. They could see that Prsedi was beyond comfort. She was not so far away that Welo could not try to reach her if the cat moved, but he wished he were a few steps closer.

But suddenly Prsedi was beyond their grasp. Chermesh had returned, so she was no longer bound by her promise to keep her distance from the leopard. Her emotions were towering above her, and she was overcome. Before any of them knew she was moving, before they could see her shift or think, she was in the field running to the huge, injured cat. She came within a few steps of the leopard with her bit of mutton in her hand, with Welo far behind her. And as she had three years before, she tossed the food to the cat, who smelled it, and licked it, and then looked back at Prsedi with those wonderful eyes. This time, though, the leopard did not want to eat.

Welo had run after Prsedi, and now he was too close. The cat growled at Welo. Prsedi turned and yelled at Welo: "Stay there, stay where you are! You are scaring her!" She walked to Welo, reaching high to push the tall man back. She told him to stay away and that the leopard wouldn't hurt her. She knew it. After a few seconds, Welo did as she asked, and backed away. The leopard stopped growling and chuffed again at Prsedi.

The crowd from the village had grown. There were now two men with bows, plus one a with the spear. The forest man had one too. Prsedi put herself between them all and the leopard, holding her hand out, telling them to stop. When they moved anyway, she did, too, blocking them from harming her cat. Standing in front of the leopard, Prsedi watched them all.

She edged backward a little to shield the cat behind her. After a moment, a rustle moved through the crowd.

Then she felt the bump on her buttocks.

When Prsedi looked back, the cat was standing on its front legs, the rest of its body still limp. The bump Prsedi had felt was its paw, pressed against her. She was not at all afraid. She crouched slowly and held out her hand to the cat. The wounded leopard sniffed Prsedi's hand and licked it. Then it lay down where it was, exhausted. Prsedi sat next to her.

Welo, who could see what all the others could see and could sense even more, was still as a rock, watching. This made no real sense. But nothing had to make sense here; it was what it was. He watched with others from the village, along with Prsedi's new forest boy and the boy's father, as Prsedi sat beside the leopard. The cat stretched its back against Prsedi's hip and placed a paw across her ankle.

Moments passed. Time seemed irrelevant. Then Chermesh was there with a large fish. When Chermesh saw where her daughter was, she too approached the cat. Slowly, gently, she laid the fish down before backing away a few paces. The leopard watched her with its great yellow eyes but made no growl against her. It sniffed the new fish, but still did not want to eat. Chermesh, reluctant to move away at all with Prsedi and the leopard so close, squatted but did not sit, concern plain on her face. She was still, silent, watching as her daughter stroked the cat's head and back, careful not to touch any wounds.

The wind moved the grass around them and felt very cold against Prsedi's skin where it was bare. She listened to the song of the wind, the hiss through the grasses and the shush around rocks, sometimes rising so that there was a tone in it. The wind's song reminded Prsedi of the songs that were sung to comfort the dead, although she was sure leopards would not have the same songs. Prsedi listened and, hoping to comfort her leopard, she began to sing softly. She did not sing the dead songs because the leopard was not yet dead, but instead sang festival songs. She didn't know what the leopard would make of that. She didn't know how to speak to cats so they could understand, but she hoped the leopard would be soothed.

Then she heard a sound from the leopard's throat, a humming sound of a sort. The leopard had joined the song. For several moments they sang three together, Prsedi and the leopard and the cold wind.

Then, the cat suddenly yelped. Prsedi shifted, ready to gather legs under her in case she needed to run. But the cat showed no claws, and no teeth toward her. Prsedi relaxed again and sat still. The leopard's great head stretched back to her, laying against the top of Prsedi's thigh. The leopard chuffed once, twice, and then was quiet.

And then she was gone. Prsedi felt her go.

Tears erupted from Prsedi's eyes, and the sound of her grief rolled across the field, and all the field was quiet, and all the people watching were silent with awe at what they had seen. Welo came forward, knowing the cat was dead, and placed a hand on Prsedi's back. He didn't try to comfort her. He could see that no comfort he, a strange gangly man, could offer would be of help. Chermesh came too. They simply sat with Prsedi to be a presence, so she wasn't alone.

Prsedi leaned against Chermesh, trying to sing the dead songs now. She couldn't. She was unable to find all of her voice.

The songs did come, though. Belisse saw what had happened, all of it. She saw what Prsedi wanted to do. She, Belisse, sang the proper songs, softly, but with a voice very clear, very open. Very elegant. Prsedi barely glanced up when Belisse began. She was grateful to her friend. Grateful *for* her friend. Akesh was there too by then, but did not sing; she saw that this was a moment between Belisse and Prsedi—and she also heard the clean, soft elegance of Belisse's voice, and had no wish to disturb it.

Prsedi's grief went on, to her it seemed to go on for a very long time. Finally, gradually, it slowed. Then Welo put his arm around her. Chermesh put an arm around her from her other side. The three sat together with the limp and liquid beauty of the leopard, draped across Prsedi's lap, while her tears subsided. Her morning friend, the forest boy, had come close, sitting with her and wondering what kind of friend he had found that day. And Belisse came, crossing the field with astounding grace and beauty for a child of nine winters. She sat with the forest boy to be near Prsedi.

Welo wanted to say many things to Prsedi in her grief. He wanted to say that the death of anything was sad, that all animals die, and even humans you love die. He wanted to tell her they all go to the earth, that Dhegm takes them all, and that she, Dhegm, is the earth and this beautiful cat was hers now, and Dhegm would take the leopard in her care.

He wanted to say that. But he was almost a stranger to Prsedi. It was of no use. He was of no use. His voice would not rise in him to say those things. He watched her, silent, and watched Chermesh, feeling out of place here. But he couldn't leave Prsedi, or Chermesh, alone with this much anguish wrapped around them.

Prsedi stroked the cat's head and back. She looked up at Welo, putting her hand to his cheek. *She* was comforting *him*, he realized, and was startled by it. She put her hand on his cheek and spoke to him, a child of nine speaking from deep inside to a grownup.

"I know" she said. "I know what you want to say. I know all of that. I love Dhegm, who takes us when we die. Us, and animals, and everything, and who cares also for the beauty and wonder of leopards. Of this leopard. Dhegm is wonderful and beautiful, see?" Prsedi swept her arm around her, showing the world to Welo who lived so constantly in it, showing him the wind, and the trees, and the grass bending and bowing and full of life.

Prsedi looked again at the leopard whose head still rested on her legs. Tears stood on her cheeks, but she made no crying sounds. She stroked the leopard's neck.

"She was my friend," she whispered to no one. "She is my friend."

⚏ ◌ ⚎

The whole Téuta heard about Prsedi. The story of her crazy bravado, of her run to an injured leopard, was across the village in minutes, and everyone who was not asleep or bedded with a friend, or too drunk to care came to see this girl, the girl who stroked the back of a leopard as it was dying, and who wept with grief for its death. Prsedi was lost in her grieving. She paid no attention to the whispering crowd.

But to the Téuta she was no longer just Prsedi. No longer a simple girl, wise among her peers. That day, and for all the rest of the days of her life among the Téuta, she was the girl who sang with leopards when they died.

Among the Kujoté, she had a different name. They regarded her with less reverence than the Téuta, treating her with great respect but also with humor. It was the name Welo's forest friend had used for her, drawn from the sounds the leopard had made when Prsedi first approached—sounds whose meaning he understood. He had whispered that meaning to Welo as they watched together.

Among the forest people, they called her the leopard's daughter.

CHAPTER 38
6226-6225 BCE

Long after the leopard's death, the Téuta treated Prsedi with awe. Even grown adults would sometimes bow their heads to her in respect, which made her social life awkward.

A few friends treated her differently. Belisse—herself regarded with a certain respect as Akesh's child, and with some nervousness as Welo's—treated Prsedi as just another girl. Belisse's friend Uébe did the same, partly because Belisse did, and partly because that was simply how Uébe treated everyone.

Uébe was beautiful and knew it. She treated no one as less than herself, and her beauty ensured that no one treated her as less in return. The complexity of that, Prsedi thought, was too much for Uébe to bother with, so she set status aside and treated everyone the same. Beauty could be a gift, or a burden—or something to ignore. Uébe chose the last.

However, most of the children her age found it hard to play with the girl who sings with leopards, so Prsedi spent more time alone than she liked.

Her new Kujoté friend Nemas came to see Prsedi and Belisse at festival times. Sometimes, in between festivals, Nemas came with his father when he visited the village to see Welo or Akesh. Slowly, the children learned to speak to each other in a mixed language of their own, half Téuta and half Kujoté.

The year Prsedi had passed her fourteenth winter, Nemas came five times. He came to the spring festival, and again three times in the summer, and also to the fall festival. Whenever he came, Nemas spent some time in the morning with the adults. But in the afternoon, he generally came to Prsedi to play or talk, or to do whatever she did in their time together.

At fourteen winters, Prsedi did not play hide-and-find much anymore, but she and Nemas did have contests. Who could throw farther (Nemas). Who could spear a fish (always Prsedi). Who could run fastest? (As children, Prsedi won. But over time, as Nemas practiced and grew, he began to win that contest.) They also competed over who could swim fastest in the river. (Prsedi always, since Nemas did not live near a river big enough to practice in.)

On the day of the Téuta fall festival in Prsedi's fourteenth year, after they climbed wet out of the river on the far side, Nemas challenged Prsedi to climb the steep rocks that led up to the plateau.

"Let's climb to the top of the rocks, to the top of the slope there."

"That is the plateau where we grow our grain and keep our sheep," Prsedi said. "There is a path to get there."

"Can you climb up to it instead of using the path?" Nemas was apparently intent on this idea. "Have you ever done that?"

Prsedi had not done that, and in fact had rarely visited the plateau even by the path. But the challenge had been made, and she accepted it. For Prsedi, it was not really a challenge, though. On this side of the river, the rise was not really a cliff. It was steep, but not vertical. She climbed to the top with ease and grace.

Then it was Nemas' turn. He too was a climber, so he did not find the climb difficult. But halfway to the top, a small rock under his foot slipped from under him, and his hand did not have a firm hold above him. He was not at the top, only about halfway there, but that was far enough over the rocky ground below. Prsedi watched him tumble backward, rotating in the air. Shocked, since the climb had not been difficult for her, and frightened for him, she held her breath.

Nemas was agile. He righted himself as he fell, and managed to land on his feet on a rock only a man's height above the ground. Prsedi breathed again. The fall itself had only been the distance of four men's height. A long fall but not dangerous if the landing is good. And if the rock he landed on had been flat, Nemas' landing would have been perfect.

The rock's surface was not flat, though. It had spots higher and lower, with no order among them. Nemas' ankle bent with the impact.

By the time Prsedi reached him, Nemas had climbed down and was sitting on the ground. His ankle was swelling fast. When he stood, he could walk, but it was more of a step-then-hop-then-step.

It took some time for the two of them to get back to Chermesh, who immediately sent Prsedi to find Akesh, then to find Welo and Nemas's father, Newir.

When she arrived, it took Akesh only a short time, gently probing the injured ankle, to come to her conclusion.

"Not broken," Akesh said to all the assembled watchers. "But not good either. Badly injured. I should bind it. And he should not walk on it."

That was a problem. Akesh knew. The Kujoté would be traveling down the river very soon.

"How long?" Newir asked in Téuta, just ahead of his son who was asking the same question in Kujoté.

"Half a moon." Akesh said. "More, maybe. Maybe a whole moon."

"And, if he walks on it?" Newir asked.

"It might take many moons after that to heal, and might not heal completely. Maybe not ever heal like it was before, after a walk that long."

"We will take him on a travois," Newir said.

"Yes," Akesh agreed. "That would be better."

The planning between Akesh and Newir about how to transport the injured boy would have continued if Chermesh had not spoken up. "He can stay here this winter," she said. "He can stay with us."

"Here?" Newir looked at her. "In this hut?"

"Yes. Why not? There is room."

The conversation continued, everyone taking part in it. Newir argued against it. But it was utterly simple, and utterly practical. After a few moments of thinking about it, Nemas thought it sounded fun, and spoke in favor of the plan. In the end, Newir agreed. When the plans had been made, Nemas said, "I have always wondered what the Téuta do over the moons of winter. And of course it would be a great honor to stay a whole winter in the hut of the leopard's daughter." Calling Prsedi the leopard's daughter was a joke between them. Nemas smiled when he said it—his first smile since his ankle was bent.

⚏ ⚉ ⚎

Spring has come too soon, Prsedi thought, and realized she had never before been sad to see the spring festival arrive. It did arrive though, and with it Newir and others from the Kujoté bearing their spring gifts to the Téuta people. Newir also brought shells of a kind they had never seen before and presented them to Chermesh and Prsedi. Both women loved the gift, but to Prsedi, what he gave was not a sufficient compensation for what he took. Early the next morning, the Kujoté left for the walk back to their camp in the forest. Nemas, fully healed, went with them.

Before he left, Nemas asked if Prsedi would like to come to the camp with them, to visit, or even to stay if she liked. It had happened before. Téuta girls sometimes went to the Kujoté for love or adventure.

"Nemas, I want to," Prsedi replied. "I don't want you to go. And I want to see the Kujoté, I want to know your people. But I will stay forever if I do that. I know I would stay. To leave the Téuta, that is a big thing. To leave my ancestors, leave the cliffs, the great cliff-wall with its carvings for the dead, and the river. To leave all of that is hard. Tell me," she asked him, "when will you be here next?"

"I don't know. Not long, I think. We come often in the summer, don't we?"

"Let me think about this until the next time I see you."

So Prsedi stayed with Chermesh. But she cried sometimes, thinking of Nemas, and all they had done together. Chermesh became tired of her crying and gave her daughter chores to do to keep the tears away.

One day Chermesh came back from a visit with a friend, intending to make something for them to eat. At fifteen winters of age, Prsedi was more than capable of making dinner, but Chermesh was not sure she would. Maybe she would be too sad to do that even for herself.

I am glad I am not that age anymore, Chermesh thought, when she entered and found Prsedi with teary eyes and no dinner.

"Why are you crying now?" Chermesh asked. "He will come back soon, Prsedi! It has been a moon only. He will be here. What are these tears for?"

"The day we met," Prsedi said, "Nemas and me. I'm thinking about the leopard. About its beauty."

Chermesh was exasperated with that. The leopard was a beautiful thing, a wonderful thing, for both of them. For everyone, really. But it had been six winters since the leopard died.

"Prsedi," she said. "No more tears for now, OK? Make dinner. I will be back in a moment."

Then she walked to the doorway, bending to go out, and stopped abruptly. Standing tall again, Chermesh turned back, looking closely at her daughter. She walked back to the girl, the young woman, Chermesh reminded herself, and squatted on her heels so she could look Prsedi in the eye.

"Chermesh," Prsedi said, puzzled. "I see your tears too, now that you are so close. What is it? Are you also crying for the beauty of leopards?"

Chermesh laughed softly at that. "No, Prsedi," she said. "No, not leopards."

"What then?" Prsedi asked, baffled by her mother's behavior.

"I am laughing and crying for the beauty of my daughter," Chermesh said. And as she spoke, she put her arms around Prsedi in a hug so the glad tears that trembled in her eyes would not fall down her cheeks. Or at least if they did, Prsedi would not see, and laugh about them. While she hid there, holding Prsedi, Chermesh thought silently, *And for the beauty of you, too, Nemas.*

Because for now, nothing seemed more beautiful to her than these two friends. *More than friends now*, she thought. *More than just friends.*

Then she explained to Prsedi what she knew.

Prsedi showed little change. Others would not notice. Yet. Not for a moon or two. But the changes in Prsedi had been enough already for her mother to see them long before Prsedi herself did. To see, and to know, unexpectedly, suddenly, standing inside the doorway to her hut, what they meant.

In fact, Newir and Nemas did not come back to the Téuta until the middle of the summer, and by that time Nemas needed only a glance to know that he would be a father, and Newir only a glance to know he would be a grandfather.

Almost before Nemas was close enough to greet her, before he did greet her, Prsedi called out to him.

"Yes! If you still want, I will come with you to the Kujoté!"

And she did. When Newir and Nemas left the following morning, Prsedi went with them. Chermesh and Belisse and Uébe and Welo and Eini and Akesh and many others all watched them go. The girl who sang with leopards was leaving the Téuta.

She would not be completely apart from her Téuta life, though. Before the year was out, a friend she knew well joined her. Uébe, the beauty, had also found a young Kujoté man, and when the fall festival came she went with him to the wandering people to travel down river to the warmer plains below.

⚘ ⚘ ⚘

For two years Prsedi travelled with the Kujoté. Each year when the forest people returned during the summer, she came with them, bringing her child to the festivals. And she visited in between, sometimes staying with Chermesh for a half-moon at a time before leaving at summer's end to travel to the Kujoté's winter camp on the plains.

But after two years, at the start of the third and before the time for the Kujoté to come for the summer moons, Prsedi walked into the Téuta alone, walking up the river alone. And that year the Kujoté did not come back to spend their summer at their camp in the forest.

Prsedi said nothing about what had happened. But there was not one of all the Téuta who did not see these things as portents, as changes in the foundations of their world.

ꝑ

All the hut was active. They had spun their views out at length for many moons, for many years really.

Nothing worked here anymore. The crops were failing. Everyone knew, because the Kujoté had told them, that there were better, safer, warmer places. That the Kujoté no longer came to them in the summers was terrible, but also in a way, good. Because at the end of summer, the Téuta no longer had any spare grain to give their friends. By winter's end, before spring arrived later each year, there was deep hunger in the village.

And everyone knew also that the displaced, the hungry, were getting bolder and more desperate in the mountains all around them. Raiders were no longer a problem only for others in places far away. Violence was well settled in among the mountains now. There were rumors that the groups who lived by violence were larger, perhaps simply growing or perhaps joining.

Many among the Téuta felt that this place was theirs, that neither failing crops nor violent people should be enough to drive them away. This place on the river was where Saurig had brought them. It was the place their ancestors knew, and where the wall of the dead called out to those same ancestors to help the living when help was needed.

Yet Eini, her visions pushing her, was sure it was time to go. She argued that at least some of the village should find a different place. She had been hinting and hedging about this for many years. Now, finally, there was a growing number in the village who listened and agreed.

For those who stayed, Eini argued, perhaps the crops would be sufficient, and perhaps the remaining numbers would be great enough to keep violence away, or to turn it away if it came. She loved the ancestors too, and the river. Eini loved the plateau, and the cliffs, and everything here. After fifty winters, it was hard to imagine any other place to live. But her stumbling, foggy dreams were pushing the Téuta people, and she said so to others. Why? They asked. And again and again, as she had throughout her life, Eini had to tell those who asked that she didn't know. She only knew it was time.

And so, the Téuta would gather today to discuss these things. And maybe, to decide.

Every voice mattered at a gathering. Those who had other work stayed away, but all who were able would come to listen or to speak. Eini would tell again of her feeling that those who felt they must stay could stay, but most should go, down river to places they had all heard about but few had seen.

She was sure of that. But as she looked around her in her hut, as her eyes fell on the familiar faces, Eini was also sure of something else.

"You must stay. Akesh," she said. "And Belisse, and Sntodi. You must stay here. Senne, too. You must care for Chaisa, and stay with Nedeh and care for her child as well."

Eini spoke with power and conviction. But the others were puzzled.

"Why?" Sntodi asked. "The whole of the Téuta will be there to hear the talk and speak their feeling. Why must we stay here?"

Sntodi had spoken for all of them when he questioned her. Now, Eini replied to all of them as well.

"I don't know," she said. "I only know that it matters. Akesh, Senne, Nedeh, you are Téuta and have been for a long time. Nedeh, since you were a child you have been Téuta. Now I think the Téuta need you to be here. And maybe you need to be here, to show the Téuta how to leave a place that is rooted in them."

Even to Eini, it made little sense. But all those in the hut had watched her for many years. They knew her, and knew that it was good to listen, even when what she said was hard to understand.

"I will go," she said. "I will speak. We have talked, and I can say what you would want to say. I will speak for myself, and also for you."

Nedeh looked hard at Eini, then at her feet with a frown. And then, slowly, she sat, cradled her infant in her arms, and held him close to nurse. The others looked at Nedeh, then at each other. Then, one by one, they sat too. Eini watched them. When all were seated, she nodded, seeming withdrawn into herself.

But Akesh stood again.

"I will go with you," she said. "I will tell them that raiders come like wolves. I will tell them that this place will travel with them, even if they live somewhere else. These are things that Senne and Nedeh and I know. They are things I can say for you."

After staring at her friend, Eini accepted this. There was truth there.

Eini and Akesh left the hut. They went to speak to the Téuta.

CHAPTER 40
SPRING 6222 BCE

All the words, Prsedi thought, *all the same words, the same arguments, again and again.*

Much of the Téuta had gathered to discuss what they should do. The only place inside the village big enough for a gathering of this size was the wide sandy ground under the wall of the dead. Here, the ancestors could listen to what the people said, and could know what they decided. It was proper that so great a decision should include them. *It should,* Prsedi thought, *include Saurig, the most ancient ancestor, who brought us here, who made this place ours. We need her approval of so solemn a choice.*

When winter was done, the Kujoté did not come. Even the oldest Téuta could not remember a year when they had not; their parents, and their parents before them, said the Kujoté had always come, as far back as memory reached. No more. Prsedi knew why, but she would not explain.

It felt like traditions no longer mattered. The old stories no longer bound them. Something new had to happen. Even Eini, the keeper of the past and the visionary of the future, said so. But Eini was an old woman now. Her stories of the past were still wonderful to hear, but her visions of a vague and troubled future were often dismissed. Perhaps they would be dismissed again today, but Prsedi did not think so.

Spring, the time for a new year, new work, was here, and if a decision was going to be made, this was the season to make it.

Rain fell, but small rain and soft, and in the spring it was foolish to wait for a time without rain. The meeting went on. Eini had argued again for sending much of the Téuta down the river to find a new home, and having others wait if they wished to wait. No one else really had a plan at all, so Prsedi assumed that Eini would win the day this time. This time, most of the Téuta adults were there to hear her. Not all. Some were on the plateau caring for the grain and the sheep or keeping watch for danger around them. And many of the very old and the very young, and those who cared for them, waited in their huts.

It had been decided, Prsedi was sure; everything had already been decided, although the talking still went on. Soon the split would happen, and those who wished to go would go. Prsedi was saddened by it. It seemed wrong to her. She thought the Téuta should stay together, here or there, but together wherever they were. Together always, as the Kujoté had done. So she rose and left the meeting and walked slowly along the cliffs, near enough to touch them, simply for the comfort of feeling their high solidity.

Earth sodden from weeks of rain was soft under her feet. She walked on, moving farther away from the assembled Téuta because she didn't want to listen to this talk anymore. She'd had her say. Now, she wanted to be apart, to hide from what was about to happen. So, she found a place where the cliffs hollowed a little. The hollow didn't really hide her, it wasn't deep enough for that, but it was mostly out of the rain. Prsedi leaned back against the wonderful, the ancient, the always cliffs, and closed her eyes, letting her mind drift.

The meeting was just sound now for her, and she ignored it to feel the day. But try as she might, she could not relax. She did not know what it was, but something troubled her.

⸙

Eini too was distracted by something, some inner disturbance she could not quite see and could not quite discard. She set it aside. She had to convince the gathered Téuta it was time to leave the place where their ancestors had lived for more generations than could be counted.

She felt it even more strongly now, and her dreams showed it coming closer, looming over them. But she had talked about it for so many years that now when Eini tried to warn them, they laughed, or were curt, not angry, just impatient. Then they walked away to do whatever it was they had meant to do before she talked to them.

And so, she spoke at the gathering, and the Téuta listened politely, as they had listened to the others who spoke. It was the duty of all Téuta to listen here. This year, several had suggested that the people should go south to lower ground, at least for now, while the winters continued so cold and the summers so dry. "Why is this happening?" They had asked. "The gods have abandoned us. What are the shamans doing about it?" Some had argued, as Eini did, that they could return to this, to their home, when the gods relented. "It is not forever," they said. The most adamant of them always said that. It is not forever. Just for now.

Eini wanted to say what she really believed. She wanted to tell them that the weather was not the problem. Instead, she just repeated the arguments the others had used. And she did it badly, which was unusual for her. She was the storyteller, the legend teller. She always spoke well.

What was distracting her so much?

Then the earth trembled, only a little, but enough.

Abruptly, she knew. The dream-thing that had stumbled toward her for so long showed itself huge, leering and vulgar. The Téuta grumbled at the trembling earth, but this small trembling had happened before.

Eini knew, though. She knew the terrible truth had come at last. And now she saw it clearly.

She knew that those who had gathered near the cliff were doomed.

She turned in fear, not for herself, but for the Téuta. Akesh and Belisse! These two, Eini had felt for many years, were the safe path, the only safe path for her village. But Akesh was here by the cliffs. For a moment, that realization felt like panic to Eini.

She thought of others who felt like safety to her. Prsedi was here, somewhere. Welo was nearby, but he did not like crowds, so he would be standing at a distance from the meeting. Sntodi had said he was going to stay near the hut. And Belisse, Eini remembered with relief, was in her hut with her child. At least they were safe.

The Téuta were watching Eini, standing quiet while the trembling ground simmered and stopped. They expected her to continue, to make her argument. They did not understand when she turned to the wall of the dead, which rose to the sky above them, and spoke, not to them, but to the cliffs.

I see you! I see you, she thought. *But you will not get the thing you want! You will take me and also Akesh. But I feel a safe path still. There is Chaisa still, cared for now by Belisse and by Nedeh along with her own babe. And Senne. Sntodi is with them. All of these will live. And Welo has long legs! He can run, and might live. You can take us who are here beside the cliff. But these others still here among the Téuta will defeat you! They will defeat you!*

Eini thought all this, but she said only one thing.

"You have come at last!" she shouted at the cliffs.

The watching Téuta thought she must have more to say. But in the next instant, the ground lurched like a leaping fish, and the cliffs above them cracked with the loudest sound any of them had ever heard. Suddenly, everyone was running. Fleeing the cliffs that had been their protection forever.

But Eini could see that there was no path that would save any who had been seated along the cliffs. No path. Those at the outside of the crowd, those closest to the river, might survive, but those here at the cliffs would not. The wall of the dead leapt out of its place, slid down toward the wet ground as though it were kneeling. Then the base of it struck the ground, and the top tilted toward them. All the gathered Téuta ran toward open ground. But most realized, even while they ran, that the open ground was too far.

It was too far.

The great cliff tilted, its shadow racing ahead, covering them.

Eini did not move. She simply stood and watched the wall of the dead loom over her, bending and falling, closer and closer.

Nothing to do. Nothing.

So Eini closed her eyes, spread her arms wide, and danced. She twirled like a madwoman, dancing with Dhegm, with the world, with the ground and everything.

But her mind went on, repeating her thought as a mantra as the shadow came across her. Eini lost herself in her dance. Her dance was what she felt. But her mind continued to repeat its last phrase.

They will defeat you! They will defeat you! They will de—

And then the wide, beautiful white and coral face of the wall of the ancestors smacked hard down on the ground, and all the Téuta under it were gone.

† ⬭ ⱶ

Sntodi stood outside the hut watching the cliffs fall, watching all the havoc, all the death. The rocks crashed down through the village; the great cliff dropped its face to the ground. It did not drop across him, or the hut behind him. But there were great rocks that came after the cliff, that tumbled and rolled across the earth, herds of them crushing whatever they met.

And one of those came to Eini's hut.

Nedeh, and Senne, and Sntodi, leapt aside, but Belisse was slower. She was seated, holding and nursing Chaisa. The rock that came toward them did not roll directly through the hut, but it crushed the wall behind her. And that wall fell toward her, burying her under bricks. Chaisa wailed in fright. Seeing that Belisse was trapped and limp, with everything below her chest pinned beneath the fallen wall, Nedeh handed her own child to Senne. She then took the Chaisa from Belisse's slack hands.

In the next moment, another great rock smashed into the side wall, which collapsed as well, burying Belisse completely.

Belisse, Eini's great hope for the Téuta, was buried under the rubble of her hut, under boulders that kept coming, rolling one after the other across the ground.

The whole hut was collapsing. Belisse was trapped beneath it, insensible. She seemed dead, and likely was. There was nothing to be done for her—nothing except to save her child.

So Nedeh, Senne, and Sntodi, sharing the same thought and needing no words, took the two babies and ran toward the river, the best chance of safety. They ran hard, then splashed through the water, then swam, then ran again, until they crossed the river and stood on the far bank.

Then they looked back at the awful tumult. They looked back at the end of all the Téuta they had known. The two infants cried and shivered hard from their time in the cold river water. Sntodi took his parka off to cover them, to warm them. To keep them living. Even now, with death all around them, he acted to keep the infants safe.

But in everything else they were lost. Without Akesh, without Eini, without Belisse, they were lost.

PART V

A New Téuta

CHAPTER 41

Prsedi, so close to the cliff that her hand was on its face, felt a tiny tremble in the earth beneath her, and in the rock behind her back. She put a hand against the rock to steady herself. The tremble stopped, and all was quiet.

Then, without further warning, the whole world shook hard, as though a bee was biting it. The shaking paused for a moment, but there was thunder under the ground that she didn't really hear; she just felt it deep inside.

The gathering was not quiet, but no one was speaking, or too many were speaking. Prsedi did not watch them or hear them, but she had the idea that they were confused and held each other. That they turned this way, and that, bewildered. The people shouted all at once, but she heard only the sound, not the words. She felt in some deep place inside her that the words made no difference.

Prsedi reached again for the cliff to steady herself. She didn't know where the danger was or what it was, only that it was there. She crouched, leaning close against the great rock wall. And that was what saved her.

Thunder rode up from below her, and then came hard, sharp, loud thunder from above, and the cliff that had always been there seemed to move away from her hand. She jumped from the motion, toward a part of the cliff that seemed to stand still, as it should. She looked up and flattened herself against the mass beside her. The cliff she leaned against seemed steady, but nearby sections buckled outward, and when she looked up, the cliffs above her were leaning.

The ground was trembling, shuddering, twisting, and her feet sank into it up to her ankles. Then the top of the cliff broke away high above her head, and the whole face of the cliff seemed to slide outward and down. It stabbed and cut the ground like a giant knife. Then it leaned out above her. The weight of it pulled it free.

It fell away—slowly, then faster, then fast—falling toward the center of the town, toward the great, crowded heart of the Téuta. It slammed into the ground so hard that the earth leapt around it, tossing Prsedi backward like a rabbit skin along what had once been the base of the cliff.

After the great slab fell, the cliff kept breaking. New slabs slid loose above her, then shattered. Boulders bounded down the face, bounced, and fell away, until at last only pebbles came, pouring down over her.

Prsedi lay on her side, curled tight against the deepest part of the cliff—the part that seemed, so far, to be still, or as still as anything could be in that stone storm. Great rocks piled around her, and smaller rocks, pebbles, and sand buried her. Somewhere in the clear part of her mind that was always with her, she knew that the chaos was a fleeting thing. But that part of her mind felt distant while she was being buried alive.

To her senses, to her fear and her hope, the rumbling seemed to go on for days, perhaps for years. In each instant, her life felt divided into two parts: a small part that was all her life before this, and a far larger part—the longest and clearest part—which was this time of chaos, as debris rained around her and she waited for one of the huge rocks to kill her. All the rest of life had shrunk to a tiny memory beside it.

The rumbling and shuddering finally ended, but the fear stayed. Prsedi pushed dirt away from her face so she could breathe. She tried to stand, discovering that she couldn't. She was caught in a space, tiny, and tight. Even with the mud cleared from her face, she could barely breathe at all with the dust clogging her lungs and drifting around her. As dust settled, though, she could see an opening in one direction. By squirming along between the dirt and the rock above her, digging the mud away in front of her as she went, she could move toward it.

Again, her life had two parts. The first was all that had gone before in the years of her life. The second, the largest part, was this slow, impossible squirm along the ground towards open space. Squirm and dig and squirm, sure always that this was what her life would be until the rocks and mud took her. Prsedi moved hand-length by hand-length along the ground.

She made it through. Coughing, scratched, and sweating hard from fright and exertion, she reached an opening where she could stand and take a few steps, if she leaned against what was left of the cliff to slip past the boulder lodged against it. By squeezing herself small, she scraped through into a wider hollow, one where she could take several full steps and where the rock above her rose well over her head. Here she could breathe a little more easily. The walls did not press so close around her, and the dust from the avalanche was finally settling.

There was a faint light, reflected through small openings to the distant world outside. A few were as large as a fist, but those lay far above her. Looking around, she saw there were many of them. Two narrow threads of dim light reached the ground, but most ran low through the rock.

From far away she heard wailing from what remained of the Téuta —a sound she recognized as massive, hot grief, thinned and cooled as it snaked through long, wet channels between the rocks.

None of the gaps were large enough to climb through. There were three dark holes that she could put her arm into up to her shoulder, and many that were big enough for several fingers. But none big enough for all of her. Rain came sliding down the rock walls of her room, washing them, washing mud from the floor that flowed out around the rocks.

Watching the water made her realize how thirsty she was. The water was brown as it washed over the rocks; it was thick with dirt from the stones above. She reached toward the water anyway, before the clear center of her mind came back to her. She was thirsty, it told her, but she should wait. The rain seemed to have increased. It fell hard above her, though she could not hear it. The sound of the breaking cliff had dulled her ears.

Prsedi sat, and waited. In an hour, the water would be cleaner. In an hour everything would be cleaner.

ⱶ ⱷ ⱶ

To those still alive, those in what remained of their great village, the rest of the afternoon seemed silent. The rain fell, and the wind blew, and trees loosened by the rocking earth fell against those around them. But no sound seemed to matter to the villagers. The forest was quiet, with all the animals, all the insects, seeming to hide and tremble at the knowledge that the earth could do a thing. The villagers who had stayed in huts that were closer to the river than to the cliffs, came out when the thunder of falling rock died away. They gazed at the cliff's former top, which had been high above them and flat to walk on before this, but now stood vertical and far too close, and at the great boulders that had rolled across the ground to the river, crushing everything in their path. All the Téuta that were left simply stood in the lonely day, knowing but refusing to see what had happened. Unable to absorb it, unable to feel it, the day passed. The sun lit the new tumble before them and sank in the west. Evening came, and in its calm they finally heard a sound that they understood. In the distance, wolves sang their songs to the sky, or to each other. They sang their sudden fear of the earth into the night.

For three nights, the wolves sang. By the third night, the Téuta found a solace in their song. In the song of the wolves, they found another song, a remembered song. They heard the song of grief and resilience that Akesh had given them from the clifftop after Senek's death, the song she had sung standing on that same clifftop that now faced them, upright like a wall, and taunted them. They heard what Akesh had told them. They heard the strength of the earth.

They heard it. But for now, they were too numb to feel it. Three days was not enough time to recover from a grief this deep.

ⱶ ⱷ ⱶ

Night was frightening for Prsedi in her little tomb. She slept, and woke, and slept again, and woke again, and waited for her thirst to kill her, but otherwise she seemed surprisingly well. A few deep bruises, some scratches and nicks, but well enough.

The rains had continued through the first day, and toward late evening the water seemed clear, but she still waited. She didn't trust the water coming down through the rocks.

Waiting had been a mistake. The rains stopped overnight, and then there was no water at all, only mud beneath her feet. But as she explored her little space, she found several depressions where water had collected, including two deep ones where all the dirt had settled, and the surface water seemed clean. She took a sip and waited, then drank again when the first sip didn't make her sick.

I will die of hunger, not of thirst, Prsedi thought. Rain would come again, without doubt, at this time of year, and it would fill her new water-bowl.

Death was near. She knew that. She had no reason to think that anyone or anything could change that. Each boulder in the mass above her was too large to move, too large for the village together to move. And even if one could be moved, the result would only be that the others would collapse and crush her. And in any case, although she could not see them, Prsedi knew that the people of the Téuta had to have lost so many, that the town must be so disarrayed that no one would think of looking for her. She was only one of many under the cliff.

Through her small channels of light and sound, Prsedi had heard a little. She knew there were no real leaders left, because the cliff had crushed them. She had called out, loudly she thought, but no one seemed to hear her.

The first day after the cliffs fell, Prsedi spent an hour remembering to breathe, waiting for the dancing dust to settle. The new rains helped; instead of dust in the air there was mud on the ground and clinging to the rocks. She was cold. Her cloak must have come off in the landslide, or been lost as she dug her way into this place.

She remembered the fear of that tiny, wet tunnel where she had been when the boulders finally stopped falling. She did not want to go back there. But she was chilled through, especially at night. If she meant to stay alive, she needed the cloak. So she went back.

The tunnel was cleaner than before, the mud washed thin by the rain, and it seemed less tight than she remembered. Still, it closed around her enough to stir panic. She backed out several times to calm herself before returning to search. The cloak had to be there; it was nowhere else. When her hand finally brushed it in the dark, it was sodden with mud—so heavy it seemed almost made of it.

She cleaned it a little under the flow of rainwater, a kind of a minor waterfall at her tiny tunnel's opening.

It was worth the effort. The work warmed her, and even though the cloak was wet, it was still something to wrap around her shoulders. It kept the chill and the rain out and the warmth of her body in, and soon the part next to her skin was cool instead of cold, and no more than damp. And so Prsedi wrapped the damp cloak close around her and slept.

When she woke on the third day, the rain had stopped. The waterfalls had vanished. She draped her cloak inside-out over a stony shelf and explored her tomb. Nothing had changed now that her lungs and her mind had cleared. There was the chamber she slept in, the one she could stand in easily, and a second smaller room, and in the smaller room the hole she had climbed from as though emerging from an underworld. That tunnel went back into darkness and ended in a distant wall of dirt.

This was her space that no one else in all the life of the world would ever see. Her living room. Her dying room. Her tomb.

CHAPTER 42

Dreams about life, about memories, about those crushed under the cliff. Their lives were gone, and soon hers would also be gone. What *is* life? What is it for? Memories discarded. Memories separated from you and blowing away like chaff, others like leaves lifted by the wind of life under them, or birds lifted by flying against the wind. *Dhegm, Dhegm,* Prsedi thought, *I will see you soon. Very soon I will see you. I will be happy then.*

"*Yes,*" she heard Dhegm reply in many voices. Some had serious purpose in them, but others also seemed like humor, like laughter. The goddess had one voice like a wild storm blowing along the river canyons, and one like a hand smoothing a soft pelt. "Yes Prsedi, we will be together soon." This voice was like a grand echo sounding down the length of the long earth, the always earth that endured forever. The earth that produces everything and consumes everything. The earth spread out around Prsedi and above her. She had walked on the earth, and now she was beneath it, and it contained her, and Dhegm's echoing voice washed across it and was heard by everyone. Even by Prsedi in her tomb.

This sound makes me think of wind because it is wind, Prsedi thought in her sleep. *It is the wind blowing across the rock above me.*

But it was not just sound. She felt Dhegm all around her. She felt the immensity of the goddess, and the goddess spoke to her in all those voices, and in others. *Am I asleep?* Prsedi wondered. *Am I dreaming a dream of Dhegm against me? Am I dead already?* She asked this because she felt the goddess like a physical thing near her.

As she roused herself from her dreams, Prsedi felt her hand being held by another hand, a tiny hand. The touch warmed her. "Wake up Prsedi," the voice said. It was an old voice, high and soft.

Prsedi came awake, bewildered. Nothing had changed. She was in her tomb, where she would be forever. But no, something had changed. As her vision cleared from sleep, she knew she was not alone anymore. Someone immense was there, or someone tiny was there. She rolled over to see what hand it was that held hers.

Beside Prsedi, holding her hand softly, was the smallest, oldest woman she could imagine.

"Good. Be awake Prsedi. It's time to go," the old woman said.

"Who are you?"

"It's time to go."

"There is no way to go."

"Come, Prsedi." The tiny creature tugged at her hand. "I will show you something."

This woman is a dream. Prsedi thought. *I am still asleep. Or dead, and this is what the dead see.* But dream or not, dead or not, the woman's presence was compelling. Her voice was compelling. Prsedi could not hear that voice and fail to act.

So Prsedi followed an impossible old woman who was not there, who *could* not be there, and watched as the woman crawled into the tiny tunnel clogged with dirt.

At first she thought it was the same. But when Prsedi crouched and looked into the tunnel, it seemed wider and taller than before. The rain had washed much of the dirt and mud from the floor away. Though the far end still looked like mud, there was now a dim light there. And the old woman was gone.

Prsedi did not want to enter the tunnel again. She did not want to follow the old woman who had seemed to feel no fear, who had slipped through the narrow passage without difficulty, as lithe and eager as an infant. Yet then the old woman called to her, and her voice was like a rope, pulling Prsedi toward her.

Prsedi crawled into the space.

With the mud and dirt washed away, it was no longer so tight that she had to squirm on her belly. She crawled along to the end, and reaching it, found she could stand. At the top was a small opening, too small to get through, where a small shaft of dusty light could enter.

Prsedi pushed at the pile of dirt and gravel above her and found she could make the opening wider; the mud moved easily out of her way. She pushed and dug until she could finally squeeze through into a long, narrow tunnel, not much wider than her shoulders but four times as tall as she was. There, a massive slab of rock leaned against another—or perhaps against what remained of the solid cliff itself.

No, against what is the new cliff.

"Go on, Prsedi," the old woman's voice said behind her. "Here is the path."

She turned and saw the old woman both there and not there. For a moment, she seemed like a shadow. Then she was gone.

Prsedi turned again to the long tunnel and began to walk. She had to climb over boulders, and up and up closer to the top of the tunnel, until she had to stoop to walk, but she continued, because the light was stronger as she continued. It looked like a dead end, but light was on it, light that seemed strong, wildly strong to Prsedi's eyes that had been in her dark tomb for so many days. When she reached the end, she saw why. There was a nearly vertical shaft there, and at the top was daylight.

Beside her, the old woman stood, solid and easily seen in the light.

"You see, Prsedi?" she said. "It is not so long a climb. You can get out. You were a good climber as child."

Prsedi turned and looked again. It did look like a long climb to her, too long and steep for her to try. She was hungry. She had not eaten in days. She was too weak for a climb like this.

The woman's hand pushed her, and there seemed to be strength in it, a strength that poured from the woman into everything around her. Prsedi turned to look at her, to look down, because the woman was so small.

"You are not coming, are you?" She asked.

"I will come for some of this climb, but in the end I will stay. Don't worry about me, I will be fine."

Prsedi smiled at that, because by then she knew who the woman was, or what she was.

"I know," she said. "You live here."

Prsedi looked up to the light, to the thing she had wanted for all of her days in her tomb. She was gathering her strength. Gathering the strength to climb back into the world. Or gathering the strength to decide not to climb.

"If I stay here," she asked, "will we be together?"

The woman, who was there and not there, who was older than anything could be old and still always young, seemed to smile a smile that creased all of her face in the dim light. Her ancient smile showed the lines of all the thousands of thousands of laughs that had preceded it.

"Who is this woman who asks me such a question? Is this the always wise Prsedi? You know the answer, Prsedi," she said. "Here or there, we will be together. Whether you stay or go, we will be always together. Don't stand deciding when there is nothing to decide. Go."

"I don't want to leave you," Prsedi said.

Again, the woman chastised her.

"You can't leave me, Prsedi. You know that. The girl who knows how to sing with leopards must of course know that." The old woman paused, watching. Then, seeing Prsedi's reluctance, she said, "I'll visit you, Prsedi. I'll visit at your breakfasts, if you want."

"You will visit me?"

"Yes." The old woman nodded. "Like this, and we can talk with each other."

"You would truly visit me?" The idea seemed preposterous. "Of course, I would be glad, and honored, to share my breakfast with you. But it's not really mine to share with you, is it? The only breakfast we have is from you. It's always yours. As we are always yours, Dhegm," Prsedi said, giving the older woman the only name she knew for her.

Then Prsedi knelt, and tried to bow her head to show Dhegm her respect, but Dhegm took her arms and lifted her up. The woman's hands were soft and quiet, but they pulled Prsedi to her feet with strength beyond all resistance.

"There is no need for that between us, Prsedi," she said. "How would you eat breakfast when I visit if you are always kneeling and bowing? We are friends. Stand now. Climb."

So Prsedi climbed, slowly at first, then faster as the wide world, Dhegm's endless, beautiful world, felt possible again. She had thought she was too tired, too weak, and too hungry. But before she was ready to believe it could be done at all, she was out, standing in the open, in a brilliant evening, breathing the clear air. She smelled water, and trees, and the droppings of animals that had passed here, and the pungent scent of growing things. Prsedi turned in a circle, taking in everything around her. The air was clean, the ground was clean, the water was clean, the trees were clean, and Prsedi realized that she was not. She was filthy, and starving, and exhausted.

And alive.

CHAPTER 43

Prsedi stood for a moment, taking in what surrounded her. She had much to think about. She had survived, but her village had been crushed, and many she had known all her life were dead. The knowledge pressed hard on her. The grief pressed too, though she could not yet say for whom she was grieving, or which deaths she was grieving for. It was grief already days old, and it had drained her, along with everything else that had happened. She did not have the strength left to think about it.

So, she pushed it away and instead tasted the life that remained. She was grateful for that life, and she felt embarrassed to be so grateful for something so temporary, then embarrassed to have thought that it was temporary at all. *Eini has told me this. She is right. The living die; each of us dies*, she thought. *Our days tumble by us like rain in the storm, like leaves, or like rocks in a landslide, and in the end we die. But life is always here. New life is here, and life is always new.*

Prsedi spent a few minutes reveling in that thought before she realized that she knew where she was. She was at the top of the cliffs, what remained of them, and everyone knew Welo and Akesh had a hut just a few steps from here, with a pool of water fed by a spring next to it. The hut might have food, some grain in a jar somewhere. Prsedi started toward where she thought it might be. Almost before she started to look, she found it.

Welo was not there. Or Akesh. That was not surprising. But the jar of grain was there, and a crock for cooking, and a fire-pit still warm and easy to light, and a store of dung to burn.

Prsedi ordered her tasks. She went first to the spring and drank, not too much, although it was hard to stop. She washed her face, scrubbing hard at it to get rid of all the dust. Then she started the fire in the hut, went back to the spring to fill the crock, placed the crock beside the fire pit to warm, and put a handful of the grain in the water.

When that was done, she returned to the spring, took her clothes off to wash them, and entered the pool herself to make herself as clean as she could. It seemed to her that both her body and her clothes were so filthy that they would be soiled forever no matter what she did, but she did her best.

Her clothes were easier, in a way. She submerged them whole into the pool and let the spring that fed it flood the mud from them; there was a long dark tail to them as the water flowed past. She pressed them and soaked them and pressed again until the water flowed clean through them. They were clean enough at the end, but they were sodden and almost too heavy to lift, since she was weak with hunger. She did lift them, though. She set them on some rocks to dry and returned to the fire to be warm.

Then, for the first time in days, she ate. Her bath and her washing had taken so long that the grain was very soft, and the water completely gone.

If I had taken much longer at the spring, this grain would be dried and hard again, she thought. *And probably burned and stuck to the crock.*

Then, finally, after she had eaten and was warm again, the calamity, the deaths, losing the village, the blood and anguish, all found their way to her. Deep loss found her, and she sat crying alone in Welo's old hut, by Welo's fire pit, with only her grief to cover her because her clothes were still drying outside.

Prsedi did not know how much later it was when she was startled awake by something—a shadow, a silence, a noise, she was not sure what. She could not have really slept. She was still sitting up, leaning against the wall of Welo's hut. She still felt the warmth of Welo's fire pit.

But the fire was bigger, and she had a goatskin draped around her, and her clothes were spread on the floor near her.

A darkness filled the doorway, and Welo entered, his face dark with mixed emotions. Grief, of course. His face was heavy with it. But there were other feelings, too, especially relief and concern for the young woman he had watched grow from childhood. He came in with the bowl she had been using, now clean, and set it down.

"Are you well?" he asked. "You look thin, and very tired, but generally well."

"I am wonderful," Prsedi replied. "I am alive, and that is wonderful. I want to remember forever how wonderful it is to be alive."

"Yes." Welo nodded. "I felt you, sensed that you were buried but still whole, and that there was no way to get to you. So many are dead," he said. "No more than one in three of the Téuta still live, and those mostly the very young and the very old. I thought you couldn't help but join the dead soon. How did you get free? But no, never mind. We can talk about that later. First make sure you are well."

Prsedi laughed for no reason at all. She laughed simply because the world was joyful to be in. Immediately she felt the grief again, for all who had been lost, then with effort pushed that away to find the joy. That was the wisdom Akesh had given once to all the Téuta. There is joy even when it's hard to find it. *How astonishing to have known both Eini and Akesh. I know both are among the dead,* Prsedi thought, and grief came again, and again she did her best to push it away and remember life. This time though, she failed, and grief took her. Tears came and went on. But she couldn't cry forever. Finally, she could breathe again, and feel life inside her, and all around her.

To Welo she said, "I am well, Welo, yes. More well than you can imagine. But I am hungry too."

"Wait some time," he said, "to eat more. I have fish, and I will get more if we need it, but I'm also cooking more barley grain for you. It will be ready soon. You're sure you are well?"

In the chaos of her emotions, grief had gone again, and joy was here.

"Yes. I am very, very well," Prsedi assured him. "Very very very! I have never been so well."

They sat and talked as the fish cooked, and talked more than they ate. Food twice in a short time after so many days without it did not rest easily inside Prsedi, but the discomfort was small, and she didn't mind. After dinner, her clothes seemed dry enough to wear, so she laid Welo's cloak on the sleeping platform, dressed, and retrieved the cloak for warmth.

She was entranced with the surprise of being alive. She wanted to celebrate life, to create more life, but she also felt grief for all the death around her. These two feelings nestled close and blended together with no seam. She was sure that should have surprised her, but after crawling and climbing with Dhegm the goddess through the tumbled rocks, nothing could really surprise her. *With Dhegm! With the goddess, the mother, the earth!* She had *held Dhegm's hand.* Nothing could surprise her after that. Nothing.

Except maybe Welo.

Except the hut, and the fire, and the smell of food.

Except the wind and the trees, and beetles and lizards and dust.

Nothing at all could ever surprise her again, except everything, everywhere, forever.

She was wrung hard with grief, but she could not stop her smiles.

"Thank you for all of this," she said. "For the hut, the shawl, the food. And for talking with me. All of it amazes me now."

Welo nodded, but said nothing. Prsedi, sitting near him in the small hut, leaned against him, and Welo put his long arm around her shoulders. She felt the hugeness of him, his long, strong arm around her, the muscle in his chest. *Welo,* she thought. *Long, beautiful, bony Welo. My wonderful, beautiful friend.* She put her hand against his side. She turned her face, and smiled. She felt his warmth, and the joy of him, and of life.

Then, exhaustion and stress overtook her, and she was asleep.

Prsedi woke to the smell of deer stew and bread, instantly aware of her hunger. A moment later, Welo came with a bowl of water from the spring. He nodded to her before adding it to the stew. She watched his long, hard back as he worked.

They sat together, eating from the same bowl. Clean, warm, and well fed, Prsedi felt the hut was bliss after living in her tomb. But the quiet bothered her. It had been quiet in her tomb for so long.

"We should talk, Welo," she said. "I haven't been able to talk to anyone for many days."

"I know." He looked at her. "You never told me how you escaped from that place."

"No," Prsedi agreed. "I didn't. But you could not have helped me. It was impossible. Someone did come to help, though. She showed me how to go, where to go, and where to climb."

"Someone came to you? Who could get into that place?"

Then, after a pause, because she was not sure he would believe her, Prsedi told the story of meeting Dhegm, of Dhegm taking her hand to lead her out of her tomb. Welo accepted all she said. If Prsedi could hold a leopard's head while death came to take it, then she could meet Dhegm. She did not have to convince him. After she had finished, she spent some time in silence, then she spoke again.

"You have seen that I am sometimes sad for all the lost, and sometimes very happy. Meeting Dhegm, finding myself alive at the top of the cliff, this is why I am sometimes happy. But you, Welo, I don't think you are happy."

"No," he said quietly. "It is hard to be happy."

They sat for a moment without speaking. Then Welo took a deep breath and spoke again.

"There's much to be unhappy about," he said. "Akesh is dead under the cliff, and Belisse under her hut. Eini, too, lies under the cliff, and many others are dead in many ways. That was hard—very hard. The first days were terrible. And thinking of you trapped there, sensing you, knowing you would die there—that was hard as well. Others were trapped alive, but you were the only one who seemed trapped whole. The others were injured, or broken, or fading, but…"

Welo paused, not wanting to say the rest. Prsedi had to ask.

"But what, Welo? But not whole?"

"No, not whole." he said. "Injured. Some of them were missing parts of themselves. I don't want to remember."

Prsedi sat for a long time, frowning. It was very easy for her to imagine what it would have been like for the others, not only trapped, shocked and thirsty, choking from dust and in pain. She understood not wanting to remember. She didn't want to think about it either. Welo was right; it was hard to know these things.

But she did think about them, because she felt a kinship with them. The family of the buried. The family of the frightened, choking with dust and drowning in mud. The family of the dead.

Then she thought about the other thing Welo had said.

"Belisse?" she asked. "She is dead?" This was a grief she had not known or expected until now.

"Yes," Welo said. "She is dead. Her hut fell on her."

"And her child? Chaisa? Is she also dead?"

"No, Chaisa lives. Nedeh with her new babe nurses both."

Prsedi let that knowledge settle.

"Where are the others," she asked. "The other living buried ones?" It was a question, but it didn't sound like a question when she said it out loud. She already knew the answer, but she had to hear it.

"They are dead. It has been many days, Prsedi. Most died quickly. After the end of the first night, perhaps three or four remained still living. But by the end of the next day, the day after the shaking land, only you remained alive inside the fallen rock."

Now, Welo too was looking at nothing and frowning at nothing. Both of them now carried scars in their hearts that would never heal, maybe as disfiguring inside them as those fire-made scars that Akesh had carried outside on her face.

Welo recalled himself to the moment first.

"Let them go," he said, breaking the long silence.

"What?"

"Let them go. Let go of the dead. We can't save those who are dead already. Dhegm has them. The songs Akesh sang for us told all of us that. But the others, the living of the Téuta, are still down there. My granddaughter Chaisa is there, alive. Very alive. Alive and fussing and pestering Nedeh or Senne or whoever is taking care of her."

It took Prsedi a moment to understand what Welo said. Slowly she accepted it, and her naturally practical nature, still dim from her emotional journey, returned.

"What can we do for them?"

"I'm not sure," Welo said, "that I can do anything. They blamed me for bad news before this happened. They will blame me even more for this."

"Why would they blame you? What could you have done to be blamed?"

"I have done nothing. But people heard that I went chasing stranger gods. They will not believe me when I tell them there are no stranger gods, and I didn't chase them anyway."

Prsedi sat quietly for a moment, thinking about this.

"They do this, don't they?" Welo continued. "You have lived among them. You have heard them chatter among themselves."

Part of Prsedi was shocked to hear him say this, even though she knew it was true. It had been true for most of her life, people in the village blaming Welo for bad things that happened, large and small. He was strange, too tall and socially clumsy. He saw things they could not. And when he was exploring the world, when he was far from the village, he was not there, so it was easy to blame him. This was not a new thing, but it had always shocked her when people did it. It was unfair and made no sense, so always before she had dismissed it.

"Well, what can I do then?" She asked. "I am not Belisse. Or Eini. Or Akesh. And I am not you. Who is left that can help them?"

"I don't know." Welo shook his head. "They seem confused. I don't think the people down there have bathed, and some have eaten only a little. You can tell them to bathe, and to eat."

Another silence came over them before Welo spoke again. "I think," he said, "that you must tell them that they should go to where the Kujoté spend the summers. They will listen if it is you who tells them. They remember the leopard. They will hear you."

"And you can't tell them. Because of the stranger gods."

"No," Welo agreed. "And also I can't go. I will stay here, with Akesh and Belisse. I don't think I can leave them. I can't."

He paused, turning his face away, and then he went on.

"The Téuta should not stay here. In the mountains, that way and that," Welo pointed in two directions, "there are warring people. Violent people. They too, are shocked by what happened. But sooner or later they will forget their shock and think of the Téuta, of the rich prize that was always too big for them."

There was a long pause before Welo continued.

"And when they do," he said, "they will come to scavenge. All of them will come. And the Téuta as they are now can't stand against them. I know. I know what can happen. I have seen it. So you must go to them and convince them. The Téuta can't survive here. There must be another place. And you are the only one among us who has seen it."

CHAPTER 44

Oł

Hewsos still painted the sky when Prsedi rose. Welo had risen before her, so she was alone. The hut was warm. A simple breakfast of fish and onions and barley-mush sat by the fire.

She ate while she waited for Welo to return. She didn't want to leave this place. Here with Welo, the world was quiet, and simple.

When he did come, he seemed gruff. Prsedi had seen him like this before, many times. She knew it only meant that he felt as she did, that he wanted her to stay, that he would be alone when she had gone, and that there was really no good choice.

They had watched for two days from the clifftop. The people below still seemed dazed, unable to unite, unable to be Téuta. They simply sat and waited. Waited for what? Prsedi did not understand them.

There were still many people in the Téuta. But the Téuta were dazed, and too many of them were very old, or very young. In truth, their only real defense against the violent people was that they had nothing left worth stealing, or even scavenging. They had barely enough food for themselves.

Even so, the raiders had attacked poorer targets than the Téuta with great brutality. And Welo could sense them. They were moving in different directions, ranging across the mountains. They were not close enough to worry about yet. They had never truly attacked the Téuta before because it was too big for them. But now, if they could see what he and Prsedi had seen over the last days, they would know it was safe to come. Welo knew they would learn of it soon. And when they did, they would come.

Prsedi accepted that she was not Belisse, or Akesh, or Eini. She was Prsedi, though. She had been a friend to Belisse since childhood, and had been close to Eini, and to Akesh. Maybe the Téuta would listen to her.

It was still early when she started down the path to the Téuta. That path pushed her away from the Téuta for some distance, but there was no other path that could get her to the river more easily. She walked through trees, across what seemed like undisturbed forest until she found the game trail leading down toward the river. The walk was not difficult, but she was filled with misgivings about what she would find at the end of it. By mid-morning she had reached the river and turned upstream.

The river had changed since she had been here last. Many great rocks had fallen into the current and been strewn along the banks. In one place, the river had been blocked completely, and had found a way around. In another, the ground had cracked open, forming a deep pool that had not been there before. But even if it had changed in some places, the landscape was familiar. Prsedi knew where she was, and where she had to go.

The clouds were like feathers across the sky as she walked upstream on a calm, bright day.

When she turned around the last cliffs, rounding the final bend of the river, and saw that the village was mostly gone, the sight of it up close shocked her. Prsedi stopped where she was. For a time, she just watched with wide eyes. Where most of the Téuta had been, there was nothing now except a great and empty mass of stone. A large section of cliff had vanished, replaced by a rubble of huge boulders, and smaller boulders, and dirt.

And the wall of the dead, the great and ancient wall of ancestors, was gone. It lay face down on the ground.

A week after the event, dust was everywhere, covering the houses that remained. Even far from the fallen cliffs there were houses half collapsed, and others crushed or half-crushed, buried under the cascade of the catastrophe. Rubble was everywhere, and the sight of it, the familiarity of it, took Prsedi's breath away. She knew that rubble very well. She had been under it, and would still be under it, if Dhegm had not come to guide her out.

The people who remained still acted dazed. There was no organization among them. No one seemed to know what to do. They wanted to fix things, but there was no way to fix what had happened. In one way, Prsedi thought, she was luckier than these left-over people. She had been buried deep, hidden from much of the sound of the aftermath. She had not heard the calls and the crying of those who were trapped, or the silence of the dead. Instead, down in her tomb, she had mourned them, thinking she was one of them. That she was among the dead. But the barrier of rock around her in those first days muffled the pleas for help from those who were injured. She had not heard them.

Many of these ragged people sat staring at the ground, or at the cliffs, or at anything that moved. Some seemed to gather around open outdoor fires, simply gazing into the flames. Others walked, although they seemed to walk at random, without a destination.

Some, Prsedi noticed, clustered around a young man with immense shoulders, as if they were looking to him for direction. She recognized him as one of those who tended the fields in the summer, furrowing, and weeding, and carrying water up from the river to the planting ground to keep the barley alive during the dry days. It was hard work, she knew, and those who did it grew strong. Prsedi had known him a little when he was a child. He was not that anymore. Now, he was an adult, bigger than any other among these survivors. Not as tall as Welo, she thought, but heavier, and young enough that he would still grow for several years.

Krepus, she thought. *His name is Krepus. His mother is Cenakrot.*

She watched him pacing, restless, waiting for some sense of what to do, for some choice to be made. Krepus was more alert than most of the others, although he too, seemed dazed. Stunned and bewildered by what had happened. Paralyzed by this latest calamity that had come on top of the long misfortune of the changing world.

The survivors might have continued this way, wandering aimlessly, sitting and staring, pacing in frustration until the afternoon passed and the sun went down. They might, and perhaps, have carried on unchanged until night fell over them, with Prsedi watching from the far rocks downstream. But they did not. As she watched, Prsedi became aware of a buzzing among them. People were standing and turning toward her.

She had been noticed.

She had thought, with good reason, that she would be dead by now, and clearly the remaining Téuta had thought so, too. Seeing her standing alive and healthy, and more than that, clean, as many of them still were not, seemed to them like an act of the gods. And so it was, she thought. Of one goddess, at least, and of one man. Dhegm and Welo had put her here.

Jarred from her thoughts by the wave of recognition among the Téuta, Prsedi stepped off her rock and started toward the village. As she drew closer, all eyes turned to her, which disturbed her. Did they expect her to know what to do? Did they really think that because she was the girl who sings with leopards, she could guide them? Rescue them from this calamity? What could singing do to help these people now? Maybe Akesh could have saved them with singing, but what would Prsedi's singing do? She was not Akesh. No one could be saved by her singing.

There is nothing I can tell them, Prsedi thought. A real leader would know what to do and say, or a shaman, or a god, or the dead. But I am not any of those things. I am only Prsedi.

But there seemed to be no leader. There was no shaman, none that she could see. And the gods were silent here. Everyone who had been at the gathering had been crushed under the cliffs, and they and all the rest of the dead were silent.

Prsedi watched as a shift passed through the crowd, and eyes turned toward her. The young man—the large one—noticed her at last and understood that she was the source of his restlessness. He walked toward her. It was a long walk, but he was quick, and as he advanced, she moved slowly to meet him.

He came closer, standing facing her, and bowed slightly to her for respect. He had been among the old since the cliffs fell, and they had been little help to him. They had looked to him for leadership, even though he was only fourteen winters. He felt that he was far too young to be expected to lead, but he was strong enough to do the work that had to be done. He had some who could help, particularly the men from the plateau and the women who had been caring for children, but those in the prime of adulthood were too dazed to make choices of their own. All were in deep disbelief about what had happened. So Krepus had made the choices as well as he could.

But now Prsedi had come, as though returning from the dead. He wanted to show more respect than he did, because at eighteen winters she was older, and because she was Prsedi, and because her appearance seemed like an act of the gods since she had surely been crushed by the landslide days before. She was here, and Krepus was grateful, and for the first time, he was also hopeful.

"Prsedi. The leopard girl. We thought you were dead," he said. "Everyone thought you were at the meeting, under the cliffs."

"I was."

"Then how are you here?"

Knowing the story would take time, Prsedi sat on the ground, motioning him to join her. It was the first time since the catastrophe that anyone had made a choice for him, even so small a choice as that.

Feeling a wave of relief and gratitude, Krepus knelt to listen.

Prsedi told about her days in her tomb. And about her escape to the cliff top with Dhegm's help. About washing and eating at the pool and the hut, and finally about her walk here. As she did, she watched his face. And she watched the faces of the ragged, dazed villagers, and saw the sullen anger there, and knew she should not mention Welo.

When she had finished, Krepus looked at her closely. Then, he did bow down to honor her. He bent lower than her age would have warranted, because she was Prsedi, and at last he had an adult who would take the burden of the Téuta from him. And Krepus bent low in her honor because to him, she was hope to him. He felt her honor like a flame in front of him.

Pressing him to sit up again, Prsedi looked past him. She was not worried about honor or age.

"What are they doing?" she asked. "Many have not bathed. Some of the old will need help, and some of the people look like they have not eaten much for many days."

"Yes," Krepus said. "It has been hard for me to get them to do anything. Their grief is too big for them."

Prsedi shook her head, taking a moment to think.

"Do we have grain?" She asked. "Meat? The sheep should be living still, if they've been cared for. Have they?"

"I did feed them. I took them to fields to eat," Krepus said, "each day except the first. We have some men who are not too old, and many women who can help, are glad to help, but do nothing except care for the children unless they are told what to do. For that they need no instructions, and I would not know how to give them, anyway. There are houses that still stand, the houses where some of these, the survivors, were when..." his voice faltered. "When it happened," he said finally. "There is grain in them," Krepus added, "and we have eaten some of that. There is also grain in the hut on the plateau next to the fields."

Prsedi was quiet, considering how to bring these people back to the world. Finally, she held her hand out to Krepus.

"Come," she said. "We must help them be Téuta. Perhaps I can make them wash themselves and stand up again. Bring a sheep, two sheep, or three, but no more because we will need them. Bring grain and many large pots to cook with. We must have a feast, a feast here, outside, together. Because the Téuta must make a decision. All of us."

Prsedi stood, and Krepus stood after her. Together they walked toward the ruins of the Téuta.

CHAPTER 45

All the Téuta were clean at last, and fed. Those who tended the fields were back at that task, even though that work would probably be left behind. Those who tended the sheep and the goats had done their jobs. Still, there was a great deal to do, and too few remained for all the work that needed to be done.

Some of the plateau had also collapsed. Much of the fields that remained were cracked or tilted and unusable, so repairs were needed if they planned to work any of the plateau fields again. New fields would need to be cleared if the people chose to stay here. For days they had feasted, because the number of sheep and goats were far more than the survivors needed.

Everyone knew what had to happen, but no decision had been made before the thundering earth, and none since either. So after the fourth feast in as many days, Prsedi stood, and all the eyes of the Téuta turned to her, waiting for her to say the thing they would hate to hear, and against which some would argue with terrible grievance, but which they knew, every one of them, was right.

They are not ready yet, Prsedi had thought through the days of feasting. *They must be satisfied, or they will not choose the right thing.*

Now, at last, she stood, waiting until every remaining Téuta watched her and was quiet. They had known that she would say what must be said, but her first words were not what they expected. Her first words were questions.

"What have you done for the dead?" Prsedi asked. "How have you honored them? Helped them?"

Many of the people watching were puzzled. What had they done? What could be done? But some nodded in agreement. These, she thought, might help her lead, and she was grateful that they understood her.

"Have you spoken to them? Provided for them? Have you sung the songs for the dead, so that they might find comfort? Have you taken what they might need to them?"

The people were silent, looking at each other.

"Why not?" Prsedi demanded. "We are Téuta! We are *Téuta!* We can't bury them any more than they are already buried. But we can't just leave them as they are. We can make offerings to the gods, and leave what the dead need on the top of the fallen cliffs. Make bread, soak it in whatever honey, or anything else sweet, that can be found. All of them will need to cross to the land of the dead. Help them!"

Prsedi paused, letting them think about that for a moment.

"And sing for them," she said then. "Sing. These are our dead. Téuta dead. Sing the songs that will comfort them."

No one had given Prsedi charge of them, but every one of the Téuta knew she was telling them what they should have done many days ago. So, they did as she asked. For the rest of the afternoon, they sang. Then they worked to give the dead that lay under the cliffs everything they might need. The Téuta still living scavenged through their huts and through all the others that were still standing to bring food for the dead, and spears, and bows, and clothing. And most of all, sweets rolled inside flats of bread to pay for their trip across the water to the land of the dead.

They brought these things to lie on the fallen cliff as tribute, and as preparation for the hard journeys these dead must make. And they brought them also, knowing that their own hard journey, the journey of the living, was still ahead of them.

Many were glad to sing the Téuta songs, but some also remembered the song Akesh had sung for them when Seneks died. It had been a song from a distant place, sung in a strange language, and those who remembered wished she were here to sing again.

When they had finally finished, Prsedi again stood quiet until the Téuta gathered to hear her. And this time she said what they knew she must say.

"You know. All of you know. I hardly need to say this. We must go as Eini said we must. The fields are ruined. The cliffs lie flat on the ground. The wall of our ancestors has fallen. The river still runs, but it is changed. All is changed, and we must go."

The arguments came then, as she had known they would.

"Where would we go?"

"We are Téuta, this place is the place of Téuta!"

"Saurig led us here! *Saurig!* It is not right. It is wrong to leave Saurig!"

"How can we leave the dead behind us? All the ancestors, there, there! They are there. We can't leave them!

Many voices, many protests, all loud, all filled with deep feeling. And all false. They knew. They all knew what they had to do. But, despite her call to send some people to the plains, all Eini's teaching of the old stories had done nothing except bind the Téuta more firmly to this place.

Prsedi simply listened, waiting. When the voices dwindled enough for the people to hear her, she spoke again.

"Hush, all of you. Stop this. Saurig was right when she brought us here. This place was good when Saurig led us, and good through all the years since. But now the earth has told us, the gods have told us, that it is no longer good for us. The fields are ruined. The cliffs are ruined, and few huts are still standing. You all know what we must do. It does no good to protest and sound your voices like this."

Only one voice responded, and it was the right one. Krepus, the young giant, spoke, and his voice silenced every other.

"Where, Prsedi?" He asked. "Where will we go?"

"There is a place, Krepus. You all know that I traveled with the Kujoté for two years. I saw many things. I have seen a place that would be good for us. It is on the plains, not in the mountains. It is warmer there than here in the winters, and there are wide fields down near the river, not on a plateau but down beside it where the water is easy to bring to the summer crops. It is a good place."

"We just leave our ancestors? Just leave the dead behind us?"

"Can we take them? Of course we must leave them here. We don't need to abandon them, Krepus. They are here and will be here forever. Look," Prsedi waved toward the ruined cliffs. "Who could move them from under all of that? We can return to speak with them sometimes. We don't abandon this river, or this place. We keep it. But we can't live here now. If we want to save the Téuta, the people who came from our ancestors, the people of Saurig - if we want to save the Téuta, then we must go where the Téuta can live."

There was not much more to say after that. The people sat silent, waiting for someone, Prsedi or Krepus, to tell them what to do. Prsedi made one last effort to move them.

"You all mourn the village," she said. "I mourn it, too. I wish Akesh were here to sing for us. I want you all to remember her song, though. I want you to hear her song, and to remember that it's possible to live even while you are mourning a whole village. Akesh told you that. Listen to her song. Listen now to it."

But Akesh was part of what the Téuta mourned. She had become something important to them, and now, like everything else, she was gone.

Many were too tired to think. But for others, thinking about Akesh made their bitterness bubble up inside them. Voices from the crowd called out. "Akesh can't sing anymore!",

"Akesh is dead!",

"Akesh is under the rocks with everyone. Everyone! Maybe she can sing to them!"

"Akesh is only bones now!"

Prsedi stopped, knowing they were right. Akesh was there, under the cliffs, along with Chermesh, and Eini, and everyone. She was not bitter, as the crowd was. But she was tired, and these voices discouraged her.

There was someone pushing through the crowd. Two people, one gently pushing to make a path, and the other behind. Nedeh came, with her baby in her arms, and behind her was Senne carrying Chaisa. Carrying Akesh's granddaughter.

As they pushed through the last of the Téuta and reached Prsedi, Senne turned to the crowd, and spoke to them. She was old, more than sixty-one winters, and was not used to speaking in any voice but the softest, the voice used to speak to those near you. Now she spoke to all the Téuta still living, and they had to cluster closer to hear her.

"I know!" Senne told them. "I *know* what it is to lose a whole village, your whole village, and everyone that matters to you. I lost the village I was born in. Terrible violence came to us. Since then, I have become Téuta. I have learned to love the Téuta. Now I have lost the Téuta, too. Twice! Twice I have lost my village!"

Senne paused, gripped by a grief she had thought long past. The people watched her. They all knew the story of her village. They waited for her. When she could manage to speak again, she took a long breath, then another, and continued.

"So I know," she said. "Remember that I know. Remember when I speak, that I know what this is to you. You say that Akesh is dead. Yes, she is dead. I loved her. Through all of her life, I loved her. I grieve for her more than I know how to say. I wish she was here, alive, to sing to us."

She paused again, for so long that some in the crowd thought she might be finished. But she was not.

"You say Akesh is bones. Yes, let us say that. She is bones. So listen to those!" Senne said. "Listen to Akesh's bones singing to you. Or listen to her singing in your own bones. And pick yourselves up. You are Téuta, and only you can be Téuta. And the Téuta matters. So be the Téuta. Decide how. I think Prsedi is right. But you must decide. Hear Akesh's bones sing to you. Then decide. Many are dead there," she said, pointing to the catastrophe of fallen rock. "But you are not dead! You are not! So the Téuta is not. Do you wait here for Akesh to take your hands for you? She lost her village, the one she grew up in. I lost mine. I know what you feel. I know, I know, I know. What you feel, I know. But look around you. See how much of the village, how many of the people are here. Decide something, some way for you to keep the Téuta from being dead. Then do it."

Senne could not be Akesh. Who could? But with her old voice she did sing songs then. Songs that Akesh had also sung in a language strange to the Téuta, but one that she had used.

Most were still dazed. But a few did hear the songs, and even tried to imagine they heard Akesh singing from the cliffs. Some even turned toward the fallen cliffs, as though they heard her there. As though they heard the bones of Akesh singing to them, telling them that it would be alright.

As she spoke, Senne had held Belisse's tiny child. When her speech, the longest of her life, was done, she and Nedeh carried the infants back through the crowd. They went to sit by the river and care for the babies while the people all drifted off to do simple things they knew how to do.

And they might have kept doing them forever. They might simply have waited to die there under the fallen cliffs. Except for the wolves.

That evening, the wolves sang again. This time they were close enough to capture the Téuta's attention, and all of them listened, even if they were doing other things. They seemed, at first, to be just wolves in the night. But then, again, the people began to hear Akesh sing too.

She sang with passion and loneliness and strength, and Prsedi walked back to the place where she had spoken to the Téuta earlier, and waited there. Her heart was full of the song she heard. She was sure that others would come.

They did. A few who were near saw Prsedi there, and they told others. Then word spread from fire to fire that Prsedi had heard the wolves and had more to say to them. So, everyone who mattered gathered around her.

The bones of Akesh truly were singing then. Singing to the people, telling them about the joy that was still there, even if for now they could not feel it. And about the beauty still there, even if they could not see it. She was telling them that they would feel and see those things again, as she had, as Senne and Nedeh had. They would see them in a future too far away to understand, and a future that would be strange to them.

In the late evening, many gathered again around Prsedi who spoke reluctantly, saying what she needed to say and what the people gathered around her needed to hear.

"We are Téuta. We will always be that. But it is my belief that we must be Téuta in another place now."

She paused, looking at the crowd that watched her. They were restless, they were uncertain. But it was Prsedi who spoke. Prsedi, who sang with leopards, and as everyone had heard by now, it was Prsedi who was not a shaman but had still seen a living Dhegm with her own living eyes.

Prsedi saw that they were ready.

"Go to your huts," she told them. "Or to whatever place remains to you. Gather what you need, what you really need and no more. Because we will walk for a long way down the river. I have travelled with the Kujoté. They travel light, and so must we."

People rose. Earlier, they had eaten their fourth feast in as many days, so they were slow to move toward the places that held whatever they still had. Prsedi smiled, and stopped them.

"Sleep now," she said. "We don't have to leave today. But we must leave very soon so we can build what we will need to survive the winter. But now, sleep. We can gather our things in the morning."

The Téuta dispersed to their chosen places. They went to their beds. All reluctant. Some resentful. Some simply tired. The decision had been made. That decision, the one they all knew had to be, had finally been said out loud. Their time of lethargy and confusion was done. Their time of work and walking would begin in the morning.

CHAPTER 46

Prsedi had little to gather for the walk. She had a parka, and a cloak, and some wrappings for her feet and legs. She had a warm sheepskin she could take with her. She gathered a large bag of grain. She had nothing else to take.

Then she thought about what else they might need.

For a moment her hut was almost dark, with only the soft light from the fire-pit reflecting from the walls, and then the sun came through the doorway again. *Krepus*, she thought. *No one else is that big, to douse all light as they come through the door.*

When she turned to greet him, she saw that he had someone with him.

"Prsedi, this is my friend Raghe," Krepus said. "He is a shaman, or almost. I think he is the only surviving one. All the others died under the cliff. At least, I have not seen any of the other shamans since the cliff fell."

We will need a shaman, Prsedi thought.

"What does it mean that he is *almost* a shaman?" She asked.

It was Raghe who answered. "My father was a shaman. Senyan. You knew him."

"Yes," she said, remembering. "I do know who you are." Then she asked again, "Why almost?"

Raghe shrugged. "I am only twelve winters. But I have been trained to be a shaman since I was small. I know how, it is only that I am too young."

Prsedi watched the boy for a moment. He was barely able to stand, so deep was his grief. But he did stand, and he offered what he had to the Téuta.

"Do you know healing?"

"No, not very much. Seneks did that, not my father."

One shaman, and too young. And not a healer. And Akesh and Seneks were dead. *Akesh is buried here,* she thought. *Belisse as well. Welo will stay with them even if that means he is alone for the rest of his life. And the Téuta have somehow turned against him.*

Somewhere she had to find a healer, because there would be scrapes, and spring was full of coughs and running noses.

"Raghe, you will need to be our shaman, even if you are too young. We don't have another. Will you be able to do that?"

"Yes," the boy said. "I know how. I will do it."

"But you grieve your father."

Raghe nodded. "And my mother, and my sister. Everyone here grieves. I am no different in that." There was silence in the room for what seemed to Prsedi like a long time.

"There is something else?" She asked.

She was looking at Krepus, but it was the boy, Raghe, who answered.

"There is a way into the temple," he said, finally. "Maybe. I'm not sure. I'm small, I might be able to get in. There is something there that might help us."

"Yes?"

"You remember when there was a crack in the Wall of the Dead, when Seneks died?"

"Yes. I remember."

"The shards of the wall that fell, they are in the temple."

Prsedi looked up at that. Yes, the shards would help; the shards would be a way for the Téuta people to keep their past with them, to take the place with them, and to take the dead with them. It could solve something that had concerned Prsedi too. They had to leave. There was no doubt in her about that. But she, and everyone, hated to leave their ancestors behind.

"Is it safe to get them?"

"I don't know," Raghe said. "Maybe. I think I can do it."

Prsedi studied him, remembering her own experience. He was only twelve years, and this could be dangerous.

"Can no one else do this?"

"Many probably could," Raghe said. "Probably better than me. But no one else is allowed. I am the only shaman left."

The boy was very near tears. Prsedi watched him. He wanted to do this, and, she thought, he felt he had to do it. If he did not try, it would haunt him for the rest of his life.

"Alright, Raghe," she said finally. "Thank you. But don't risk too much. Don't get trapped. I have been under the rocks. I have been where I thought there was no way out. It is not a good place to be. Please be very careful. The ancestor-stones matter, but so do you. You are our only shaman."

The rest of Prsedi's early morning was spent in preparation for the walk, and in goading and prodding others to prepare. There were things that troubled her, so she was relieved when Senne also came to talk. Prsedi greeted the older woman with respect and waited for her to speak first.

"You are sure this is right," Senne asked. "This journey?"

"Yes," Prsedi said. "I'm certain. This, here, has become too hard for us. It was hard before the shaking ground, but now half of the village is crushed, and half of our grain fields have fallen into the river. And the years keep getting colder and the summers drier, so even with whole fields, the crops are hard to grow. There is a better place for us. I've seen it."

When Prsedi had finished speaking, the two sat quietly for a time, simply listening to the day. Listening to the preparations of the Téuta to leave their home. Then Prsedi spoke again.

"Eini used to say that the past is what we are, and the future is what we have. It is an interesting idea to play with, isn't it? Now this place, the

Téuta here, is the past. But it is still what we are. And for us, the future isn't what we have. Right now, we don't have anything. The future is what we have to do."

Prsedi walked to the hut door, watching the people outside, busy with preparations.

Words, she thought. *Just words. I say them to encourage Senne, and to encourage everyone, but I'm not sure what any of the words mean. Not sure what anything at all means.*

She turned to Senne.

"Senne, here is something that is troubling me. A question."

"What question?"

"Why did Dhegm save me? She even told me that I would be with her whether I lived or died; it didn't really matter. And there were others she could have saved. But she saved me, so I would live longer on the earth. Why did she do that?"

Senne did not answer. Instead, the two women sat watching a beam of sunlight as it fell through the doorway and tracked slowly across the floor. Prsedi loved the fact that this was something she could do with Senne, sit and talk. With Senne, she was not a leader. She was just Prsedi, Senne's friend.

"It is the second time I have lived when others died," Prsedi said. "Why does this happen? Why should I live when others don't?"

"I don't know," Senne replied after a moment, "why a goddess does what she does. Maybe she saved you to do this, what you are doing now for the Téuta."

Then she continued, "This is the second time for me, too, to live when many others didn't. The first was the raid on the village where I lived. What was the first time for you, when you lived and were surprised?"

"Oh," Prsedi frowned, still watching the sunbeam. "I lived then," she said. "But I was not glad about living."

Senne watched her silence. Finally she said, "You don't want to tell me. You don't like to talk about it. I know that feeling, too. The fear of looking at what happened."

Prsedi turned to Senne, seeming almost surprised to see her, as though she had been lost in distant thought.

"You're right," she said. "It's not something I like to remember, but I will tell you. In the Kujoté, there were great times, they are a wonderful people. And they have wonderful feasts with other groups of wanderers when many are together, as many as all the Téuta, with a great deal of eating and drinking beer, and many other things. After one feast like that, sickness came. Terrible sickness. Some of the groups survived, but many died, including many of the Kujoté. Nemas died, and our son. And Nemas's father, Newir. I was sick too, very sick. But I did not die. And I don't know why. I don't know why I was one of those who lived, now or then. And this time, Dhegm herself came to help me."

"Some Kujoté did not die? Why did you not stay with them, then?"

"After Nemas, and Newir, and my son were gone, I felt strange there. I began to think more and more about the Téuta, about my own people. I wanted my own ancestors, and the huts, and the wall of the dead. Uébe lived, and stayed with them. She had a child, who also did not die. But I wanted home. I wanted the Téuta."

Here Prsedi began to feel emotions she did not want, grief not only for the people who died here but also for Nemas, for the Kujoté, and also for this place and the wall of the dead that now lay on the ground. Too much, too much grief. She pushed it away. She had no time for it.

She stood, shaking off the past, and turned to her friend. "I walked a very long way to get back," she said. "And now, I must walk again. We all must. You should prepare, Senne."

"I think I will stay," Senne said, "That is what I came to tell you."

Prsedi stared at her. "Senne, no! Why?" she asked. "We need you!"

Senne looked up at her. "Welo also needs someone, Prsedi," she said gently. "He had Akesh, and Belisse, but they are dead. He is grieving for them. He is grieving as much as any of these people here around us. He needs someone alive to talk to. He came to us, to me and Akesh and Nedeh, when we had no one, when our village was gone." Senne gestured out the door at the Téuta, busy with their preparations. "These people speak against him," she said. "And I don't want to listen to them. And also, I am too old for a long, hard walk. I will stay here, with him."

"I hear them talking, too," Prsedi said after a moment. "I hear them saying strange things. Even those who have known him well now think of him as bigger and harder than he is. They say he chased alien gods.

Even those who know it's not true say it. I think they must need an explanation for what has happened to the Téuta."

"Why don't you tell them to shut up?" Senne asked with some heat.

"I do!" Prsedi said. "I have argued with them. I told a few, when they said these things, that I don't want to hear any talk against Welo. I have told them it's all nonsense. And often, while I am speaking to them, they agree. They see the stupidity of what they are saying, the falseness of it. And then, the next time I hear the same people talking to others, they are speaking against him again. I have tried, but I can't make them stop."

"Then stay with us, with Welo and me."

"I want to," Prsedi said, and even as she spoke, she knew it was true. *I want to!* "Welo knows I want to stay. He knew that when he sent me down here to try to get some sense into the people. Welo gave me this task, Senne. Save the Téuta. And, if you were right before, then Dhegm also gave me this task. If I thought I could let them go on their own I would stay here. But right now I need to make sure the Téuta finds a new home, a safer home, where the raiders won't find us until we have regained our strength."

For a moment, both of them were silent.

Then Senne said, "OK. But I will stay. You don't need me. You think you do, but you don't. Even Nedeh doesn't need me. She is in shock. Everyone is. But she has her own babe, and she has Belisse's child, Chaisa, to care for. Sntodi will help her with both, along the walk and after. She will be fine. Better than most of these," and Senne pointed out toward the Téuta people. "And she will never believe the things they say against Welo. No one loves him more than she does. Maybe she can help you convince them."

Prsedi heard the truth in what Senne said. She thought for a moment. Then she opened her arms and held Senne close, knowing she would never see the old woman again once the people began their walk.

⊤⊤ ⍟ ⊢⊣

After Senne left, Prsedi was alone until Raghe returned to her. He was covered with dust and mud, but he held two white sculpted stones, each as long as half of Prsedi's arm and as big around as her tight fist, clearly part of the ancient carvings on the wall.

"I could not get all of the pieces, but I found these."

Prsedi recognized them. She had looked at them many times when she was a child, and knew exactly where they had been on the wall of the dead. They had fallen from the wall ten winters ago, when she was eight.

It was long ago, she thought, almost as though her thoughts were speaking to the stones. *And I was young then. But I remember you. I remember.*

CHAPTER 47
SPRING/SUMMER 6222 BCE

In mid-morning, the people began to gather. Standing with Raghe, Prsedi spoke to them.

"This young man," she told the assembled crowd, "Raghe, will be our shaman. He is not yet a full man, so not a full shaman, but it will not be long before he is grown. Next year he will have thirteen winters. And he has risked the shadows under the cliffs to bring us these." She held the carved stones up. "These are part of the carvings from the wall of ancestors. While we carry these, we carry some part of this place, some part of our past. And with these, maybe our ancestors can find us."

She was not sure that last was true, but she said it loudly because the people needed to believe it.

She handed the stones back to Raghe and told him to keep them, to guard them. It was a heavy responsibility. But it was his responsibility to carry.

Then she started the process of herding the Téuta away. Herding them down the river to whatever new home they could find. A home where their wheat and barley could grow down next to the river, not on a high plateau where it was hard to bring water to them. The Kujoté had shown her that such a place was there for them.

There were some who were not yet ready, so there were delays. Neither Prsedi nor Krepus was surprised by this. But they did want to start. Even if they only went around the nearest rocks to camp for the night, they needed to begin the journey. By late afternoon, they had managed that. Several people wanted to go back to sleep in their huts, but Prsedi told them that the group would leave early the next morning. "Sleep where you like tonight," she said. "But we will not wait for you tomorrow, so you will have to catch up." Still, a few went back. Eventually, they all returned to the group, but some did not catch up until the next camp was made, a day's walk downriver.

As they moved off on the second day, herding their flocks of goats and sheep, Krepus suggested to Prsedi that some of the healthy adults, and even perhaps some of the older children, might walk at the top of the ridges above them to keep watch, and be sure that raiders were not following.

"We are still hundreds," Prsedi said. "And I have heard that there are not that many raiders together as one group. Surely, they would hesitate to attack so many?" Yet, even as she said it, she saw Krepus's point. Despite their numbers, they were vulnerable.

"Lead them, then," she said at last, and Krepus agreed.

For the rest of the trip, the people would at least know there were guards keeping watch above them. Maybe, Prsedi thought, that would help. Or maybe not.

The people walked on. A full moon came and passed, and the moon waned to nothing, and started to swell again. If it had been only Prsedi who drove them, or only Krepus, the people might have turned around and returned to the cliffs. But together, they were strong and organized. Despite his youth, Krepus was large, and reassuring. And Prsedi was the girl who sang with leopards. She was the woman Dhegm had come to help inside the cliffs. It was Prsedi, not a shaman, who, without a shaman trance, had spoken face to face with Dhegm. That alone was enough to keep the people walking downriver, to keep them driving their herds and camping each night along the shore.

As the journey became the life they knew, resistance faded. Slowly, people began to think a little less about the home they had left, and wonder a little more about the mysterious home ahead of them.

The walking was not difficult. Food did not become a problem on the trip. There were plenty of sheep, and many goats, and the river gave them fish, and those who walked at the top of the ridges gathered the new spring plants. They were alone with the world around them. It was enough.

Prsedi did notice, though, that strange new tales were arising, new stories of the past that were full of imagination. Some were stories the adults told, but the children also had their own stories. Many were about Welo. About his size, and how tall he was. As the trip continued, Welo seemed to get bigger and bigger in the memories of those who had not known him well.

Soon he will be the size of a tree, Prsedi told herself when she heard these tales. But she did not contradict them, because there were other stories too—stories more important to her, and far harder to argue against—that claimed he had brought the catastrophe on them by chasing stranger gods. He *had* chased stranger gods; that much was true. But the stories went further, insisting that those gods had long memories and mischievous natures, and that by following them Welo had angered the Téuta's gods in turn. Those gods, the stories said, had taken out their anger on the village. More and more people began to say that the cliffs themselves had fallen in punishment for what Welo had done. Raghe told these stories, too, and seemed to believe them. Since the Téuta knew him as a shaman, a speaker-to-gods, since they now knew him as their only shaman, they believed the stories he told so often.

Prsedi loved Welo. Remembering him as he was, she hated these stories and struggled to stop them. But in this one thing, the people listened to their shaman and not to her.

She had a village to save. Both Dhegm and Welo had given her this task, and she had accepted it. Welo had Senne to keep him company, and the memories of Akesh and Belisse and all the Téuta's ancestors as well. Those companions would not believe such stories. Welo would be fine. And if she could keep them together, the Téuta people would also be alright. Maybe the stories of Welo would help them survive.

As they neared the next full moon, the hills became gentle, and low.

One night, when she had kept them walking beyond sunset, Prsedi climbed to the top of a hill and stood there for some time while behind her, Krepus and the others made camp. When they were finished, many of the Téuta came to join her. Spread below them, they saw in the moonlight a great expanse of small hills, and beyond those, fields of grasses so wide they could not see the end of them. The river flowed through them in a deep, wide bed. Prsedi knew this view; she had seen it before. But those who came to stand with her that night had not, and they felt awe that such a place existed.

They slept then after a long day. In the morning they walked on until they had reached the last even of the smaller real hills. A few climbed to its top, from the last peak overlooking this astounding landscape. From there, they saw aurochs grazing in the fields and along the low hills on the far side of the river. Below them, a wide field blooming with tall grasses seemed to go on forever. There was no human presence they could see, not so much as a single hut.

Prsedi stood there on that last hill and looked out across the grasses and traced the river as far downstream as she could see it. It came down from the hills behind them, from the mountains, and made big curves across the flat lands, heading who knows where.

In the middle of the day no wolves sang, but Prsedi heard them anyway. The lonely strength of the singing wolves held her, the memory of Akesh held her, and she took both inside to keep them.

Krepus came to stand beside her.

"What do we do now, Prsedi?" He asked.

She looked at him and smiled. "Now that we have brought them downriver," Prsedi said, "we figure out how to live here"

Prsedi was eighteen winters, Krepus only fourteen. They were not really sure how to go about building a new life. But all of the Téuta were standing with them, including some who had far more experience in the world. A voice arose behind these two young people.

"Where will we find mud? Good mud?"

Prsedi turned to see who had spoken. It was an old man she recognized, but did not know well, a man of forty or fifty winters.

"I think," Prsedi said, "that a morning's walk downstream the river is wider. There are flat areas that look like they flood in the spring when the snow melts. I only saw them in the late summer, so they were dry.

But the silt along the river edges looks like it would make good mud when it is wet."

"Then go there," the man said, "and make bricks."

"Make…?"

"Yes," he nodded. "All these people, even the children who are old enough. We will make bricks, for huts, and long houses for the animals. We need to build our new Téuta. So, making bricks is the first thing to do. Set up our camp, and eat, and sleep. Then, make bricks."

The man was small. Krepus was half again as tall. The people behind them had not heard much of what was said. They still looked to Prsedi and Krepus to tell them what to do. But the man was right. Krepus began walking through the people, repeating what he had said. They would walk half a morning downstream and set up camp. Then, tomorrow, they would find the place where there was good mud, and make bricks.

"We must build huts to keep us warm next winter. And we must make places to keep the sheep safe. And also, we will build a wall, a high wall around our new village to keep us safe when violent men come to find us."

"Will the violence come, even here?" The people asked.

And Krepus, with all his fourteen winters, replied, "I don't know. I hope not. But we will be ready if it does. We will be strong."

After that, everyone stood on the hilltop for a few minutes, looking down on the beautiful emptiness.

It was evening before they reached the place where they would build their village. First in the brightness of the moon, and then in the dawn, the weary and grieving Teuta had seen the bounty and the great beauty of the place that would become their new home. The place that was now, even before they made their first brick, already their new home. It was just a camp when they first slept there. But in its long fields of waving grasslands, in its herds of aurochs and the shelter of its hills and the cradling bend of the river, it was now the Téuta. And the people knew this, and they slept satisfied.

In the morning, they went to work.

CHAPTER 48

SUMMER 6222 BCE AND ON

There was, of course, much more for the Téuta to do that summer than make bricks. Although the plains were warmer than the mountains, winters would come there too, deeper and colder than they had forty years before. The Téuta people needed shelter and food to survive them.

Their first weeks were spent as Prsedi had been advised, making mud bricks, as many and as fast as possible. Everyone who could be spared from other tasks helped, including all the children who were old enough to play in the mud. They found it fun and quickly became experts. For everyone, it was a happy, messy diversion, generally encouraged by the smell of roasting or boiling or baking foods in the temporary firepits erected near the mud flats.

Five buildings were finished that first year, all of them wide and tall and very long. Four were for the people sheltering in over the winter. One was for the animals. More could have been built, but Krepus insisted that they should use the time and bricks instead to build a sturdy wall around the whole of their camp, tall enough so that it would be difficult to climb over. The elders who had survived the cliffs and the journey to this new place saw the wisdom in this, and agreed with him.

The raiders from the mountains did not yet know exactly where the

Téuta had gone. But their whereabouts would not be secret for long. It might be a year, or even two, or it might be only a moon. Krepus and the elders told the Téuta that they had to prepare. Everyone could see that, even though their village was large, their strength was thin. So, they worked hard, and when winter finally came, there was ample shelter for everyone inside the village wall.

The following summer, Krepus and the elders insisted that they work on the wall, making it thicker and taller. But many smaller dwellings were built as well, with bricks newly made or scavenged from one or another of the long huts they had built so quickly the year before, and when winter came again, everyone slept in a cozy mud brick hut, most in small groups as they had before the cliffs fell across their old village. By the time all the Téuta people had built new huts to live in, only two of those first long houses remained intact. One had been built as a place to keep the sheep and goats, and the other was kept for ceremonies, meetings, and feasts—and as a shelter for any animals that could not fit into the places meant for them. Krepus continued to live there, as well as several of those who cared for the sheep and goats.

The people became used to their life on the plains. They improved the fields of grasses, planted wheat and barley seed from the old Téuta, and made gardens, all easily watered from the river, which ran along the fields so close that carrying water to them on the dry summer days was easy—at least it was easier than it had been to carry it up the trail to the plateau in the mountains.

And the following year they again built and improved their dwellings and their crops. It became routine. The Téuta people were becoming well settled in their new home. They were glad there in the milder weather, and for the large fields of grain, with great herds of aurochs just across the river and other game all around them.

Luck was with the Téuta, although they did not recognize it as luck. The raiders, busy in the mountains, did not look for them for the first few years. Krepus' wall seemed, for a time, like a foolish extravagance.

Raiders did come in the end though, in the spring of the fifth year, when winter was just fading. And then both the wall and the long plains around it suddenly seemed to matter. Because of the plains, the raiders had no forest to hide in; they could be seen coming from a great distance. And the wall kept them from surging through the Téuta huts when they came close. The people in the village who were skilled with the bow could crouch on the tops of dwellings near the wall, watching the raiders outside it as they came across the fields, firing arrows when the raiders were within range.

The raiders were a band of about thirty men and two women, but many were dead before they reached the wall at all, and many more died trying to climb over it. The raiders that lived after that, about half of their first number, hid behind the outside of the wall where the Téuta arrows could not find them.

Krepus, then eighteen and full of strength, vigor, and foolish confidence, climbed the wall from the inside along with two others. With knives and spears, they drove at the remaining raiders, rousting those who stayed and pushing them back from the village wall. Krepus was wild, huge, and strong, and seemed to be everywhere at once. The fight was brief, and the few raiders who remained alive fled across the plains and back into the hills.

Not a single life was lost among the Téuta, not even a sheep. But the raid did show that the wall mattered, and that peace was still tentative even in this wide and plentiful land. Why? No one really understood that. There was game everywhere. What might the raiders need that they did not have or could not take from the land itself instead of bringing violence?

When the fight was over, all the enemy dead were piled far outside the village and burned. The flames of their funeral pyre rose higher than any building in their new home, burning from early morning until the day was nearly spent. The next day, everything that remained was pushed into a pit and buried. No one wanted to remember these dead.

But everyone remembered Krepus' foresight in championing the wall that saved them, and his strength and courage as he fought.

No raiders came again for many years. In their new village on the plains, the Téuta people flourished and grew. New children were born, adding to the great number who had come with Prsedi and Krepus down the river from the mountains, and this abundance of children grew older, and had children of their own.

The imperfect turbulence of human life continued. Raghe found a place where the remnants of the wall of the dead could be displayed so the people could embrace and remember their history and their ancestors. And they did. They remembered and repeated to their children all the ancient stories that Eini had taught them. Now they had new stories of the history of their people to add to the old ones.

Wolves still sounded in the mountains, and they sometimes could be heard even on the plains. This ancient music helped the new Téuta people settle and be satisfied on the flat lands by the river.

For those old enough to remember, the tragedy of the cliffs remained a wound that could not be completely healed. But those old enough for that were also old enough to remember something else. The lonely, glad music that the wolves gave them held something else within it, heard by those who needed it. It held grief and also joy. It held solace.

It held, for those old enough to remember, Akesh singing.

It held within it the strength of all the earth.

For them the distant music of the wolves was a promise from Akesh that her bones would sing forever for the children of the Téuta.

The End

AFTERWORD

A Note from the Author

Dear Reader,

I want to thank you for picking up your copy of *Singing Bones* - readers are everything to authors, and I appreciate you more than I can say.

As an author I depend on you to leave an honest review on Amazon and Goodreads. Your reviews matter. Other readers will appreciate hearing your opinion on the book before they commit to it—and of course I would also like to hear from you about my story, or my characters, or whatever other thoughts the book raised for you. Please leave a review to let me know what you think.

Warmest Regards,

Stuart Ullman

THE TÉUTA'S CHILD
LATE SUMMER 6192 BCE

Prologue: Welo and the Neolithic Earth

Long before Kaikos, before Chaisa or Sntejo, even before Prsedi—before any of the people in the new Téuta village—there was Welo the giant, and the curse of him lay miasmic across the whole of the Téuta. It lay across the village and across the people. It lay across the fields and across the mountains around them. Maybe it even lay across everything beyond.

And it lay with particular venom across the girl, the blind child; it wrapped thick around Kaikos. Twelve years old and small for her age, she looked harmless. But the curse contained her like a cocoon from which, even after all the tranquil years, an implacable anguish might still emerge.

Or so the Téuta people thought. So they felt, and the oldest among them had reason to feel it, although no one, not even Kaikos, could sense the curse. They couldn't taste it or touch it. They couldn't see it.

Kaikos, since it wasn't her nature to worry, ignored it most of the time and behaved as though it didn't exist. She played and hunted with Sntejo. She cared for her garden and did her chores without dwelling on the curse. Kaikos and her mother ate in their hut together in the evenings and bathed in the river together in the dark mornings without feeling the burden of it.

They swam hard in the mornings to warm themselves. The water they bathed in was cold because it was new from the mountains, and it was clean because the Téuta village was a half a morning's walk downstream from where they lived, so there was no one above them to soil it. In the autumn or the spring they ran back to their hut to stay warm in the cold morning air. Kaikos had reached the age when she could just outrun her mother, so now she had to slow from time to time to let Chaisa catch up.

The hunting, the running, the swimming all felt good. The air and the water felt good. Nearly everything felt good to her, so it was hard for Kaikos to remember the curse that the Téuta seemed to understand as a toxic mist seeping from Welo and flowing toward their village across time and distance. It was hard, since she was so young, to remember why they said so. To her, Welo seemed no more than an old story from a long-faded past.

Chapter One

"Kaikos, slowly! Be careful," Chaisa called out after her daughter, but laughed even before she said it because she knew it was no use. Kaikos burned the joyful, eager energy of childhood. And Chaisa's shouted caution to her daughter was only habit; she didn't really worry about her blind child running hard across the earth. She knew that somehow Kaikos could sense everything around her.

So Kaikos ran, racing up the slope toward home. Chaisa ran too, but Kaikos ran faster, and Kaikos had cheated at the start. She had simply scooped up her belt and waistcloth from the ground and started off straight out of the water, fastening her clothing around her on the run, while Chaisa, laughing about Kaikos' boldness, took the time to quickly dress before she started. The distance between them had extended far enough that Chaisa had to call loudly for Kaikos to hear her. But there was no slowing her daughter now, refreshed in the dark by her swim in the river, and now running in the cool, clean morning with the sun already awake.

Chaisa watched her daughter's dark, late-summer back as she ran ahead, watched the small humps of muscle in it shift from side to side as her arms moved with running. Kaikos ran until she reached the hut, then she turned her face to the sun to catch its warmth and waited for her mother.

How could Raghe even think about killing something so wonderful? Chaisa thought, remembering how close that danger had come. Remembering how close it still could be if the issue had not been submerged by neglect, buried beneath the placid rhythm of daily life. But not gone. It was not gone. The layer of neglect that lay over it was not so thick that it couldn't be broken.

Some dream in the night had pushed this memory toward her, so as she ran her mind strayed back to the time of her daughter's birth, the time before Kaikos even had a name. The shaman had wanted to kill her, probably at her birth, but certainly a week later, and by then he had many who agreed with him. It had taken Chaisa only hours to know her baby was blind. After a week everyone knew.

A child born blind was a bad omen, a curse from the gods, Raghe had said, and as shaman he was an authority on gods and curses. And on death. He seemed to like it, Chaisa told herself bitterly as she ran.

Chaisa brushed Raghe from her mind and watched her daughter.

When she reached the hut Chaisa put an arm around Kaikos' shoulders, and they walked toward the doorway of the hut, both still laughing and warm from their run and still slightly damp from their river-bath.

"I'm hungry this morning," Kaikos said.

But it was late. The sun's lower edge was fully above the horizon when they reached the door.

"Get started on your work, Kaikos. I'll bring bread out to you when it's done. It won't take long; the stones are hot, and the dough is ready."

The hut seemed close and warm when she entered. Chaisa, coming in from the bright early sunlight, waited a moment for her eyes to adjust to the room where the only light was from the small door, the firepit and, dimly, the smoke hole in the roof. She had put some moss and dry dung on the fire and blown it to life when she woke, and she had added some wood just before they left for their bath. She had mixed water and wheat and barley flours, and a little salt, the night before; the dough was waiting in a crock. Now she only needed to form the flat loaves and put them on the stones.

While she worked her mind still watched the girl running ahead of her. The vision made her happy, so she added some walnuts to the dough to please Kaikos. Bathing and running were good, the first cold and the second warm, and she had the pleasure of both still with her. But her mind was restless. While she waited to turn the bread her mind returned to that danger time, twelve years ago. She didn't want the thought, but she couldn't stop it. She often remembered that single moment, in her mind the most important moment, the most important single act of her life.

Even then Raghe had seemed to love death. Bulls and babies, the strong and the weak: death, the shaman said, to prevent greater death. Death to preserve the living. So when the rumors came to her that Raghe was on his way to take her child, Chaisa had done the only thing that she could do: she lifted her naked baby up from the ground and ran hard toward Prsedi. Only Prsedi could stand against the shaman.

She came without warning into Prsedi's hut, hardly aware of the flagrant impertinence of approaching the woman without permission or any gestures of courtesy. Prsedi was honored and important among the Téuta, and even more so among those who lived outside the wall. Prsedi was old, even then more than forty years, and Chaisa was young; Prsedi spoke to gods and they spoke back to her, and Chaisa was just another Téuta woman with no distinction. She had always kept a respectful distance from Prsedi before that moment. But Chaisa had ducked through Prsedi's door on the run without thinking of any of that.

Prsedi had barley flour on her wrists and bread dough in her hands, and when she turned to see who had come there was that single moment that returned to Chaisa again and again: Chaisa simply put the baby in Prsedi's arms as she turned.

Of course Prsedi was startled, and of course she was charmed; how else could she respond to the surprise discovery that she was holding a baby? Prsedi couldn't keep from covering this sudden child with flour, and even a little sticky wet dough on the child's ribs. She had dropped the dough into Chaisa's waiting hands, and Chaisa flattened it and went to the firepit to put it on Prsedi's oven stones then, which was why making bread now reminded her of that moment. She had been embarrassed to keep Prsedi from her breakfast, but there was nothing else she could do.

When Raghe finally realized where the baby was and came through the door of Prsedi's hut, ready to demand that the baby be given over to him, Prsedi was sitting with the baby in her lap, smiling and stroking the baby's feet to watch her toes flare. She was absorbed in that diversion.

"It belongs to me."

The voice was abrupt and abrasive in the small room, and Raghe stood just inside the doorway looking entitled, looking imperious, and looking directly at Chaisa—and the room became very still. Prsedi's laughter stopped before her head rose to look at him. When she did raise her eyes, Raghe stepped back to press his shoulders against the wall above the doorway. Those who had gathered outside, crouching to look through the entrance, stepped back too. It was a shock to them. Prsedi was never angry, and no one in the village thought she could ever be fierce, but the fierce anger in her face when she looked at Raghe would have frightened a leopard.

Raghe recovered from that first fright, though, and stepped forward again to assert his rights. "The baby is mine," he insisted.

Prsedi had almost laughed at that, but her fierceness never left her.

"Stop staring at Chaisa, Raghe, as hard as that might be for you. Look at me." She waited for him to do that, to turn to her, so she could see his eyes when she continued.

"This baby is not yours, Raghe, in any sense, although I know you wish it were yours in every sense. Don't deny it; everyone has seen how you watch Chaisa whenever you walk outside the village wall. But resenting the mother is not a reason to kill the child."

"You know that's not what is happening, Prsedi. You were there. *We* were there. We know what the gods can do."

He paused, looking at the baby in Prsedi's arms, and continued, "The child is blind, Prsedi. It will be a burden to us as it grows, but even that is not the worst. It's a cursed child. Cursed. It's Welo's family, born blind; you know it's cursed. We don't want it among the Téuta, among the people, to curse the rest of us; we don't want Chaisa's curse to stay among us to make other women bear blind children. And we don't want to anger the gods again. You may regret the loss of a single child, but better the loss of one life than the lives of all the Téuta. You know that. You know it must come to me. I'll get Krepus to enforce this."

Prsedi had smiled at that and relaxed a little. Krepus, at least, was not a fanatic.

She knew Raghe watched Chaisa only partly because he found her attractive, but also because he was afraid of her. He was afraid of everything that raised his memory of the old Téuta, of what had happened there. So perhaps her accusation had been a little unfair to Raghe. But only a little, and he needed that. No one else could stand up to him except Krepus, and Krepus rarely did. Raghe needed to be brought to earth sometimes.

"Yes, good. Get him," Prsedi said, and Raghe left.

Krepus, when he came with his strong young friend Sntejo, darkened the doorway as he squeezed his shoulders to get through it. Sntejo, behind him, was also big, but not so big that he blocked all light; he was a smaller, younger and happier version of the Téuta leader. Krepus was irritable, as he often was, and stood with his usual frown looking over the scene. He had been pulled from other business, other demands of leadership, at the request of Raghe, his shaman, his speaker-to-gods. But he knew Raghe was not the only one who spoke to them. Prsedi spoke every day to Dhegm, the earth, the mother. It wasn't his purpose to anger Dhegm. It wouldn't help the Téuta to do that.

Krepus consulted briefly with Sntejo, who responded with some unexplained and whispered vehemence, then chose diplomacy rather than decision. He found a compromise between his god-speakers, between Prsedi and the shaman: Prsedi and Chaisa would keep the child; they would guarantee it would add no burden to the Téuta. But Chaisa must leave the village, so that this child didn't live among the Téuta, so that if there was a curse at least it was a curse far away. "Go a proper distance away", he said, "and take the blind child with you."

Krepus softened when he looked at the baby and had asked what her name was. Chaisa hadn't chosen a name yet. Krepus watched the baby for a moment and called her "kaikos" meaning only that she was blind, and Prsedi smiled at the word. And so Kaikos it was; a strange name, but one given by the king, and blessed by Prsedi.

Krepus asked Sntejo to walk with Chaisa and Kaikos when they left so Raghe's adherents wouldn't attack them on the way. Sntejo and Chaisa left without waiting, before Raghe could protest; she left her hut behind, with everything in it. Better to be far from the village while Krepus' decision was fresh. Sntejo said he would bring what he could from her hut over the next weeks. And after a long walk they found a place near the river but hidden behind some hills, so the Téuta didn't have to be reminded of her every day.

While they walked Chaisa talked with Sntejo, for no reason other than that he was there. It felt strange to speak so casually to him. He was close to Krepus, the king. He lived inside the wall, and she did not, so she only knew him a little. She was nervous talking to him. But she was also grateful.

"Thank you for saving my child," she said. "I know you spoke for her."

"She's beautiful," Sntejo replied.

Chaisa looked at him then, a little puzzled. "You're not afraid of her curse?"

"Prsedi wouldn't have held her or defended her like that if she were cursed."

"And Raghe? You're not afraid of him?"

"Maybe that. He has power. But I—I don't like Raghe."

"Why?"

But Sntejo simply walked ahead with a sour look. He didn't want to talk about why he didn't like the shaman. Chaisa had not asked him again then, and she had never asked in all the time since then. It seemed a long time. Twelve years.

And now Kaikos was nearing the end of childhood, bright and quick, and it made Chaisa happy just to watch her run. Still blind. Nothing would change that. But she ran without any concern about what might be in her way; she knew what was in her way and ran around it.

How she knew was a little mysterious. She sensed things. Chaisa knew the word Kaikos used to explain her sense. "Bholos" she said. Chaisa could never completely understand what that meant. It was something like fog settling into the landscape. But Kaikos couldn't see the landscape, so what she sensed was this fog with the landscape's shape under it. Chaisa couldn't really envision it, but she accepted it. She believed the words. She believed them because Kaikos proved them every day.

Kaikos sat on the far side of the hut and began her task for the day. After a time, Chaisa brought the barley bread with walnuts out for her, and a little honey to dip the bread in. She brought a woven grass shawl too, to keep Kaikos warm in the early morning. They sat and talked in the sun while they ate.

When they were finished Chaisa went in to begin her own work, and she sang to herself.

Inside again, tidying the area near the firepit, she thought again about Prsedi and Raghe. They were not friendly with each other before that encounter, the moment when Kaikos' life or death was decided. An old difference, a leftover grievance from the old Téuta, gnawed at them. But after that day there was animosity between them, because Raghe still wanted death for Kaikos, and Prsedi still wanted life for the baby she had covered with barley flour before it had a name.

Chaisa wasn't happy about the animosity. What was the good of it? What was ever the good of it? But she did not regret the action she took that created it. Prsedi's friendship, and Sntejo's, had come from that moment, and both had high value. Chaisa felt honored by them. But it was still true that Prsedi's goodness and Krepus' decency were all that stood in Raghe's way. Chaisa watched the balance of power between them carefully; a little change, a little carelessness, might give to Raghe what he had wanted for so long.

Again Chaisa shook her head to brush all the old memories from her mind. Prsedi was far away. Raghe was far away. But here—here there was Kaikos, alive and quick and young, quietly working just outside the hut.

Read more at Amazon

ACKNOWLEDGMENTS

Writing this book has been a long and hard effort. I didn't realize before I started how much would be involved in writing a prequel to a book already published, creating a history that had to match, perhaps not in every single detail but as completely as I could manage, the events and relationships and implied histories in the book already out.

Three years. It has taken three years since the publication of The Téuta's Child to get to this point. And I admit that during those years, when something in the book was not going as I wanted it to, I was even more difficult than usual to live with. Taciturn, solitary, frowning. Pacing in silence through long afternoons as I contemplated problems in the plot, or the characters, or in the house and the yard, or the world.

So again, my first thanks have to go to my wife, who endured all of that, and who in spite of it gave me her support in writing this.

I thank also all of my beta readers (friends, relatives, and others who read the book and gave excellent and useful critiques and suggestions). And finally, importantly, I want to thank Kathryn Johnson and Lucretia Grindle Lutyens who gave me extensive, professional critiques pointing out some real flaws in an earlier version. Lucretia also gave a very detailed, and very valuable, line edit to the final version. I thank all of these people for their help in getting here. This book would not have been possible without them.

AUTHOR'S NOTES

The 8.2K Event: The setting for this book

The event that set the stage for the story in this book began almost 8,300 years ago, on a day when the southern edge of the Laurentide ice sheet at the top of the world collapsed and created havoc across the earth.

The *whole* earth.

A sea of meltwater lay behind the ice dam. For a year the icy water drained into what is now Hudson Bay in North America, and from there into the North Atlantic. By the time it had drained completely the level of the oceans of the earth had risen by more than a meter, and the mass of frigid water caused, abruptly and without warning, a period of rapid global cooling that lasted 70 years—and then the climate trend reversed, and the world warmed for another seventy years, until it returned to its prior level and continued its long, natural trend.

This cataclysmic event is not fiction. This is a real event in the geological and meteorological history of the world we live on. It's now called the 8.2k event. It was not benign; it is known to have created massive flooding in any low-lying areas near any coast, and sometimes far from any coast. It is the event that created the English Channel and so separated England from mainland Europe. The redistribution of weight across the surface of the earth created volcanic activity, and very probably earthquakes, wherever the earth is prone to them.

The global cooling was not the ice age. Don't confuse it with that. The last glacial maximum ended nearly19,000 years ago, and the Younger Dryas, which was the last gasp of the deep severity of the old ice age, ended officially 11,700 years ago, nearly four thousand years before the events in this book. But the 8.2k event was nevertheless an abrupt and serious climate crisis for the people who lived then.

The important thing about the event, at least for the story told here, is that it happened after at least some of humanity had settled into permanent villages. They farmed the fields around them. They lived in the same homes summer and winter, raised their families in the same place they themselves were raised, generation after generation. What could they do when the whole earth cooled for decades? When we were hunter-gatherers it was easy to adapt when the weather turned. We could just travel to find more congenial climates, south for warmer and north for cooler. But once we had spent hundreds or even thousands of years building a village and improving fields, once our local ground was rich with the graves of our ancestors, moving was a much bigger investment, adopted at a much higher cost.

The entire central episode of the 8.2k event lasted about 140 years, but this book covers only the first forty of them. Still, several generations appear and grow old, and within the story there are births and deaths, and a slowly changing cast as the crisis evolves. Eini and Seneks and Sntodi, Welo, Akesh, Belisse and Prsedi, and others, all appear in their turn, in their own generations and at their own times, and each has a role in the story of the Téuta facing those first troubled years of the event.

The Téuta was a very big village for the time; a village of just over a thousand people. They lived by farming wheat and barley, by gardening peas and lentils and vetch, by raising sheep and goats, and also, still, by sometimes hunting and foraging in the forests around them.

They were a settled people. They were fat and secure. This sudden climate event must have come to them as a constantly deepening, and deeply disturbing, surprise.

Archeological / Economic

As I did for my first book, I should explain right away that I am not an archeologist; if any actual trained or experienced archeologist ever reads either book that will be clear to them from the start. But I did do a good deal of reading when I wrote The Téuta's Child and gave what explanations and excuses I could to justify the lives and structures I described there for the Téuta people. I won't repeat all of that here. But I do want to address one complaint that I heard from some early readers both of that book and this one.

There is a belief, long held, that primitive people had to work ceaselessly to fend off starvation, that they lived in dire poverty scratching (a frequently used word) a meager living from the earth. There seems to be a belief that because their lives were so filled with work they were, from lack of time, less capable of intellectual pursuits, or art, or social events.

None of that is true. None of it.

I think this image was first adopted because we want to believe in progress. We want to believe that our lives are better than theirs, that even the early civilized world was better than the presumed deprivations of a hunter-gatherer existence. We want to think that the emergence of agriculture, and the long path of technological advancement, somehow improved things, that they not only improved our standard of living but also improved *us*, so that we are in culture and morals and even intelligence better than men and women who lived in the stone age. We want to think that this long progress has provided us with leisure time not available to those who lived before.

In 1972 an ethnologist named Marshall Sahlins, who had spent a lifetime observing primitive cultures, pointed out that the people who live in those cultures, modern hunter-gatherers, were rarely hungry for long, rarely froze to death, and worked on average much less than we do in the most advanced cultures today. A typical hunter-gatherer might work 4 to 5 hours on those days when he or she worked at all, and they might take between a third and a half of their days off. Even when working their time was often interrupted by social interactions, occasional naps, and so on.

Sahlins' book, titled Stone Age Economics, seems to have taken some time to have an impact on the beliefs even of archeologists in the last decades of the twentieth century. It came, I am told, as a great shock to them to understand the significance of Gobekli Tepe, a megalithic structure that must have taken a great deal of time to build—but which was constructed more than 11,000 years ago, long before the emergence of agriculture. How, people asked, did they manage to take enough time away from the desperate struggle to stay alive to build such a massive structure, with huge stone pillars that had to be chipped from the bedrock with flint tools and transported to their place in the monument? Those who were so deeply surprised that the hunter-gatherers who built Gobekli Tepe had the time to do it must not have read Sahlins' Stone Age Economics book. What is perplexing is not that these hunter-gatherers had the time, it is that they had the motivation to do it. Something in the world made this massive, hard, time-consuming project seem important to them.

Those who settled down and depended on farming and domesticating animals worked harder than the hunter-gatherers, but there's no reason to believe that they were without leisure time; in fact, although it was seasonal, they probably had a good deal of leisure time. They did not produce cars or even carts, they did not have indoor plumbing or electricity, or any of the vast variety of things we in the modern world cannot seem to live without. They produced only what they needed to eat, dress, and stay out of bad weather. And (this is important) there weren't many of them. They did not have to feed great masses of people. 8,000 years ago, at the time of the stories in this book, the whole human population of the world was probably less than ten million. Give that some thought. Something on the order of one quarter of the population of the Tokyo metropolitan area spread out across the entire land surface of the earth. What would that be like?

There were cities that must have seemed enormous for the time. Chatal Hoyuk in Anatolia, in modern Turkey, was a neolithic village that would have existed at exactly the same time period as the Téuta in this book, and it is estimated to have had a population of between 3 and 8 thousand people. They worked, sometime hard. They lifted heavy things, and the bones that remain there show that. But I don't know that there is any reason to believe that they worked without rest, or without leisure, or without recreation. No reason to believe that every person had to work without cease. Just the opposite. They seem to have had a great many feasts, judging by the number of aurochs bull skulls displayed in their homes.

Humans are human.